St. Augustine Academy Press

About *Msgr. Raymond J. O'Brien:*

Born in Chicago in 1892, Raymond O'Brien studied for the Priesthood at St. Mary's Seminary in Baltimore, MD and was ordained in 1921. He was then appointed teacher and spiritual advisor at the newly established Quigley Preparatory Seminary, where he taught high-school age boys who were considering the priesthood. During these difficult years of Prohibition and Depression, he became intimately familiar with the temptations and discouragement experienced by young men. He dedicated himself to this cause, establishing numerous youth groups at Blessed Sacrament Parish, where he was transferred in 1936, and where he was known never to turn away troubled youths. He also served as auxiliary chaplain at the Bridewell and County Jail. He was honored with the title of Monsignor in 1949 in recognition of his humanitarian work as well as his promulgation of the faith, and he died in October 1963, a most beloved pastor and friend of boys.

About **Nice Going, Red:**

Set in 1930s Chicago, *Nice Going Red* is the tale of "Red" Devlin, an 8th grade boy who has his heart in the right place, but a little embarrassment is all it takes to overcome his resolve. When the boys from St. Mary's get embroiled in a street fight with the Dodgers, Father Walsh is deeply disappointed. He applauds their courage in standing up for what's right, but true moral courage means fighting with more than just fists: it means knowing when to walk away, without fear of being called "yellow." Will Red finally manage to find his way...or will misplaced pride lead him astray?

Dixon must have suddenly thought of his secret boxing practice, for he jumped away from Red and assumed a ring pose; then, with much bobbing and weaving, that he assumed was the proper ring technique, he came toward Red again. (*Page 252*)

NICE GOING, RED

The Story of a Boy Who "Couldn't Take It"

by

Rev. Raymond J. O'Brien

with new illustrations by

Erin Bartholomew

2016

ST. AUGUSTINE ACADEMY PRESS

HOMER GLEN, ILLINOIS

This book is newly typeset based on the edition
published in 1935 by Benziger Brothers.

All editing strictly limited to the correction of errors in the original
text and the updating of outdated spelling for some words.

This book was originally published in 1935
by Benziger Brothers.

This edition ©2016 by St. Augustine Academy Press.
Editing by Lisa Bergman.

ISBN: 978-1-936639-71-7
Library of Congress Control Number: 2016951840

Illustrations by Erin Bartholomew ©2015
Frontispiece redrawn from original found in the 1935 edition.

Contents

Dedicated to
Bishop Sheil
and the
C. Y. O.

CHAPTER I

Red Has Another Fight

RED DEVLIN walked slowly down the alley toward his home. The scowl on his face plainly showed that he was worried. He had just been in a fight; that, too, was plain to see. But that didn't worry him; he had been in lots of fights. Trudging along, he pulled his cap down a little farther over an eye that was beginning to swell; then he tenderly touched his handkerchief to his lip, and his frown deepened when he saw that his lip was still bleeding. He glanced at his bruised knuckles and—grinned. Boy, what a fight! If the fellows in his room could have seen it.

Suddenly his grin gave place again to a deep scowl as he muttered: "They'll kid the life out of me—fighting for a girl." That is what worried him. Poor Red was easy to tease. As the boys said, "he couldn't take it."

Red, in the eighth grade at St. Mary's, was a traffic officer of the school police. His station was at the Lincoln Street car line, a block from the school. This afternoon, having seen safely on their way the last of his schoolmates who crossed "his corner," he slipped off his Sam Browne belt and started home.

Three girls, dressed in the school uniform, were a short distance ahead of him. Coming toward them were two young rowdies of the neighborhood, Dixon and Small, whose chief occupation seemed to be dodging the truant officer. Red saw Dixon deliberately trip one of the girls, then turn and laugh as his victim stumbled and fell headlong to the sidewalk. Just what happened after that even Red could not well explain. Nor could the young ruffian who tripped the girl; he suddenly heard the tattoo of racing feet behind him, and turning quickly to see who was coming, received Red's fist full on the mouth. Red was beside himself with rage and contempt. Without a glance toward the girls, he tore into the surprised bully with all the fury of an angry tiger. But it was two to one. Red could have thoroughly licked either of the young toughs in a fair fight; but, with both of them coming at him, he was almost certain to get the worst of it. The uneven odds made him fight all the more fiercely. He swung viciously at the head nearest him, trying all the time to keep either of the pair from getting behind him. Suddenly Dixon lunged for him, disregarding Red's blows in an effort to get his arms around him. Just then Red heard a shout and a shriek of automobile brakes as a car slid to a sudden stop at the curb. The driver jumped out, flung Dixon one way and Small the other, and stopped the fight.

"You come with me," he ordered, as he grasped Red's shoulder and shoved him ahead of him into the car. "You young Indian," he said, with a smile, "you can't lick them both. What was it all about?"

Red was puffing from exertion and his eyes were still ablaze with anger. "One of them tripped a girl," he answered hotly. "Let me out. I'm not afraid of them."

"I'll let you out at the end of the next block," said his rescuer, as he started the car. "Get them some other time, one at a time," he continued, smiling. "Who was the girl?"

"You saw them standing there, didn't you?" asked Red, gruffly.

The man recalled that he had seen the three girls watching with dismay the unfair fight. "Yes. I saw them. They hurried away when I jumped out of the car."

"Well, he tripped one of them, and she fell," said Red. "They go to our school."

The man laughed. "Well, you're their hero now," he said. "I'll let you out here. See that you go straight home. You look a bit messed up."

He stopped the car and Red got out, frowning.

"Good-bye," called the man, but Red didn't answer. The words, "You'll be their hero," were still ringing in his ears, and he was thinking of what the fellows in school would say. Red blushed. "Shucks," he muttered, "they'll peddle it all over the neighborhood."

Red was almost home when suddenly his face lit up with a smile. "By Jove," he exclaimed aloud, "that was Jim Blake's sister. That's who she was." He quickened his pace. Jim Blake was captain of last year's baseball team, and although he was now in high school, Red knew that all his friends in school remembered Jim. "I can say I did it for Jim. He'd do it if anybody tripped my sister." A few feet ahead of him a gate opened, and Bill Harte, one of the boys from the second division of the eighth grade, which occupied a room next to Red's division, came toward him.

"Wow," he cried, as he saw Red. "Another fight? Boy, look at that eye! What happened ?"

"Aw, that wise guy, Dixon was walking down Lincoln Street with that other goof, Small, and Dixon tripped Jim Blake's sister." Red watched Bill intently to see how he received this explanation. "Jim would stick up for my sister, wouldn't he? So I sailed into him and Blake. I had to fight 'em both. I was alone."

"Did you lick 'em?" Bill asked excitedly.

"A fellow goin' by in a car stopped us," Red answered. Bill grinned; he guessed the true answer to his question.

"Where was it?" asked Bill.

"Near my corner," Red answered. "Jim Blake's sister was going home from school with two other girls from your room, and this guy tripped her."

"Jim Blake's sister?" asked Bill. "Why, she wasn't in school today. She's home, sick."

"What?" exclaimed Red, in surprise.

"Sure!" answered Bill. "She sits in front of me." Bill was laughing at Red's surprise.

"Well, they were from your room," declared Red. Then he suddenly realized he wasn't even sure of that. "I didn't take a good look at them," he said, "but they're from our school. They all dress alike." The correct identification of the girls was not a matter of importance to Bill, so he came back to the fight.

"Dixon and Small, hey?" he asked. "Part of that Dodger outfit."

"Yeh," declared Red. "You know them. They're always hanging around the corner up near the movie theater. Dixon always wears a dirty, old red sweater."

"Oh, I know them," said Bill, with a toss of his head. His lip curled with contempt. "They think they're hard boiled. Want to take a walk up that way tonight?" he asked, and Red knew instantly the purpose of Bill's proposal.

"And how," exclaimed Red. Then he gently touched his swollen eye. "But what about this?" he asked sorrowfully. "I don't want them to see the shiner. Let's wait a while."

Bill understood. "Guess you'd better take care of that. I'll get one of the other fellows and we'll drift up that way anyhow." Then he thought of his reason for being in the alley. "S'long," he said quickly. "If I don't get to the butcher's, we won't eat tonight."

"I'm glad tomorrow is Saturday," said Red as he moved on. He tried to recall the faces of those girls. After a moment he admitted to himself that he did not know who the girls were. "Aw, heck," he muttered. "She's from our school, anyhow." His shoulders squared. Bill Harte didn't seem to think it strange that he should fight for a girl. Red grinned. "Bill would fight for any old reason, though," he said to himself.

As Red entered the kitchen, his mother turned from her work at the table. "Well, for heaven's sake!" she exclaimed. "Fighting again! Look at your face. Look at your shirt. Now, you just wait till your father comes home. You're a disgrace."

Red tried to speak; he wanted to explain. "But, Ma," he began. His mother continued sharply. "Oh, I know it wasn't your fault; it never is. Somebody else always starts it. Who was it this time?" she asked.

"A tough guy tripped a girl from our school," explained Red, "and—"

"What's that?" quickly asked Mrs. Devlin.

"And there were two of them," continued Red. "One of them tripped a girl from our school."

"Yes," continued his mother, rather cautiously. "Then what?"

"Well," answered Red, "then I hit him. Then they both started at me, and I hit them both. Then some fellow stopped us."

"Who was the girl?" asked Red's mother.

"I–I don't know," answered Red, weakly. "You see, I–I didn't get a good look at her." Red saw the shadow of doubt cross his mother's face.

"Francis," said Mrs. Devlin solemnly, as she raised a warning finger. "Are you telling me the truth?" Mrs. Devlin knew that Red would not deliberately tell a bare-faced lie, but long practice in making excuses had given him a certain skill, annoying to his mother, of rearranging parts of his story of what happened so that while everything he said was true, indeed, it may not have occurred in just the way he permitted his questioner to assume.

"Yes, ma'am. Honest," declared Red.

His mother hesitated. If Red had fought in defense of a girl from his school, she had no word of reproof for him.

"Go upstairs, wash your face and change your clothes," she said. "We'll see about this later."

While Red was carrying out his mother's directions, his older brother, Arthur, came home from work. Mrs. Devlin quickly told Arthur about Red's latest fight. Arthur's eyes glistened. He was proud of Red.

"He's a good kid," he exclaimed. "I'm going to take a look at him." He started upstairs.

"Hey, Red," he called. Red was "Frank" to his older brother only in the presence of company or when a state of war existed between the two brothers.

"What d'ya want?" demanded Red, as he opened the bedroom door. He was anxious to know what Arthur would say about the fight.

"Wow, what an eye—and a peach of a lip!" declared Arthur. "Atta boy! How about some first aid? Want a piece of beef steak for the eye?"

"No. It's all right," said Red.

Arthur couldn't resist the temptation to tease his younger brother.

"The Red Avenger flew to the defense of the fair maiden, hey?" he said laughing. "Boy, won't Father Walsh be proud of you? What's your lady's colors, Red? You know the knights of old always wore the colors of their beloved when they went forth to battle."

A dangerous glint showed in Red's eyes.

"Now, cut out the funny stuff, you big stiff," he exclaimed. He brushed past his brother and started downstairs. Arthur followed whistling, "Come, come, come, be my hero."

Red's sister, Rita, was setting the table for supper and his young brother, Bobbie, was out in the yard. By this time, both of them knew about Red's fight. Red grinned at Rita, and Rita smiled back proudly. Then Red caught the meaning of the tune that Arthur was whistling. He appealed to his mother. "Say, Ma, make that big stiff keep still," he pleaded.

"Now what's the matter?" she asked, as, slipping her hand under Red's chin, she raised his face for a close inspection. "You're going to have a black eye tomorrow," she said.

"Some little hero, isn't he, Ma?" asked Arthur, gaily. Then, turning to his sister, he asked, "Rita, did you ever have a boy get marked up like that over you?"

Rita, always Red's champion, turned a withering look on her older brother. "Never mind, Mr. Smarty," she said. "I hope that if some day I need help, there'll be somebody like Frank around. You *might* do," she said meaningly, "but I'm sure of him."

"That's enough now," said Mrs. Devlin. "We'll see what your father will say when he hears about it."

When Mr. Devlin came home, he found the youngsters on the porch, strangely quiet and expectant.

"What's wrong?" he asked, smiling.

"Red had another fight," promptly and gleefully answered Bobbie, for Red was somewhat of a hero to his nine-year-old brother.

Mr. Devlin passed into the kitchen and saw Red. He greeted Mrs. Devlin and noticed the twinkle in her eyes. Then he turned to Red. "Well?" he asked sternly. Red quickly gave him an account of the fight. Arthur listened attentively.

"I see," said his father, as he passed into the living room.

Arthur smiled. "Well, that's that," he said, with a wave of his hand to show that the hearing was over and the defendant declared "Not guilty."

When Mr. Devlin returned, the evening meal was ready. Bobbie "said grace," a privilege he enjoyed ever since he made his First Communion.

Mr. Devlin took his place at the head of the table and smiled genially at Red. "Well," he said, "you finally got into a fight for a good reason, hey, Frank?"

"Yes, sir," answered Red, well pleased that his father was not at all displeased with him.

"You've got a bad eye and that lip must be pretty sore," continued Mr. Devlin. "Did you let those other fellows know that they were in a fight?" he asked, good naturedly.

"I tried to," quickly answered Red, extending his right fist across the table to his father. Crimson dabs of mercurochrome covered several scratches and one rather deep cut.

"Won't he be the idol of the girls Monday morning, though?" exclaimed Arthur, between mouthfuls. "Be sure to paint that fist up again, Red," he added with a laugh. Mr. Devlin saw the hurt look that instantly clouded Frank's face at Arthur's sally. He looked sternly at Arthur.

"Just forget the teasing, Art," he ordered. "Frank will probably get enough of that from the boys for a few days."

Red's eyes began to blink. His father had put into words the fear that gnawed at Red's heart. The boy saw his sister looking at him with eyes full of sympathy. He laid down his knife and fork and left the table. Tears started from his eyes as he left the room. A short while ago he was fearless in an unequal combat; now he was all but crushed with the fear of the taunts of his school fellows. They would make fun of him. He could stand blows, but he couldn't stand that. He had yet to learn life's hardest lesson— not to fear being laughed at.

Arthur, thoroughly repentant, jumped from his place and started after his younger brother. Red ran upstairs. He wanted neither sympathy nor company. He loudly ordered Arthur away from him.

Mr. Devlin called Arthur back to the table, and in

a few moments, repeated that command to Red. The lad returned, dry-eyed but embarrassed. No further reference was made to the fight.

The next morning, Saturday, Red, examining his reflection in a mirror, was pleasantly surprised to see that neither his damaged eye nor lip were as noticeable as he feared they would be.

Bill Harte, eager to have Red out for the usual Saturday ball game, called at the Devlin home with two others of St. Mary's team, Jack Clemens and Steve Nolan, the captain. Red was hesitant about appearing in public, but his friends convinced him that "you can hardly notice it at all." Bill then told Red how he and Jack Clemens had spent the previous evening trying to find Dixon and Small, but without success. Bill was disappointed.

"Maybe they stayed home doctoring their faces, too," suggested Steve Nolan.

"Well, we certainly looked all over the neighborhood for them," said Bill, "and just for the fun of it, we're going to keep looking until we run across them."

"Well, then," said Steve to Red, "you and I, Red, will make another pair of 'lookers,' too. O.K.?"

"And how," answered Red, laughing.

"If those fellows see you two together," declared Bill Harte, "they'll run for cover, sure." It was frankly admitted by the boys of St. Mary's that Steve was easily the fastest boxer and hardest hitter of them all, and Red, a pretty close second.

"Well, let's get over to the field," said Red. He was secretly pleased that "the girl" was not mentioned at all. These boys, however, were his "buddies." He still had to face the crowd at St. Mary's.

CHAPTER II

Lieutenant Carroll
Speaks Out

MONDAY morning found Red at his post at
the Lincoln Street crossing. The only trace of
Friday's battle was a somewhat discolored left
eye. With the exception of a few boys about Red's
age, none of the youngsters who crossed Lincoln
Street under Red's protection paid any attention to
the personal appearance of their traffic officer. The
boys who did, however, had heard about the fight and
wanted the details from Red. They gathered around
him each time he returned from the middle of the
street and plied him with questions. Red answered all
with patience and kindness; he knew from experience
that by so doing he could prevent or, at least, postpone
any teasing.

"Who were the girls?" asked one of his questioners
eventually.

"I don't know," Red answered, but another boy
quickly gave the desired information. "My sister was
one of them," he said. "The girl who was tripped is
Irene Moore. Here they come now."

The boys turned in the direction indicated by the speaker and Red blushed as he saw the three girls looking directly at him and smiling cheerfully. He saw that they were from his own class. Then the horn of an oncoming auto sounded, and Red swung around to give his attention to a few children waiting on the opposite side of the street for the signal from their traffic guide. He guided the youngsters safely across the street and found the three girls standing with the knot of boys waiting for him.

"My dad bought this for you, Frank," said Irene pleasantly, as she placed in Red's hands a red cardboard box with a picture of a fielder's mitt on the cover. Red's eyes opened wide in surprise. "And we all want to thank you," added one of the other girls.

Red's face turned scarlet. "Aw ..." he began, but whatever he was going to say was cut short by the clamor of the boys.

"Let's see it, Red. Open it." Red was all thumbs trying to open the box. He wished the girls would get out of the way and go on to school; but they, with the boys, waited to see the glove.

"Hey, Red," came a shrill call from across the street; a few more young scholars were waiting to cross and had become impatient.

"Aw, wait there," called one of the boys impatiently, but Red, glad of an excuse to get away from his admirers, left the glove in the possession of his friends and hastened across the street. When he returned, the girls had left the group, and the boys were examining with delight the new glove.

"Boy, it's a peach, Red," said one of them. "Feel the leather; it's as soft as anything." It was an expensive glove and Red's eyes sparkled as he tried it on and sunk his right fist deep into its palm.

The story of the glove preceded Red to school. When he arrived at the school entrance, Steve Nolan and Jack Clemens were waiting for him.

"So Irene gave you a glove, hey?" exclaimed Jack mischievously. "Let's see it."

"No, Irene didn't give it to me," declared Red stoutly. "Her father did." The boys grinned at Red's answer as they examined the gift.

"Boy, it's a dandy," exclaimed Steve. Then the bell rang, and they went to their classroom.

Class had scarcely begun when Father Walsh, the assistant pastor of St. Mary's, who was in charge of the school, entered the room and publicly commended Red for his chivalry. Then he added, "I know that the girls of St. Mary's will always be safe with boys like Frank Devlin to protect them."

Father Walsh was earnest in all that he said that morning, but he little knew how eagerly the boys in the class were treasuring up phrases from his complimentary speech with which to plague Red when the occasion arose. And the superior of the school, coming into the classroom a little later in the day, spoke of the incident and called Red a "little gentleman."

Poor Red! What a time he had of it. Although he was delighted with the glove, he was never permitted to forget that Irene gave it to him. Any hesitancy in loaning it to any of his crowd who wanted to use it brought a taunt that it was "all right, Red, old boy, as long as it's a keepsake from Irene." To prevent that, Red quickly surrendered the glove. He was not afraid of physical combat with any of his friendly tormentors, but that, he feared, would surely be "fighting over a girl," and would only make his present sorry plight much worse.

The following Friday evening Red was on his way home after the final baseball game of the year. St. Mary's won, and most of the team had hastened back to school with the glad news, but Red had to wait until he got his glove from one of the two "problem cases" of St. Mary's eighth grade, Clyde White and Bert Stone. These lads were not a credit to St. Mary's in conduct or scholarship, nor had they merited dismissal. Their graduation would, indeed, bring relief to all concerned. They were not members of the baseball team or of any of the school teams. The leaders of St. Mary's, both in athletics and scholarship, were Red's closest friends, Steve Nolan, Jack Clemens and Bill Harte, and their popularity, with its consequent good influence in the school, so far offset whatever bad influence White and Stone might have exerted, that Father Walsh and the Sisters in charge of the school tolerated the unwelcome presence of the pair.

"Let's cut through the alley," said Bert, as the boys left the field. As soon as they had entered the alley, Bert took a package of cigarettes from his pocket. Without comment, he took one from the package and passed the package to White. White helped himself and then offered the cigarettes to Red.

"I don't want any," said Red, a trifle embarrassed.

"Don't you smoke?" asked White, grinning at Red's refusal.

"I just don't want any. That's all," declared Red.

"Mama spank?" teased Bert Stone, trying to imitate the voice of a baby. Red blushed and smiled weakly.

"Little gentlemen don't smoke, you know," said Stone, shaking a warning finger at Bert, who by this time had recovered his cigarettes and still held the open package in his hand. "Didn't Sister say that Francis was a little gentleman?"

An angry frown quickly darkened Red's face, but as quickly disappeared. With a weak laugh, he exclaimed, "Aw, forget it. Give me one." The boys huddled together to light their cigarettes and were soon on their way. Red puffed on his only enough to keep it burning.

"Did you get the guys that beat you up yet ?" asked White, grinning. He knew that Red would not like the question put that way.

"What do you mean, beat me up?" demanded Red. "They didn't beat me up."

"Oh, no?" asked White, with a leer. "That eye you had..." Before he could finish, Bert interrupted, exclaiming, "Look. There's Bowsy and his gang; I'll bet they'll start a crap game."

The boys looked up ahead of them and saw four or five boys a little older than themselves coming toward them from the next street. Before Red and his companions reached them, Bowsy and his gang were squatting in the alley rolling dice. Of course, White and Stone stopped to watch the game, and Red stopped with them. He knew that he should not be there, and before he could think of an excuse to continue on his way, he was loaning Bert Stone fifteen cents. A few minutes later he was watching with interest the rise and fall of Bert's fortune.

"Want to get in on it?" asked Bowsy, noticing Red's interest. "Bet you a nickel Stone don't make his point."

Bert, dice in hand, looked up at Red. "Bet him, Red," he urged. Red felt the eyes of all the boys upon him.

"O.K." said Red, as he tossed a nickel to the ground near Bowsy.

Just at this point, Lieutenant Carroll stepped through the side door of the fire engine station at the end of the alley, watched the boys a moment with a puzzled look on his face, and went back into the station. "So," he mused, "Red Devlin is with them."

The Lieutenant was a good friend of nearly every boy in the neighborhood, and the boys from St. Mary's were his favorites. Red and his friends frequently stopped at the fire engine house to chat with the big, husky fireman. A little while ago he had received from some of the team a thrilling account of the afternoon's game.

"Where's Red?" he asked, as the boys were about to leave. "I want to see that eye. I haven't seen him since the fight."

"Say, Lieutenant, do you want to have some fun with him?" asked Bill Harte. "Irene Moore's father gave him a glove, but Irene brought it to school, and Red goes wild if you tease him about 'Irene's' glove."

"Well, where is he?" repeated the Lieutenant.

"He'll be along pretty soon," answered Bill. "He was trying to get his glove back from Bert Stone when we left the field."

The boys continued on their way, leaving the Lieutenant to await Red's coming. He was rather disappointed as he saw what was detaining his young friend. Some time later, when he looked down the alley again, all the boys, including Red, had disappeared.

The next afternoon, in a neighborhood barber shop, Mr. Devlin and a few other men were waiting their turn for the barber's services. Most of them were fathers of boys in the neighborhood. In a corner of the shop, Lieutenant Carroll was devouring the sport news of the evening paper. The rest of the customers were discussing local politics, when their attention was claimed by loud voices of a few boys passing the shop. Their conversation was that of a typical gutterboy, lewd and profane.

The barber nearest the door turned from his task of heaping steaming towels on the face of the man in his chair and addressed those waiting. "Every day I hear them," he said, with a gesture of disgust. "They don't work; they don't go to school. Just loafers. They must live in alleys somewhere."

An elderly, sour-faced gentleman laid aside a magazine he was holding and said, "The boys of today are going to the dogs. Heaven knows what will happen to our country when they are running it. Now, just the other day..."

The speaker was rudely interrupted by a hearty laugh from Lieutenant Carroll. "Well, believe me, they couldn't do any worse than some of those running things today," he declared. "Most of the kids around here are all right. I know them. I know the hoodlums and the fine, law-abiding, fun-loving crowd." The big fireman stood up better to address the pessimist. He shook his finger at the man and said, "Some of the kids around here are far better than any of my crowd were— or yours either. Why, I'll bet you anything you name that, for every young loafer you'll find like those that just passed, I'll find a dozen boys that are as fine and decent as any man in this shop. I'll bring you plenty of boys who are clean and square and earnest and game. They wouldn't give one Lindbergh for a dozen so-called 'big shots' of crime or politics."

The big Lieutenant's eyes were flashing and his arms were waving; he was all set for a speech, but a barber touched him on the arm and said, "You're next." The Lieutenant climbed into the chair, laughing at his own outburst of oratory in the defense of his young friends.

"You're right, Tom," called Mr. Devlin. "Put a crime magazine and a magazine about air ships before my lad, and he'll take the air every time. The way these boys can talk about aircraft has me baffled. And, as far as being decent and trustworthy, I'll stake all I have on that young red head of mine. He hasn't decided whether he wants to be a fireman or an aviator; he's got pluck enough for either job."

"He's a good boy," said the head-barber earnestly, nodding his head in emphasis.

Mr. Devlin laughed. "Why, just a week ago, he was on his way from school," he said, and then told his listeners all about Red's fight with the two young toughs.

Lieutenant Carroll didn't hear most of Mr. Devlin's story. He was thinking; thinking of "that young red head." He was a bit surprised at Mr. Devlin's lavish praise of Red. He knew Red was not a bad boy, but he also knew that lately, at least, Red was not all that his father had said. Yesterday was not the first time the Lieutenant had seen him with questionable company. The barber finished his work, flicked the apron from the fireman, shook it out, and called, "Next." Lieutenant Carroll took no further part in the discussion; he paid his check and left the shop.

"I'll have to talk to Red," he said to himself as he started down the street. "Although he doesn't know it, he's just beginning to 'go tough.'"

He had gone scarcely a block when he met Bill Harte and Jack Clemens. Both boys were laughing and gesticulating joyously. "What's up?" asked Lieutenant Carroll, genially.

"We just ran into the two guys that gave Red Devlin that shiner last Friday," answered Bill. "We've been looking for them ever since."

"Yes?" calmly asked the Lieutenant. "Then what?"

"Well," answered Jack. "They'll think twice before they jump another patrol boy from St. Mary's."

"They've both got shiners now," added Bill, laughing.

"Are you fellows trying to start a gang war around here?" asked the fireman, seriously.

"We didn't start it, Lieutenant," declared Jack. "They did, and if they want to keep it up, it's O.K. with us."

Lieutenant Carroll smiled. He was pretty sure that no group that he knew in the neighborhood could stand up against the crowd from St. Mary's.

"Well now, forget it," he cautioned. "Don't go around with a chip on your shoulder."

"O.K.", the boys answered and continued on their way.

"By the way," Lieutenant Carroll called after them. "Tell Red I want to see him after Mass tomorrow. I'll be at the Engine House."

Red answered the summons eagerly. He had served the seven o'clock Mass, and had seen the Lieutenant, in uniform, at the Communion railing. By eight-thirty, Red was on his way to the Engine House. Lieutenant Carroll was sitting at his desk, reading the newspaper, as he waited for Red. Red came into the station on the run. "Looking for me, Lieutenant?" he called, as he spied his friend at the desk.

"Yes. I want to talk to you, you young Indian," answered the Lieutenant, with a broad smile. "Come here. Sit down there," he said, motioning Red to a chair.

Red sat down and looked at the big officer before him somewhat puzzled. When he received word from Bill Harte that Lieutenant Carroll wanted to see him, he assumed that he was to be sent on some errand. The Lieutenant looked at the paper before him for an instant or two, then turned to Red and asked bluntly, "Red, when did you have your last smoke?"

Red blushed and grinned nervously. "My last smoke?" he began guiltily, "Why, I–I" he stammered.

"Be on the square, Red," urged the Lieutenant. "When did you have your last smoke?"

"Friday, after the game," answered Red. Lieutenant Carroll frowned.

"What's the big idea, Red?" he asked. "Getting hard-boiled? Does your dad know you smoke?"

"No," answered Red, the trace of a whine in his voice.

"Does Father Walsh know?" asked the Lieutenant.

"No," said Red, beginning to pout under the questioning.

The fireman hesitated a moment; then, "Does Irene know?" he asked, maliciously. He knew well that that question would sting Red, and it did.

The boy quickly rose from his chair, resentful and sullen.

"None of your busi..." he began, but Lieutenant Carroll interrupted him.

"Sit down, Red," he said quickly, putting his hand on the boy's arm and gently forcing him back into the chair. "That was unfair. I take it back."

Red's glare gradually changed into a smile.

"Red, I just want to tell you something," began the Lieutenant, kindly. "Something that happened yesterday. I want to tell you a few things that your father said about you in the barber-shop yesterday afternoon. We fell to talking about the boys of today, and he started to boast about 'that young red head' of his. He certainly trusts you, Red. He's proud of you. He told the whole shop the story of your fight a week ago Friday. One of the things he said was that he'd stake everything he had on your being trustworthy. Do you realize what that means, Red?"

Red nodded, and a blush slowly mantled his cheeks. Lieutenant Carroll continued. "Now, while he was talking, I knew you were double-crossing him. I could have made him eat his words. Why? Because I saw you Friday, after the game; you and those two would-be toughs from your school were out there in the alley, shooting dice and smoking with the riff-raff of this neighborhood." Red frowned. "Of course, that isn't murder, Red," said the Lieutenant; "but I think that if I were you and my father was so sure and so proud of me as yours is of you, I'd get a bigger kick out of living up to his opinion of me than I would out of smoking a cigarette on the sly, or hanging around a crap game in an alley."

"What's that?" asked Red, puzzled a bit. This was a new way of looking at Friday's performance.

"I said that your dad believes you're true blue. Your mother does, too. I'm sure of that. Can't you understand what that means to them, Red? If I were you, I'd take pride in really being what I seem to them to be. Do you?" demanded the Lieutenant. Red listened sullenly, making no attempt to reply. "No," exclaimed the Lieutenant, answering his own question, as he slapped his hand down on the desk. "No. You deliberately double-cross them. They think that you're honorable. Well, there's nothing honorable in hanging out with a crowd of alley-rats, or smoking on the sly. A boy who does that and pretends at home that he's on the level is paying a big price for the satisfaction he gets out of his smoke or his 'wise guy' company. I think that I'd prefer the greater satisfaction of feeling that I was on the square with my mother and dad."

"I–I wasn't shooting dice," declared Red. "I didn't even touch them."

"No?" asked the Lieutenant, a curl of contempt on his lip. "Stop quibbling. Be a man. You were with them, even if you were not shooting dice, and—" he insisted, nodding his head emphatically, "you were smoking."

"Aw, if you don't smoke, the fellows think you're a sissy," argued Red, somewhat weakly.

"Bah!" exclaimed the Lieutenant angrily, as he jumped from his chair. "Would I want you to act like a sissy? Your father thinks you're a man! Why, you haven't the courage to be a man! If you did, you'd do the right thing no matter what the other fellows thought."

The big fireman sat down again and snatched up his paper. He was plainly displeased with Red's attempt to defend his conduct. Before Red could say anything, he continued sharply, "All right, Red, all right. Now, do as you please. I just wanted to tell you how you'll hurt your dad if he finds out that you are deceiving him." Without raising his eyes from the paper, he declared, with feeling, "And as far as I am concerned, you can stay away from here if you keep traveling with that crowd, the trash I saw you with Friday."

Red stood up. "O.K.," he said, with an insolent toss of his head. He slowly walked out of the engine house with an air of nonchalance that was intended to impress upon the Lieutenant how little concerned Red was with all that the man had said. Deep down in his heart, he felt more like crying. He knew that everything his friend had said was true, but, humiliated by the fireman's stinging rebuke and ultimatum, he was in no mood for any further parley.

CHAPTER III

Double-Crossers

RED had scarcely crossed the street when the fire alarm suddenly broke the calm Sunday morning stillness. Instinctively, despite his sulky mood, Red listened to the strokes of the bell sounding off the number of the fire alarm box from which the call was coming. "1-1-1, 1-1, 1-1-1-1," tapped out the bell. "324," counted Red. "That's for Engine 29." He turned to see Lieutenant Carroll and the members of Engine Company 29 race for their places on the fire apparatus. With a roar of the motor and the shrill scream of the siren, Engine 29 swung out of the fire station and down the street. Red dashed back to the chart behind the Lieutenant's desk to check the location of the alarm. Box 324 was at Chestnut and Rush Streets.

"That's a mile from here," said Red to himself, as he went back to his place across the street to wait and see whether any further call would come in. He and his crowd had chased too many false alarms to get excited over Engine 29 rolling out. He sat down on the front steps of a house opposite the fire station. The home of Engine 29 stood before him silent and empty. As Red waited he saw the door leading from the engine house to the alley slowly open; then somebody stealthily slipped into the station and silently closed the door. The rear of the station was in too great a shadowy darkness for Red to identify the person, but the thought slipped through his mind, "That's the fellow who's stealing their things."

Red's suspicions were aroused because he knew that for some time petty stealing had been going on in the engine house and the firemen had not been able to detect the thief. Red dashed across the street and into the station. He saw no one. Tip-toeing quietly to the rear, he stood at the foot of the stairway leading to the sleeping quarters on the floor above. Soon he heard a noise as of the catch on one of the steel lockers being lifted. Without a thought of danger to himself, Red climbed the stairway as quickly as he could without making any noise. From the locker room came sounds that Red could not mistake; somebody was rifling the firemen's lockers.

Red looked around for a weapon, but saw nothing that would do. He recalled seeing a new axe near the captain's desk. He wished now he had brought it upstairs with him. "The bats," he exclaimed to himself. He knew that there were a few baseball bats in the locker-room. They would be in the usual place in the corner farthest from the door. True to his habit of acting first and thinking afterwards, he made a wild dash across the short space between the stairway and the locker-room. Without so much as a glance at the thief, who, startled by Red's sudden and noisy appearance, whirled around with the coat he was searching still in his hands, Red dashed for the bats, seized one, and turned to face the prowler. Red's eyes opened wide in surprise. The thief was Bo Wickers, a seedy-looking ne'er-do-well, whom the firemen had often befriended.

"You lousy bum!" gasped Red, anger and contempt written all over his flushed face. "You! You double-crossing skunk. Put that coat back in that locker and do it quick! Put back in that locker everything you've taken!" commanded Red. Bo Wickers knew Red, and he knew also that Red's commands, backed up by anger that the boy could not well control and by a baseball bat that he knew Red could control, were not safely to be ignored.

"I'm lookin' for somethin'," Bo declared, but his tone showed that he was lying.

"You're looking for a crack of this bat," cried Red. "Put that stuff back." The thief hung up the coat and, gathering himself for a spring as he closed the locker door he leaped at Red. Crack! Red quickly swung the bat and the man sank down in a heap. He had thrown his arms up to ward off the blow, but Red was not fencing, and the bat came through the thief's guard and down on his head. For an instant Red was frightened. He thought he had killed the fellow. Slowly, however, Bo's eyes opened and he looked groggily about him.

"Stay where you are," commanded Red, relieved that the man was alive, and hoping that he would not have to hit him again. "Wait till the firemen get back."

Wickers rubbed his head, then his arm. Both were badly injured. He made no effort to arise.

"It's your own fault," declared Red. "I told you you'd get it." The boy's lips curled in contempt. "You cheap sneak. After all the firemen have done for you. They fed you; they gave you clothes. Then you turn around and double-cross them. Just stay where you are till they get back."

After a few moments that to Red seemed ages, the shrill siren sounded in the distance. "Here they come," cried Red gladly. "Wait till they see who's been stealing their stuff."

Soon Engine 29 rolled into the station and Red yelled: "Oh Joe! Come up here. Pete! Dan! Anybody!" A rush of feet on the stairs and Lieutenant Carroll entered the room. "What's this?" he exclaimed, looking from the man on the floor to the boy standing guard over him with a baseball bat in his hands.

"I caught him going through the lockers. He slipped in as soon as you pulled out," answered Red. "I followed him upstairs and caught him searching a coat."

"I was looking for somethin'," lied Wickers. "I wanted a match."

"Stand up here," ordered the Lieutenant. The thief got to his feet slowly. "Turn your pockets inside out," snapped Lieutenant Carroll.

As the tramp was complying with this order, some of the other firemen hastened up the stairs and into the room. One of them, Pete Davis, noticed that his locker was open. He hurriedly examined its contents.

"Did he take anything, Pete?" asked the Lieutenant.

"My wrist-watch is gone," excitedly answered Davis. He whirled from the locker to find the wrist-watch in the outstretched hand of the now-cringing hobo. Davis gently picked up the watch with his left hand, and, without a word, sent his right fist crashing to the thief's jaw, knocking him into the arms of Lieutenant Carroll.

"No rough stuff," instantly commanded the Officer, as he let the groggy victim of Pete's blow gently sink to the floor again. "He's had enough." A search of the thief's pockets revealed no more of the firemen's belongings. "Call the wagon, Pete," ordered the Lieutenant. "We'll turn him over to the police."

While they were waiting for the patrol wagon, one of the firemen turned to Red. "Shake, Red," he said cheerily. "Congratulations. We've been looking for this bird for a long time. How did you catch him?"

Red's face glowed with pleasure, as he answered: "I was sitting on the steps across the street for a while after you went out, and I saw him sneak in through the back door. I ran over and heard him up here, so I followed him. When I caught him at Pete's locker, he jumped at me, but I floored him with this bat. Then I just stood guard over him till you came back. He's surely a double-crosser after all you have done for him. I told him so, too."

During Red's explanation, Lieutenant Carroll listened as he helped Wickers to his feet. He was about to speak to Red, when he thought of the boy's attitude toward him only a little while ago. He couldn't overlook that, even now. "Come downstairs," he said to Wickers, and with the thief's arm in a firm grip, the Lieutenant led him from the room.

"Double-crosser, hey?" he murmured, as he walked down the stairs with his prisoner. "Well, if Red stopped to think a moment, he'd see plainly that this time one double-crosser caught the other."

Red was in gay spirits as he and the other firemen came downstairs to meet the police officers who had hurried to the station in answer to Pete's call. The firemen had good-naturedly listened to a longer and more vivid account of the detection and capture of Wickers, and Red felt quite the hero. He repeated the tale to the policemen. The officers tumbled Bo Wickers into their car, and telling Pete to report to the station to sign the complaint, drove away. Red glanced at Lieutenant Carroll, now at his desk—and all his erstwhile cheerfulness left him, as the big Lieutenant called out to Pete, "Double-crossers generally get caught sooner or later, don't they, Pete?" Red blushed crimson. He knew what the Lieutenant meant. Then, pretending that he had not heard, he walked quickly out of the station and down the street.

About an hour later, the Police Captain of the district drove up to the station and called Lieutenant

Carroll out to his car. "Lieutenant, this is just for yourself. We have let Bo Wickers out. He's the black sheep of a pretty fine family, and his brother-in-law is pretty strong in local politics in his part of the town. He guarantees to see to it that Wickers doesn't bother the firemen any more. Wickers himself feels that he's had enough, anyhow. His head is still aching and his jaw is pretty sore," said the Captain, smiling. "We'll keep an eye on him too from now on. I know the whole family pretty well, and, as a favor to them, I'd like to let Bo go."

"But what about Davis?" asked the Lieutenant. "He's supposed to go over to the station and sign a complaint. What shall I tell him?"

"Just tell him that I'd like to give Wickers another chance, for good personal reasons, and that I'll take the responsibility of seeing that he doesn't get into anything like this in the future," the Captain answered. "I'll tell Wickers that the firemen have agreed to give him another chance; but that the first time he is caught around the Engine House, Davis will sign the complaint, and we'll pick him up and put him away."

The Captain's plans were carried out while Red was busily entertaining some of his young friends with the story of his adventure.

That afternoon, as Red was on the way to a neighborhood ball game, he was dumbfounded suddenly to come upon Bo Wickers loitering, with a few others of his kind, in front of a garage. "How did you get out?" he demanded. In this second encounter with Bo, Red had no bat, and, as the man, recognizing Red as the cause of his painful experience that morning, angrily cursed the boy and started toward him menacingly, Red took to his heels and ran. He started right for the fire station. He'd find out there. Maybe they didn't know Bo was free. Suddenly he thought of Lieutenant Carroll, and as suddenly stopped running. He was no longer welcome at the station; at least, not to the fireman whom all the boys considered their special friend. Well, he'd ignore the Lieutenant and speak to Davis or some of the others.

Red thought of Lieutenant Carroll's remark about double-crossers, and a frown darkened his face. It was true; the Lieutenant had proved to him that he had been double-crossing his dad. Though Red felt keenly humiliated when he recalled what the man had said, he could not evade the fact that his friend had spoken the truth. His conscience whispered to him that the manly thing would be to go and square himself with Lieutenant Carroll, to admit frankly that his advisor was right, and to renew again the friendship that his pride had broken. A deep frown darkened his face. It was hard, very hard, for Red to admit that he was wrong. He thought of the happy crowd of his young friends, who so admired the Lieutenant and who liked to stop and chat with him whenever they found him on duty at the Engine House. Was it worth while to give up those pleasant meetings? He knew that, if the other boys learned of his trouble with the Lieutenant, they would not sympathize with him. Too many times, he had called one or the other of them apart and "laid the law down to them," as they put it, for them to believe that, in this case, he had acted unreasonably.

"Aw, this has gone far enough," muttered Red to himself. "I'll go right in and apologize, and start all over again before they find out anything about it." He quickened his pace, light-hearted with his good resolution, and as he turned the corner, he almost ran into Clyde White and Bert Stone, the very boys against whose company Lieutenant Carroll had warned him. The sudden appearance of the pair brought a quick frown to Red's face.

"Where to?" asked White blithely. Red hesitated a moment, and then told them of the theft and of Bo's arrest. "Now, the big bum is out again. I'm going to the station to see if they know about it," he explained.

"We'll go with you," said Stone, as the two boys turned and fell in step with Red. Immediately Red's eagerness to get to the station disappeared, but before he could devise any plan to get away from White and Stone, the three were on their way down the street. The two newcomers plied Red with questions about the incident at the Engine House and failed to notice Red's lack of enthusiasm in his answers. As they turned into the street where the Engine House was located, they heard a siren shrilly demanding the right of way, and saw Engine 29 come tearing out of the fire station and down the street toward them.

"Here they come!" exclaimed White, and the boys moved out to the curb to watch the fire apparatus pass. Red held back. He didn't want Lieutenant Carroll to see him with White and Stone. But as the fire engine came rapidly closer, the two stepped out into the street, calling to Red to come after them. Lieutenant Carroll, in his place beside the driver of the monster engine, glanced at the boys. He instantly recognized the pair, and as the big machine passed them, heard one of them call out, "Hey, Red, let's follow them. C'mon." On a run, the two boys started down the street, but Red stood still, burning with rage. He was sure that the Lieutenant had heard them call to him, for he had seen that they had his attention. Tears came to his eyes. "I know what he'll think; he'll think I was with them near the Engine House just to show him." Red was disappointed. Now the Lieutenant *would* be disgusted with him.

And as Engine 29 raced to the scene of the alarm under his command, the thought flashed through the mind of Lieutenant Carroll, "He was walking them right past the Engine House to show me he didn't care."

With drooping spirits, Red slowly continued on his way to the ball game. The thought of White and Stone brought a fresh flush of anger to his cheeks. They had spoiled everything. Then his angry mood deepened to include the Lieutenant. "Well, if he wants to think that, let him think it," he said to himself. "I'm through with him, too. I'm through with the whole gang of them. That bum can come back and steal the whole place now for all I care." He kicked viciously at a stone on the sidewalk.

The familiar sound of a shrill whistle caused Red to look up the street. He saw Bill Harte frantically beckoning to him. Then he saw Jack Clemens and two or three other fellows from St. Mary's hurrying toward Bill from the opposite direction. "Something's up," muttered Red, as he raced to his friends.

Before he could ask any questions, Bill hastily began. "Listen, Red, and you fellows, too," he said excitedly, as Jack and the others stopped before him and Red. "The Dodgers gang have passed the word around that if any of our outfit show up at the game today, they're going to jump us. They're out after us for the trimming we gave the two who jumped you, Red. Do you fellows want to come to the game?"

"No," quickly exclaimed Jack Clemens. "Let's go and get the Dodgers now."

"And how," Red cried. "Let's go and get them before they even get to the game. We can get as many fellows as they can."

"No," declared Bill Harte, emphatically. "Take it easy. We're not looking for trouble. We won't start anything. We'll just pretend that we never heard a word about their plans, and we'll all go to the game just as usual. But—we'll keep our eyes open, all of us, and if they start anything, well, we'll finish it."

"O.K.," seconded Blake. "That's better. Let's go and get the other fellows."

In a few moments Red and about a dozen of his crowd were making their plans. Steve Nolan, however, was a bit dubious about the outcome of his part in the afternoon's trouble. Though all the boys were neatly attired in their "Sunday's best," Steve was a picture in black and white; a new, snow white cap, white shirt and black tie, white flannel trousers, perfectly creased, white socks, and black and white oxfords. He looked down sorrowfully at his immaculate raiment, then grinned at the boys. They understood his predicament and sympathized with him.

"Gosh, fellows, I can't change them," he protested. "The big brother's girl is coming over for dinner tonight. He just got engaged. And I got to stay dolled up for that big event. Mom will just about murder me if I go home all beat up," he added ruefully. "I'll spoil the big bro's party."

There was a moment's silence among the boys. They realized the fix Steve was in, but, if there was going to be any fighting, they wanted Steve to be in on it. Steve was the best boxer in the crowd, and, as the boys said, "carried dynamite in both hands."

Suddenly Bill Blake exclaimed, "I got it! Steve, where were you going this afternoon?"

"Why, to the ball game, of course," answered Steve. "What makes you ask that?"

"All right," said Blake, ignoring Steve's question. "You go right ahead with your plans, just as though you didn't know that anything was going to happen. They can't blame you at home if you have to fight in self-defense, can they?" he asked triumphantly. "You beat it now, get away from us, and go to the game a little later. We'll stroll over that way now."

Steve began to object, but the boys unanimously supported Blake's suggestion, and insisted that Steve leave them and go to the game alone. He finally consented, and walked away; the rest of the crowd started off to the game... and to battle.

CHAPTER IV

The Dodgers Seek Revenge

THE boys from St. Mary's divided themselves into small groups to approach the field from different directions. There was no fence around the ball field; the teams playing were of the "sand lot" league, two of the well known freelance teams of the neighborhood, backed by local business concerns. As the boys reached the baseball diamond, they took places among the waiting spectators along the baselines. The game was about to start; but as Red and the other boys looked around the field, they could find none of the Dodgers.

"They're not here yet," quietly exclaimed Red to Bill Harte and Jack Clemens.

"Maybe they won't come," suggested Bill.

"Oh, they'll come all right. They're pretty sore," said Jack.

Red looked down the street. "Here comes Steve," he said, and the boys with him turned to see Steve calmly strolling toward the field. "Look who's following him," exclaimed Bill, excitedly. "Don't let them see you watching them." Quickly the boys turned back to the field. "They're Dodgers all right; two of them have

As the boys reached the baseball diamond, they took places among the waiting spectators along the baselines.

Dodgers' jackets," said Jack. "Wonder if Steve knows he's got three of them at his heels."

Bill looked across the field, nudged Jack, and said "There come some more of them out of the alley. Dixon and Small are with them. See if they stay out there on the field. They seem to be looking for us."

"If they're looking for us," said Red, "they'll come right up here."

"Three of them are staying out there," said Jack. "The rest will probably come in here and mix up with the crowd." Then laughing, he added, "The one that tripped Irene Moore is staying out there on the field. It's safer there."

Soon Steve took his place in the crowd about twenty feet down the baseline. He saw his friends and winked at them. "He knows he has been followed," said Bill Harte in a low voice. "He'll stay away from us now to see if they start anything."

Just then the umpire called "Play ball," and immediately there was a general maneuvering among the spectators to secure a full view of the playing field, accompanied by an outburst of unorganized cheers by individuals to encourage their favorite player or team. Red and his friends moved forward eagerly; fight or no fight, they wanted to see the game. They noticed that two of the Dodgers who had followed Steve now took their place right behind him, and that those who had at first stationed themselves in the outfield were now moving in to take their places along the baselines. The boys from St. Mary's, scattered throughout the crowd, knew that they had been seen and that some of them were being watched by the Dodgers. Following Bill Harte's plan of battle, they had worked themselves out to the first line of the crowd along the field, so that they could cut across the diamond to whatever point trouble might start.

For a few innings, keeping a furtive eye on the Dodgers, the boys watched the game. Then Jack Clemens noticed three of the Dodgers move apart from the crowd, whisper together for a few moments, and then with a laugh, separate and return to their places along the first baseline. One of them joined the two who were standing right behind Steve Nolan. Jack nudged Bill. "They're after Steve. Listen," he said quietly. The boys cautiously moved closer to where Steve was standing, and heard snatches of the conversation being carried on by the three young toughs behind him. It was evident that they were trying to provoke Steve.

"Naw, he ain't a barber," the boys heard one of the three say. "He's just got his old man's pants on; the old man is a street cleaner and today is Sunday." Red saw by the intent look on Steve's face that he was listening, too. Then he heard the "secret call" of the boys from St. Mary's school, the whistle of the wood pee-wee, adopted last year at Camp St. Mary and diligently practiced until most of the boys were proficient in imitating it. A lad out on the sidewalk behind the first baseline had whistled, and now merely pointed guardedly in the direction of Steve and the three dodgers, as six or seven pairs of eyes looked in the direction of the pee-wee call. Then here and there around the field the call was nonchalantly repeated; the signal that St. Mary boys were watching

"Don't you like black and white shoes?" came to the ears of Red and his friends, as one of the three Dodgers deliberately pointed to Steve's footwear and laughed in derision.

"Yeh," answered one of the trio, "they look good with black eyes."

"Oh, but he's got blue eyes, lovely, big blue eyes," added the third, with a poor attempt at mimicking a girl's voice.

Steve pretended not to hear them, but Red and Jack and Bill knew that he was not missing a single word of his tormentors. One of them was smoking a cigarette, and Red saw him blow the smoke so that the slight breeze would carry it right into Steve's face. Steve, alert to what was going on behind him, calmly shifted his position. Then two of the boys behind him whispered, glanced at the cigarette, and exchanged places. The one with the cigarette stepped directly behind Steve; the other raised his hand straight up over his head. There was a quick stir among the Dodgers in the crowd, and Red sent the pee-wee call out again; this time, not so much of a signal as a command. He saw that the boys from St. Mary's were alert and waiting; trouble was about to start.

Steve was grinning now; he had heard the St. Mary signal and saw the boys glance toward him as Red furtively motioned in his direction. Steve guessed that the boys with Red must have overheard the baiting that was going on behind him and were not waiting for the "overt act" which would start the battle.

There was silence now from the boys behind Steve. It was like the calm that precedes a storm. Without turning his head, Steve could see, from the corner of his eye, that the Dodgers had shifted their position a little to the left. He wondered how his clothes would look after the fight. He glanced down at his spotless white trousers and saw the fingers of a hand holding a burning cigarette slowly moving toward his own left hand hanging idly at his side. Instantly he sensed their plan; an "accidental" burn was to start the fight. Steve stood perfectly still. He too had made a plan.

The cigarette touched his hand, and Steve went into action. He shot his left elbow up behind him like an engine piston and caught one of the Dodgers squarely under the chin; then all in one motion he lashed out sideways, a powerful straight left that, with all of Steve's weight behind it, landed flush on the jaw of the Dodger standing next to him, the one who had burned his hand. The two trouble hunters, taker by such sudden and painful surprise, were knocked sprawling, as Steve whirled and whipped another punch into the face of the third. Before the first two could regain their feet, Red Devlin and Bill Harte were standing over them, and the rest of the boys of both crowds were streaking across the diamond or around behind the crowd along the baselines, eager for the fray. The St. Mary boys reached the scene first and before the adults near them realized what was going on, Steve, Bill, and Red, reinforced by Jack Clemens and the rest of their friends, were meeting the rush of the Dodgers with the ferocity of wild cats. The sudden excitement behind the lines seemed about to interrupt the game as some of the substitute players rushed from their benches to the fighting boys, but the fight had scarcely got well underway before the fighters found themselves being tossed right and left by a score of men who had dashed from the sidelines and hastily put a stop to the miniature riot. In less than a minute's time the two belligerent groups stood about fifteen feet apart, closely guarded by the adult peacemakers, and anxious to resume the battle.

"What the dickens is the matter with you fellows?" demanded one of the men, whom the boys recognized as Mr. Langley, a detective who lived in the neighborhood, and who happened to be one of the crowd watching the game.

"Aw, they started it," exclaimed one of the Dodgers. He pointed at Steve. "That guy started it," said one of those who had been trying to provoke a fight with Steve. "We were just standing there behind him, and he turned and poked us."

"You're lying," spoke up a youngster, not more than ten years old. "I saw you burn his hand with a cigarette.

I heard you picking on him too before you did it. You were looking for trouble."

A man standing next to Steve grabbed his hands and examined them. He saw the burn. "Yep," he called, "he's got a burn here all right. I heard them wisecracking, but..."

Steve interrupted. "I saw and heard him too," he said, glaring at the Dodgers. "So I let him go through with it and then let him have it; and that sap next to him, too, and if they want any more of it, I'll give it to them now or any other time." Steve quickly stepped out from the crowd. "C'mon," he challenged, "one at a time or the three of you." He was not bluffing; he relied on his boxing ability to make good his challenge.

Mr. Langley's eyes shone with admiration of Steve's spunk. He felt sure that none of the Dodgers would fight Steve then and there, and he wanted to show them up for the cowards he knew them to be.

"Well, go ahead," he said scornfully, "step out here, any one of you. We'll see that nobody helps him." Unconsciously one of Steve's three victims put his hand gently to his jaw. Those who had seen Steve hit him laughed aloud. Officer Langley grabbed the boy by the arm. "C'mon, you. Do you want any more?"

The Dodger tore himself from the officer's yielding grip. "No. I don't want to fight him," he muttered.

"Yellow!" exclaimed Mr. Langley, with a sneer. "What about you?" he asked, pointing to Dixon, who by this time had joined the rest of his crowd.

"I'll get him some other time," the boy answered, and the crowd roared with laughter.

"Also yellow," snapped Mr. Langley. "Hard boiled, aren't you? Like an egg—all yellow inside. Now you and your gang get out of here, and get out of here quick." The Dodgers shuffled away, whipped. Then Mr. Langley turned to Steve and his friends. "And you fellows stay right here in one crowd where I can keep an eye on you," he commanded, with a laugh.

Steve silently watched the gang depart; his fine face hardened, and his eyes showed angry glints. He was thinking of the threat to "get him some other time." That seemed to leave the affair unsettled. Steve didn't like to postpone a fight if a fight was necessary. He looked toward Red and Bill and saw them watching him. Then he glanced toward the detective, at this moment watching the game.

"Did you hear what that guy said?" he asked Red.

"Yes, but he was bluffing. That was Dixon," answered Red. "He doesn't want any more from you. I noticed he was pretty late getting to the fight."

"Anyhow, Steve," added Bill, "you're all dolled up. You can't take a chance in that layout you're wearing. We'll see them again some other time."

Steve was watching the departing Dodgers. They stopped near an alley and seemed to be making some plan. "Look at them. They're in a huddle down there now. Something is up." The boys looked around. Most of the St. Mary boys, feeling that the fight was over, had taken their places in the crowd to watch the game. As the detective had warned them, they kept, more or less, in one loose group. Jack Clemens strolled over to Steve and Bill and Red. The quartet watched the enemy group glancing excitedly now and then toward the ball field. Soon the attention of other St. Mary boys was attracted to the Dodger gang, and they took their places with their leaders.

"Let's help them out," suggested Jack Clemens as he glanced toward Mr. Langley, now evidently interested only in the ball game. Jack called to him one of the smaller boys who had seen the fight, Sonny Fields, a fourth grade pupil at St. Mary's and a friend of Jack's young brother. "Listen, Sonny," he said to the lad, "and get this straight. Take a walk down to that crowd. You saw the guy that said he'd get Steve some other time. Tell him that Steve will meet him right where he is now at eight o'clock tonight, if he wants to fight it out, and that, if any of the rest of his gang want to come, tell them just to say how many will be there and we'll meet them with the same number, and fight them man for man. Get that?"

"Sure," answered Sonny, and started off.

The St. Mary boys watched him approach the group, but didn't notice that Mr. Langley had walked over toward them and now stood directly behind them. They saw the boys down the street stop talking to listen to their messenger. Then they saw Small suddenly step from the crowd and, with a vicious slap, knock the unsuspecting boy down. With a wild yell of rage, and before Mr. Langley could speak, Red and his crowd tore down the street, followed by a score of other boys who were eager to see the interrupted battle renewed.

"They hit Sonny Fields," called back one of the boys, as like an avenging army, hot anger lending speed to their feet, the boys from St. Mary's raced to battle. The Dodgers saw them coming, turned and ran for their lives. Some turned down the alley; others dashed into nearby gangways, but after them, wherever they went, sped boys from Red's crowd, intent on avenging the cowardly attack on their little messenger.

The erstwhile peacemakers turned to see what caused all the noise and excitement. "They hit that little kid," announced Mr. Langley. "And they'll get theirs now and no mistake. It will serve them right. They've got it coming to them."

He moved hurriedly toward some automobiles parked down the street; perhaps he could catch up with the boys in a car.

Mr. Langley was right; the Dodgers that afternoon did get "theirs." They paid full price for Small's slap at Sonny Fields. Red Devlin and Steve, fleetest of foot, were out in the lead. They paid no attention to any of the fleeing boys but Small and the fellow running with him, Dixon.

"We'll get them, Steve," gasped Red. "Let the rest of the fellows take care of the others." Dixon and Small were running straight down the street. They turned and saw the two who were pursuing them, and fear increased their pace.

"The guy with the sweater on is mine," exclaimed Steve. "He wanted me."

"That's Dixon," snapped Red. "Those are the two that jumped me when I was alone. Jack and Bill trimmed them; now it's our turn."

Dixon and Small turned down an alley leading to their own neighborhood, but Red and Steve tore right after them. The two Dodgers grasped hands as they ran, afraid to be caught alone. The distance between the two pairs of boys quickly grew shorter; the Dodgers were tiring. Soon only a few paces separated them from their pursuers.

"Push 'em over first, Red," cried Steve. "That's the only way to stop them." Then both boys, within arm's reach of the fleeing pair, lunged forward and gave the two Dodgers violent shoves that sent them staggering and stumbling until, losing their balance, they fell face forward in the alley.

"Now get up and take it," commanded Red. "There's nobody here to stop us now."

"You wanted me some other time?" Steve cried to Dixon. "Well, here I am. Get up and fight.."

Neither of the Dodgers showed any inclination to get up from the ground.

Steve's face went white with anger and contempt. "I've never hit a kid when he was down," he exclaimed hotly, "but, you big four-flusher, if you don't get up and fight, I'll kick you all over the alley." He reached down to pull Dixon to his feet; the coward came up with his face hidden in his folded arms. Steve quickly backed him up against a fence and shot a stiff left to his unprotected middle. Down came Dixon's hands, and before he could raise them again, Steve's fists beat a rapid tattoo on his face, each punch carrying all the strength Steve could put into it. Steve saw that Dixon would make no attempt to fight, so placing both of his hands against the shoulders of the cringing bluffer, he pinned him against the fence long enough to say, "Well, you saw me later. How did you like it? Did you get enough?"

Dixon meekly answered "Yes."

Steve quickly flung him aside and turned to see how Small was faring. He saw Red struggling to get Small to his feet, but the fallen coward literally hugged the ground.

"Get up, tough guy," ordered Red, puffing with exertion. "It will be a long time before you hit one of St. Mary's little kids again." Steve slipped behind Small, grabbed his shoulders and lifted him from the ground. Before he could fall back again, Red swung his open hand across Small's face, a stinging crack. "That's what you did to Sonny Fields," barked Red angrily. "Now..."

Just then the boys heard a wild yell and a rush of feet at the mouth of the alley. They turned and saw coming at them at top speed down the alley two more of the Dodger crowd. These fellows had evidently escaped from their pursuers and were on their way home. Though Steve and Red were already tired from their long run and tussle with Dixon and Small, they had no intention of running away. One of the newcomers snatched up a rock and, as he approached close to the two boys who stood facing them and the two just getting to their feet behind them, he viciously threw it at Red. Red jumped aside, and the rock caught Dixon full on the side of the head. He sank back to the ground, punished accidentally but well by one of his own crowd.

Only the eagerness of Red and Steve to thrash thoroughly any Dodger who dared face them gave new strength to their tired muscles as they leaped into combat with the new arrivals. The two Dodgers tore into Red and Steve with all the fury of enraged savages, but the two St. Mary boys fought back just as furiously. Steve's opponent, unable after the first rush to cope successfully with the clever young boxer's shifting, ducking, counter- and cross-punches, and short distance jabs, suddenly threw his arms around Steve, tripped him, and threw him to the ground. Over and over rolled the two, the young tough trying to pin Steve on his back, and Steve struggling to free himself and get to his feet.

Red was battling toe to toe with the other Dodger, and Small and Dixon were up on their feet and eager to join their comrades in the hope of thrashing the two who had just whipped them. Suddenly Steve thought of his spotless white clothes now being ripped and smeared with the dirt of the alley, and, overcome with wild anger at the cause of it all, in a tremendous burst of strength, broke his antagonist's hold and jumped to his feet, just in time to swing at Small and knock him down again. Red and his opponent were badly bruised and bleeding; Red was having a tough time with his man.

Suddenly a police squad car swung into the alley and came at top speed toward the fight. The car slid to a stop, and out jumped two uniformed policemen. Behind the squad car came another containing Mr. Langley. In a borrowed car, he had been scouring the neighborhood, breaking up fights, and looking for Steve and Red. The Dodgers, seeing the policemen, started to run, but the officers collared them before they had gone ten paces.

"Into the car with you fellows," ordered one of them. "You too," he angrily exclaimed to Red and Steve.

"Why," began Red, "we...." Then he saw Mr. Langley smiling at him and Steve.

"Go with them, boys," he said pleasantly. Then addressing one of the policemen, he said, "Tom, put those hoodlums in this car and ride with us. Let those kids go with Dan."

CHAPTER V

Major Williams
Takes Charge

BY THE time the policemen and their prisoners arrived at the station, Red Devlin and Steve Nolan had convinced the driver of the squad car that the Dodgers were responsible for the afternoon's trouble. In Mr. Langley's car the Dodgers were having a bad time. The detective, who had seen Small slap Sonny Fields, laughed in derision at the battered quartet in the car.

"You thought you were tough, didn't you?" he said with a sneer. "You're tough enough to pick on little boys, but when boys of your own size went after you, you scattered like a pack of curs." The Dodgers kept a sullen silence; it was all they could do.

Red and Steve were still trying to wipe off some of the signs of battle on their faces and clothes when the car drew up before the station. Red's face was badly bruised and his lip was slightly bleeding, although a look at the boy whom he had been fighting had already told the officers who had been the winner of the interrupted fight. The policemen herded the boys into the station, and Captain Meadows rose, frowning, to greet them.

"What's this?" he asked, and Mr. Langley told the Captain the whole story. The Captain looked closely at Red and Steve. "Go back to the washroom and fix yourselves up," he said. Then he turned to the four Dodgers. "So you went to the ball game looking for trouble, hey?" He nodded his head slowly. "Well," he continued, "you found it. Put them downstairs."

When the boys were out of hearing distance, he said to the Sergeant: "Get their parents over here and call up Major Williams." The officers smiled. "Major Williams was in the other day," he said to Mr. Langley and his fellow officers. "You know that he has recently become interested in wayward boys, and he asked me to let him know when we got a few typical specimens for him to work on. We'll give him the entire Dodger outfit." Then, turning to the Sergeant, he added: "Get the Major and the parents of those fellows over here about seven o'clock."

As Red and Steve returned from the washroom, two of the officers who had arrested Bo Wickers at the Engine House earlier in the day came into the station and recognized Red. They looked at him in surprise, for there was little resemblance in the boy that stood before them now to the spic and span youngster of a few hours ago.

"Well, what happened to you?" asked one of them, smiling. Red told his story in as few words as he could.

"Are you under arrest?" asked the policeman. The boys and the officers looked toward the Captain.

"This young redhead," said the officer to Captain Meadows, "is the lad that caught the crook at the Engine House this morning."

Red smiled; it was evident that he expected the Captain to say something complimentary to him. Captain Meadows, however, merely said coldly, "We released that fellow; he has learned his lesson." Then with a gesture toward Red and Steve, he said to the policemen, "Now I'll release these fellows if you think they've learned *their* lesson."

"Well, Captain," said one of the arresting officers, "I think they have." The Captain shook a warning finger at the boys as he said, "There's nothing heroic in street fighting, boys. If you have any idea that there is, you may go downstairs with those other fellows and think it over. Officer Langley could have taken care of the fellow who hit that boy, and he wouldn't have made such a mess of it as you did. You may go now." With that Captain Meadows entered his office and closed the door.

Steve's eyes opened wide in surprise as he stared at the closed door; Red's cheeks slowly flushed; he was humiliated and confused. The policemen laughed.

"The Captain's right, boys," said Mr. Langley. "He knows how you feel. He locked the other fellows up until their parents come to take them home. You see, it is his job and ours to maintain law and order. Street fighting is disorderly conduct. You can't expect Captain Meadows to approve of that."

Steve looked at Red and smiled. "I guess the Captain's right, Red," he said. Then he surveyed his torn and soiled clothes. "But I can't go home like this," he exclaimed. "The only decent thing I have now is my cap. That fell off when the fight began in the alley. It's still clean—almost," he said, as he examined it closely.

The policemen laughed. "There's nothing you can do about it, buddy," said one of them. "Why can't you go home like that? They've seen you like that before, haven't they?"

"Yes," answered Steve. "But today we've got company. Special company."

"Oh, well, come along," exclaimed the officer. "We'll drop you at your homes. We'll square things at home for you," he added, laughing.

Steve and Red lived on the same street, about half a block from each other. When the police car drove up to the Nolan home, the boys saw that the news of the chase had reached their neighborhood. Some of the St. Mary boys and many other youngsters were gathered in small groups in the block all discussing the affair. None of them knew what had happened to Red and Steve. Now from all directions they raced to the car, all eager to find out how their two fleet-footed friends had fared, and to tell them how thoroughly the St. Mary boys routed and whipped the Dodgers who were caught before they could get away.

Red's spirits rose as he saw himself and Steve the center of interest, but, while he enjoyed his present prominence, he was eager to get home. While Steve and one of the officers were alighting from the car, Red slipped out through the door on the opposite side. "We chased two of them," he hurriedly explained to the boys nearest him, "and caught them in an alley. We licked them, and then two more of them jumped us. We were licking them too, when the squad came. They stopped us and took us all to the station. Mr. Langley spoke up for us, and they pinched the other four and let us go." With that explanation he ran across the street and down to his home.

The excitement in front of the house attracted the attention of the Nolan family, sitting, with their guest, in the front room. Steve's father and brother hastened out on the porch to meet Steve and the policeman coming up the steps.

"He's not arrested," laughingly explained the officer. By this time Miss West, Steve's future sister-in-law, joined the group, and was present to hear the officer continue. "He took the part of a little boy who was slapped by a young rough-neck. When we got to them, there were four of the other crowd to this lad and his partner. They had licked two and were working on the other two. Your boy here has done nothing for you to be ashamed of. He'll give you the details." With a wave of his hand, he returned to the car and the two policemen drove away.

With this introduction, Steve told as quickly as possible the details of the fight and the scene at the police station. The Nolans had learned from the boys in the neighborhood that there had been a fight in which Steve had taken a principal part, and they were anxiously and somewhat angrily awaiting his return. As he told his story, Miss West's eyes glowed with admiration. She liked Steve, and she knew that her fiance was proud of his younger brother. Now she saw that he had good reason to be proud. As Steve finished the story, she threw her arms around him. "Steve, you're a darling," she exclaimed, and planted a kiss firmly on the embarrassed boy's blushing cheek. Steve wriggled himself loose and, amid the family's hearty laughter, hastened to excuse himself. "I got to get cleaned up again," he said, as he dashed upstairs to his room.

In the Devlin home, however, Red was not faring so well. His family also knew from Bobbie and the boys that there had been a fight, and when Red hurried through the gang-way and into the kitchen, the whole family was there to receive him.

"Well?" asked his mother sternly. Red looked from his mother to his dad, then to Arthur and Bobbie. Rita was already brushing Red's trousers. Red saw that they had learned something of the afternoon's happenings.

"One of the Dodger crowd hit Sonny Fields, one of the kids in Bob's room. Then we chased them: Steve Nolan and I..." Red glanced meaningly at his father, for he knew that Steve was well liked by Mr. Devlin. "Steve and I took after the kid that did the hitting and another fellow. We caught them and socked them plenty. Then two other Dodgers came on the run, and we had to fight them, too." Red saw Arthur grinning at him. A flush of anger darkened his face. "Well, we did," he insisted. "Then the police came down the alley and stopped us. They let us go because we were in the right," he stated emphatically. "Then they brought us home."

"You look as though the police just stopped you in time," said his father, smiling.

"Good thing they rescued you," added Arthur, teasing.

"Go change your clothes and fix yourself up a bit," said his mother kindly. "Supper will be ready in a few minutes."

As Red started for the bathroom, Bobbie asked solicitously, "Were you losing, Red?"

Red whirled around, but before he could answer, his mother said, "Now, Bobbie, let Red alone." Suddenly the unsuspected truth broke on Red; his family thought that the policemen had rescued him from a severe beating.

"What?" he almost shouted. "Losing? Say, those Dodgers are down at the station now. Go down and take a look at them. Why..." he began, but his mother interrupted him.

"Never mind, Frank," she said gently. "Go and fix up a bit." She shook her head. "I'm afraid that you'll be a sorry looking boy Wednesday night at the graduation exercises."

Red's mouth flew open in surprise. Wednesday night. Graduation. He had not thought of that. He touched his face with his hand. Then he hastened to the mirror in the bathroom. What he saw made him share his mother's fears.

While the Devlins were at supper, the telephone rang and was answered by Mr. Devlin. "Why, no," the family heard him say in answer to the caller's question. "Red is all right." Then a moment's silence. "Oh, no," Mr. Devlin continued. "They brought him home just to save them the embarrassment of walking through the streets." Another moment. Then a laughing, "No, no. They're all right. Thanks for calling…Not at all; they did what any manly boys would have done. Yes. Good-bye." Mr. Devlin returned to the table laughing.

"Mr. Fields, that little boy's dad, called up to see how you were, Red," he said. "He heard that you and Steve were so badly beaten up by those other fellows that the policemen had to bring you home in a car."

Red laid down his knife and fork in disgust. "Now, who started that?" he asked. Arthur laughed gayly.

"That's a good one," he exclaimed. "That story will spread like wildfire around here. There'll be some tall explaining to do around the school tomorrow, Red."

Then the telephone rang again. This time somebody wanted to talk to Rita.

"Oh, hello, Irene," the family heard Rita say. There was a short silence. Red, blushing, stared straight down at his plate. Then they heard Rita laugh lightly. "I should say not, Irene," she said. "Mr. Fields heard that, too. It's not true at all. The boys didn't want to walk home all messed up, so that policeman did a little taxi service for them; that's all." Then there was a short silence, a silence that to Red seemed endless. But Rita, laughing, said: "Surely. We'll both be at school tomorrow. You can see Frank then." By this time all the Devlins but Red were smiling. Rita returned, saying, "Frank, Irene's mother saw you and Steve in the car on your way home and just couldn't wait to see if you had been arrested. Mr. Moore was at the game and saw the fight start. He said that maybe you were badly hurt, but not arrested. So they had Irene call. She said that she was glad you were not hurt badly."

"Dad," asked Red, pleadingly. "Can't I stay home from school tomorrow?"

"That will only make it look worse, Frank," answered his father. "The boys will have the true story. You fought in a good cause. What difference does it make whether your face shows the signs of the fight?"

"Aw, I'm not going to have anybody think that I got the worst of it," said Red sullenly.

"You'll have Steve with you, Red," said Arthur, encouragingly. At Arthur's remark, Red's face brightened up noticeably. Then he heard his father say, "Red, you pay too much attention to what people think. You simply must learn to do what you think is right regardless of what others think. You can't please everybody. I've told you that before."

Red said nothing. For a long time, his father had been quite concerned about Red's sensitiveness to criticism or ridicule. Red could not answer his father's arguments; neither could he steel himself to bear manfully teasing or raillery, good natured or otherwise.

While the evening meal at Devlin's was in progress, Major Williams, U.S.A., and Captain Meadows were discussing with some of the parents of the arrested Dodgers plans to take the boys off the streets and give them a chance to become decent, law-abiding citizens. Major Williams had come out of the World War with one arm missing and an enviable collection of decorations and citations for valor. A general favorite among the men under his command, his thoughts, when peace came, returned to the boys of his home city. He was in life a successful attorney, and had many times, at the request of the Holy Name Society, defended in court first offenders whom, the Holy Name Big Brothers could testify, always found in him not only a capable attorney, but a genuine friend.

Recently his interest in younger boys was awakened by a chance remark of Judge Francis, the kindly jurist who presided over the Boys' Court. "If some fairy god-mother would take these lads out of the gutter and off the streets," the Judge said, "fewer of them would be coming into court. They have the wrong kind of heroes; they see cheap crooks sneering at the law and making easy money; but they just don't see, in their inexperience, the end of the trail; the misery, the broken hearts of those who love them, and the long years behind steel bars. They see the glamour of the unarrested hoodlums' adventures; they don't see the dreary, grey stretch of years behind prison walls when the adventure goes wrong, and the law closes in upon the wrongdoer."

And now Major Williams was waiting to meet four such youths. "They belong to a gang of young toughs who are just about ripe for plucking by the police," said Captain Meadows. "Tonight is the first time we have had any of them in the station, although we have been watching them and warning them for some time. Now, we can let their case, disorderly conduct, go up to the judge, and have them officially paroled to you, or I will turn them over to you now, without booking and in that way keep their names off the police records. I have explained these things to their parents. What do you say, Major?"

Major Williams looked at the parents and saw in their faces an unspoken plea to keep their boys out of court.

"Why, Captain," began the Major, "I'd like to let these people go home feeling that the worst is over. I'll take the boys as they are."

The Captain sent for the boys. They shuffled into his office, and their parents gasped as they saw the battered faces and torn clothes of the now thoroughly subdued quartet.

"Boys, this is Major Williams," said the Captain. "He has asked me to give you another chance. I'm going to turn you over to him. I'm going to turn your whole club over to him. Play the game squarely with Major Williams and you'll never regret it. You have had a taste of cell life. Think it over. The way your crowd has been heading leads to months and years of it. Follow Major Williams and you'll never see the inside of a cell-door again. Now, what do you want? Major Williams tonight, or a trial in the morning?"

"Major Williams," the boys answered quickly. They had talked about the possibility of being sent away while they were in the cells downstairs.

Major Williams smiled. Then the smile left his face, and he asked: "Which of you slapped that little boy?"

Three pairs of eyes looked at Small, whose bruised face crimsoned with shame. "I did," he muttered.

"Do you know where he lives?" asked the Major.

"No," answered Small.

"No what?" snapped the Police Captain.

"No, sir," hurriedly corrected Small.

"Find out," said the Major, "then go to his home and apologize to him."

"Go to his home?" asked Small, visibly frightened.

"Yes," answered the Major. "Why not? Don't you think you owe him an apology ?"

"I'll get beat up," muttered Small.

"Then take these lads with you," suggested the Major, with a trace of a smile.

Instantly a chorus of protest was raised. "Nothing doing," exclaimed one of the four. "We didn't hit the kid." Then Charlie Russell, one of the two who attempted to rescue Dixon and Small, only to find himself receiving a similar dose from Steve's trained fists, spoke up frankly.

"We don't want any more of that St. Mary crowd, mister. They chased our gang all over the neighborhood this afternoon and licked us plenty. I'm for staying away from them until this thing blows over."

The Major smiled at Russell's frank admission of defeat. He could do something with that boy, he thought.

"Then you admit you're afraid of them?" he asked.

Russell put his hand up to his face and grinned. "Well, I had enough of them. I must have picked out the best fighter in the whole crowd. Boy, how he could slap them in!"

Well, I'll tell you why you are afraid of them," said the Major. "You know, deep down in your hearts, that you respect them. You know that your crowd was in the wrong, and that the St. Mary boys were in the right. A fellow always fights best when he's fighting for a good cause. Now, that unfair slap that started this thing must be squared. Until it is, I think that the boys from St. Mary's will be on the look-out for every one of you, and you particularly," he said as he placed his hand on Small's shoulder. "You can go home with your parents now. Tomorrow night, I want to meet all the members of your club. Where can I find them?"

"We meet in our basement," said Russell. "I'll have them all there."

Major Williams gave Russell his card. "Well, you call for me at 7:30 and take me there. I have some plans that I want to discuss with you."

CHAPTER VI

In Disgrace

RED spent the evening at home putting the last touches to a model airplane. His hobby for airplane construction gave him an excuse to hide his black eye and puffed lip from the boys on the street. He was still busy with his work when his father appeared and suggested—and Red knew that suggestions from his father were almost the same as commands—that a good night's rest would be the best preparation for tomorrow's work at school. Red's plea to be allowed to remain at home tomorrow met with a very definite veto; so Red, somewhat sulky, went to his room. For a long time he lay in bed wide awake, turning over in his mind the events of the last ten days.

If only that Dodger had not tripped Irene, thought Red. But Father Walsh said defending her was the manly thing. If only Sister had not spoken of him as a little gentleman....If only Irene's father had kept that old glove...But it was a dandy glove, soft and smooth; all the kids wanted to use it. He thought of Bo Wickers and how he had caught him, but the recollection of Lieutenant Carroll's coolness toward him took all the joy out of that memory. Red frowned. Well, the

Lieutenant wasn't his father…He didn't have to mind him…."I'm not a baby; I can take care of myself," Red told the darkness of his room. Then his conscience told him that the Lieutenant was right; supposing his father did find out about that crap game in the alley…"Double-crosser."…How Red hated that word now. He thought of what his father said at the telephone during supper. "They did what any manly boys would have done." Manly boys…Red saw himself again in the alley. His father would surely be disappointed…and angry. Well, he wouldn't get caught like that again….Alley rats…. What a fight that was in the alley this afternoon…. Wonder who told Sonny Fields's father that he had to be taken home by the policemen….Tomorrow….Red knew that he had to go to school in the morning. He touched his eye and swollen lip. Well, it might not be so bad in the morning. Anyhow, they'd believe Steve. Steve never lost a fight…Funny about Steve….Never looks for a fight…seldom gets sore; never, in a game…. But, boy, when somebody starts anything with him! Red smiled and found his swollen lip feeling stiff…. Maybe if he put some more ice on it….The house was silent; everybody had gone to bed. No use getting up now. Oh, heck, let it go….Red breathed a Hail Mary, turned over on his side, and in a minute was fast asleep. He didn't know that a greater trial was awaiting him on the morrow.

The next morning Red awakened and hastened to the mirror in his room. "Well, it doesn't look so bad," he told himself doubtfully. Marks of the fight were clearly visible.

Steve was waiting for him in front of his house. Red looked at him in surprise. Not a mark of yesterday's fighting was to be seen. "Boy, that's some eye," Steve's greeting. "Is your lip sore?"

"No," answered Red, "but you haven't a mark on your whole face."

Steve laughed. "No, but take a look at my arms," he said, as he shoved back first one sleeve and then the other. "Black and blue from catching and blocking his swings." Red whistled. Steve looked at Red's face again and said, "That lad you had must have been a pretty good battler. Was he?"

"I'll say so," exclaimed Red, glad to agree with Steve on that point.

"But he looked a mess," said Steve, "when those coppers came. You had him beaten." Red's chest swelled with pride. When Steve told that to the kids, they'd know who won the fight all right.

When the two boys reached the corners to which they were assigned as traffic officers, they found some of their school friends waiting to hear the details of their part in yesterday's fight. Red was embarrassed a bit as the boys peered intently at his disfigured face. He answered their questions gruffly, and then asked one of his admirers to take charge of his corner for the day. "I want to go over to the school yard for something," explained Red. The boys smiled. They knew that Red's real reason for wanting to leave his corner was his fear that somebody might think that he had been worsted in the fight. When Red reached the yard, everybody seemed to be talking about yesterday's trouble. The boys who had taken an actual part in the chase were telling others all about it. Red and Steve were the only ones who had come to the attention of the police. That they had the honor of a ride in the squad car from the station to their homes, "because they were in the right," made them the true heroes of the day. Of course, it was unanimously conceded that St. Mary's gallant boys had routed the enemy with great credit to themselves and great disaster to the Dodgers. There was but one question, a big question, in the minds of the boys. And that was: what would Father Walsh have to say about the whole affair?

As the boys expected, Father Walsh came into the eighth grade room shortly after the morning's work had started. Without wasting words, he called upon Jack Clemens to act as spokesman and tell him just what had happened. After listening, without comment, to Jack's story, he said: "Well, now, let this be the last of the affair. St. Mary's boys are not rowdies. We want no street fighting." The boys were greatly relieved to see that Father Walsh was not too displeased with them. Their relief, however, was soon cut short by Father Walsh's saying sternly, "And there is another thing I wish to talk to you boys about." He continued slowly, "I want all the boys of this class who played or attended the ball game last Friday to remain after school. The patrol boys will return to this room as soon as the school children get across their corners. I'll be over right after dismissal. Wait for me." With his hand on the door-knob, he turned and added, "And, by the way, see that all the baseball uniforms and equipment are returned not later than tomorrow."

Shortly after the patrol boys returned to join the boys waiting in the classroom, Father Walsh appeared. He saw that the boys had no inkling of why he had detained them, and by the solemn silence that greeted his entrance into the room, he knew that they had decided the matter was rather serious. He looked over the score of boys before him. "Everybody here?" he asked. "Yes, Father," the boys answered. Father Walsh then took a letter from his pocket and said, "I want to read you a letter I received this morning. I have no reason to doubt the truth of what it says. Indeed, because I know the writer very well, I have every reason to believe that what it says is true." The boys' faces lit up with keen interest.

The priest looked into the faces of the boys a minute and then began.

"Dear Father," he read, "I think that you should know that some of your eighth graders, and among them, one or two of your school baseball team, were seen a few days ago in company of some of the neighborhood toughs, shooting dice in an alley. They were evidently on their way home from a ball game. As I don't know all of their names, I shall not mention any. More than one of them were smoking. The language of the crowd was the usual gutter type.

Respectfully yours,"

Father Walsh, without looking at the boys, slowly folded up the letter and put it in his pocket. Then he raised his eyes to the boys, most of whom, he saw instantly, were thoroughly surprised. Red's face was crimson, and he looked steadily down at the desk before him. Inwardly he was boiling with anger at what he assumed was Lieutenant Carroll's way of getting even with him for his insolence.

"Well, there you are, boys," Father Walsh said solemnly. "Just a few days before you leave St. Mary's. I'm not going to ask which of you this letter concerns. I just want to say that I'm keenly disappointed in you. Evidently I don't know you so well as I thought I did. I was rather proud of you. The person who wrote this letter to me knew that. It comes from a very good friend of mine and of yours. I thought I could count on all of you to be an honor to St. Mary's, but some of you have certainly double-crossed me."

"But, Father," began Steve Nolan, with some show of indignation. Father Walsh, however, did not wait. Without another word, he turned and left the room. He knew that he could count on the good will of the majority to detect and properly rebuke the guilty ones. For a moment, nobody spoke. Then spirited declarations of innocence broke the silence, all but the guilty ones eager to prove a convincing alibi.

"We weren't in any alley," declared Steve. "We came back to the school to tell Sister we won, Jack Clemens, Bill Rogers, Tom Burke, and I."

"Well," said Bill Harte, "Gavin and I went home with Mr. Jordan. We stopped to get a 'malted,' but that's all."

All of the team but Red stoutly declared and proved their innocence.

The boys then noticed that Red was silent. He met their inquiring looks with a dark scowl. How about you, Red?" asked Steve quietly.

Before Red could answer, Clyde White exclaimed with a laugh, "Red was with us. He wasn't smoking or shooting dice. Red's a little gentleman. Didn't Sister say so?"

Red blushed even more deeply at this sally. He whirled on White, and partly in genuine resentment, part chiefly to seize the welcome occasion of changing the course of the discussion, he almost yelled: "That's enough of that, White. You bring that up again and I'll bust you in the nose. You think you're a wise guy, don't you?"

White said nothing, but just kept smiling at Red. He knew that Red was bluffing. Red saw that Bert Stone, too, was grinning at him. It was clear that they were enjoying his discomfiture. Red could almost feel the silence of the other boys behind him, a silence that told him they had guessed the truth. He knew that such conduct on the part of Stone and White had long been known to all the boys in the class. That they should claim that Red had been with them after Friday's game was good grounds for the other boys to assume that he and they were the boys about whom the letter was written. Red's team-mates were plainly surprised. Then the tense silence was broken and there came to Red's burning ears from one of the team the words, spoken quietly and without spirit, "Nice going, Red," and the disappointment and rebuke that they carried with them cut Red to the heart. He realized that his angry attack on Clyde White had not fooled his classmates.

Tears of rage and shame suddenly started to his eyes as he whirled back to his classmates and hotly exclaimed, "Well, what of it? It's none of your business." He was shouting now. "I'll mind my own business and you can mind yours. And you can go over to the Engine House and tell Carroll to mind his own business, too. He wrote that letter." With that, Red stormed out of the classroom, furious with anger and keen humiliation. He could not keep back the tears. He was in disgrace with his team and his classmates, and with Father Walsh, for Red knew that the priest would soon learn the truth. He always did. Red literally ran down the corridor. He wanted to get away from the others, from the school, from everybody. He was struggling to keep back the sobs that rose in his wretched breast. He hurried down the stairs and made for the exit, halfway down the corridor. Just then Father Walsh stepped from the Superior's room in the middle of the hallway. The priest stepped across the corridor to intercept Red's flight, but Red, sobbing aloud, dodged past him and ran out of the building, heedless of Father Walsh's call for him to "wait a minute."

Outside of the school, Red struggled to gain control of himself. He didn't want anybody on the street to see him crying. He shut his lips tightly and wiped the tears from his eyes. Poor Red's world had come tumbling down around his ears. The thought that Lieutenant Carroll, whom he had assumed he could count on to keep things to himself, had reported him to Father Walsh, almost crushed him. Grief gave way to anger as he thought of the Lieutenant. "And he called me a double-crosser," he muttered bitterly. "Then he snitches on me to Father. I'll get even with him for that." He clenched his fists as the desire for revenge surged in his heart. Then he suddenly realized that he was hurrying home with tear stained face. That would never do. He slowed his steps; they must not see that he had been crying. Things were bad enough now.

Back in the classroom things were not going so well with Clyde White and Bert Stone. As soon as Red fled the room, the boys turned their attention to this pair. "Well, what are you going to do about it, you two?" demanded Steve Nolan.

"Do about it?" repeated White, feigning surprise at the question. "Nothing."

"Oh, yes you are," declared Steve firmly. "You're going to Father Walsh right now, and tell him the whole story."

"Tell him yourself," growled Bert Stone, realizing that Steve and the rest of the boys were in dead earnest.

Steve's lip curled in contempt as he looked at Stone and said, "We're wasting time. You fellows are going to do your telling right here and now." Steve turned to Jack Clemens. "Jack, you go and bring Father over here right now. We'll all wait and get this thing over." The faces of the boys brightened; Steve's plan was enthusiastically approved.

"O.K.," laughed Jack, as he hurriedly left the room.

"Nothing doing," exclaimed White, as he too started for the door. A few of the other boys got there before him. One of them was Bill Harte.

"Take it easy; take it easy," warned Bill. "You're getting out of here after you square things with Father Walsh, not before."

"Get out of the way," loudly demanded White, trying to push his way through the guard at the door. Bill's face clouded with anger and disgust. Without a word, he shoved his open hand into White's face and with an angry push, drove White and Stone, just behind him, backward almost to the first row of desks. Then he turned to find that Jack and Father Walsh were standing behind him in the doorway. Jack had found Father Walsh just as he had been about to leave the building.

Father Walsh saw that White and Stone were, in the language of the boys, "on the spot." None of the other boys was within ten feet of them, but now their eyes involuntarily turned from the priest to the two culprits, standing together where Jack's shove had left them.

"Well?" asked Father Walsh sternly, addressing all the boys.

For an instant nobody spoke; then the crisp command came from Steve Nolan. "Do your stuff, you guys."

"That letter was about us," muttered White sullenly.

"Are you telling me this of your own accord?" asked Father Walsh.

White and Stone glanced up to the priest; then their eyes traveled to the group of boys with Steve. "Yes, Father," answered White. Father Walsh knew that he was lying.

"Then why didn't you come to me instead of sending for me to come here?" he asked.

"They wouldn't let us go," answered Stone.

"What?" demanded Steve, stepping out from the other boys. "Say that again." Neither White nor Stone spoke.

"Why did we send for Father?" demanded Steve of White. White caught the angry murmur of his classmates. "To make us tell," he muttered.

"Yes, to make you tell because you said you wouldn't," blazed Steve. "You got Red and the rest of us into trouble and you didn't have the nerve to own up to it."

"Is that true, White?" asked Father Walsh.

"Yes, Father," muttered White.

"Go home," ordered the priest. "And bring your fathers to the rectory tonight or don't come back here again."

The pair left the room, and before Father Walsh could speak to the other boys, Steve exclaimed, "Father, Red doesn't smoke and he doesn't shoot dice. He's not like those guys. You know that. He just happened to be with them and…"

"Steve," interrupted Father Walsh, meaningly, "Red is more than seven years old. Now the rest of you go home. I'm glad this thing is over and I'm glad you settled it yourselves. I knew you would."

With that Father Walsh left the room and a moment later the boys were on their way home. One thing puzzled them. Red indirectly accused Lieutenant Carroll of writing that letter to Father Walsh.

"That's not like the Lieutenant, to do that," maintained Bill Harte.

"But how," asked one of the team, "did Red know that Carroll saw them?"

Their route home took Steve and Jack past the Engine House. They decided to step in and find out if the Lieutenant wrote the letter.

Lieutenant Carroll greeted the boys cheerfully; he had not seen them since the fight with the Dodgers and wanted their version of the affair. When he had heard their story, he asked, "How are things at school?"

"Well," began Steve, "everything is all right now, but we were in trouble with Father Walsh for a while."

"Why?" asked the Lieutenant. "What was wrong?"

"Some of the fellows were smoking and shooting dice in an alley after the game Friday, and Father Walsh found out about it."

Lieutenant Carroll frowned. "What did Father Walsh do about it?" he asked.

"He didn't have to do anything," answered Steve. "He was plumb disgusted. After he left the room we found out who the fellows were. Then we sent for him and made two of them own up to it. Father is sore at them though." Then Steve looked earnestly at the Lieutenant and asked, "Did you know about it, Lieutenant?

The Lieutenant was clearly surprised at the question, but he answered, "Why, yes, I saw them myself. I tried to tell Red Devlin, who was with them, what a fool he was, but he got peeved and walked out of here in a huff."

"Lieutenant," said Steve seriously, "Red thinks that you wrote the letter about it to Father Walsh."

"What's that?" demanded Lieutenant Carroll, surprised. Steve repeated what he had said. "Red's crazy," exclaimed the fireman. "What I had to say about that I said to Red and to nobody else."

"That's about what we figured you would do, Lieutenant," said Steve, as he and Jack laughed with relief. "We'll tell Red that he's wrong."

CHAPTER VII

The Gleaners

CHARLIE RUSSELL had a hard time convincing some of the Dodgers that Major Williams was coming to their club not as a representative of the police, but as a sincere friend. Most of the Dodgers were inclined to look upon any policeman as an enemy to be avoided or outwitted. The four who had just been arrested were looked upon as heroes until their friends learned that the police had just "treated them as kids," merely sending for their parents to take them home with a warning. The older toughs of their acquaintance, their models, reappeared after arrest only when they were "out on bail," or had "beat the rap," or "served their time." The fact that the four Dodgers had been paroled, even though unofficially, to Major Williams couldn't wipe out the other fact that they had been seen being escorted "straight home" by their parents, who kept them in for the rest of the evening. That humiliating march took all the glamour out of their arrest.

When Russell told the Dodgers that the Major was coming to meet all of them tonight to talk over some plans, several of the boys expressed their intention of staying away. It was only by Charlie's enthusiastic insistence that the Major was a "regular fellow," and that there would be no harm in meeting him and listening to what he had to say that he gradually won over to his side the boys who looked upon the Major's coming with suspicion and distrust.

At the meeting that night all the boys were present except Small. The evidence of yesterday's battle was still visible in a few black eyes and bruised faces. The boys waited impatiently for their visitor. A few of them had learned something of Major Williams's war record; now they were anxious to see him and to know what he had to say. Soon an automobile drew up to the curb, and Major Williams, escorted by Charlie Russell, stepped out of the car and came into the basement.

Charlie led Major Williams through the assembled boys to the president's chair behind a battered and soiled table. The Major looked over the boys before him: friendly faces greeted him. Dixon alone, glum and scowling, loitered near the door. "Isn't one of the boys I met last night missing?" asked the Major.

"Yes, sir," answered Russell. "Small is missing; we sent to his house but nobody knows where he went."

"Perhaps," suggested the Major with a smile, "he has gone to square himself with the boy whom he slapped yesterday. I told him to do that."

The boys laughed. "No, he didn't," said one of them. "He'd never do that; at least, not alone."

"He told me he was through with our gang," said another. "He said it would be too tame now."

"Aw, let's forget him, Major," called one of the boys. "Let's get the meeting started. We can do without Small."

"O.K.," exclaimed the Major, with a laugh. "Where is the president ?"

Charlie Russell arose from his chair, stepped up to the table, and under the Major's direction, called the meeting to order. This was the first time any effort had been made to open a meeting of the Dodgers in an orderly manner. Parliamentary law had little place in their meetings. The boys looked on smiling, for it was plain that Charlie Russell was a bit embarrassed. The meeting opened, the Major arose and glanced at his watch. "There's only one or two things I want to say tonight, boys. First, how many of you have ever been to camp?" Two or three raised their hands. "Well," said the Major, smiling, "I'm going to send you all to camp just six weeks from today, provided that between now and camp time you can show me that you want to be on the square. I don't know much about you, but I'm willing to take a chance. You look like a pretty good crowd. Captain Meadows said that you're getting on the wrong track, the track that leads to trouble and sorrow. But I think we can take care of that all right."

Major Williams noted the glow of excitement that lit up their faces when he mentioned his plan to send them to camp, and knew that, under the skin, they were pretty much like the ordinary run of boys. "How many would like to take a trip to camp for a couple of weeks, all expenses paid?" he asked. Instantly every boy before him shot a hand into the air with loud declarations of their eagerness to take advantage of his offer. Dixon, still standing near the door, remained motionless. The Major decided to ignore his obstinacy, at least for the time.

"Fine," exclaimed the Major. Then he hesitated a moment, looked into the eager faces before him, and said, "Now, there's another matter that I was going to put off until we were better acquainted, but I think I'll put it before you tonight."

"Sure," cried the boys. They needed no longer acquaintance with the tall, smiling ex-officer standing before them; they knew that he was their friend.

"Well," began the Major slowly, "I'd like to bury the Dodgers tonight." He smiled at the puzzled expression on the faces of the boys at this announcement. "I don't like that name. I don't like that name because it seems to say that you are afraid or unwilling to face things as they come, duty, work, responsibility. It's just another name for shirkers, and this country had its fill of shirkers during the World War. We called them not Dodgers or shirkers, but slackers. Most of them were yellow cowards, afraid to fight, and they used every possible excuse and trick to keep out of military service. So, you see, there's something cowardly in the name of your club."

The boys listened with surprise. For two weeks they had argued and wrangled over the selection of a name for their club. One after the other, suggested names had been discussed and discarded for one reason or another. They had been rather proud of their final selection, and now their new friend in less than a minute convinced them that it was not at all a name to be proud of.

"So, Mr. President," continued Major Williams, turning to Russell with a smile, "I would like to make a motion that the present name of this club be dropped and a new one adopted."

Russell looked at Major Williams, a puzzled expression on his face. "Mr. President? Motion?" Charlie was not accustomed to be thus addressed and had no idea of what the Major expected him to do; heretofore discussions concerning matters of interest to the club were carried on by might of voice, the loudest speaker having the floor until somebody else shouted him down. It was evident to Charlie that the Major was waiting for him to do something about changing the name; so he turned from the Major to the boys before him and asked bluntly: "Hey, you guys! Do you want to pick a new name?" A chorus of "Yes" rang out in answer to his question. Then, before anybody else could speak, one of the members jumped to his feet and, ignoring Mr. President, called out "You pick a name, Major." The rest of the boys eagerly made the same plea. Major Williams laughed heartily at the result of his motion.

"Well, boys, you will want a name that begins with a D, because so many of you have a D on your sweaters."

Instantly one of the boys jumped to his feet. "Nix," he cried out. "We'll take the D off. If we don't, people won't know that we've changed our name. We'll get another letter. They don't cost much."

"That's right," came from all sides. "We don't want the D. Some other name, Major." Major Williams motioned for silence. His face grew grave as he looked out for a moment over the heads of the boys. Then he spoke slowly, and the boys listened in silence.

"I have a name. It is the name we used to call some of the men who were in my command over there. They were some of our youngest soldiers, scarcely more than boys. Only a few years older than you fellows. They were strangers to each other before the war, but the trenches made them buddies. Some of them had German names. They were German-Americans and in their hearts was a mixture of the finest qualities of both nations. Somehow or other these lads seemed to understand what many a grey head in those days didn't seem to know. They were absolutely loyal to their country, boys; no fight was too fierce, no hike too long; no trench too close to No Man's Land for them. But they knew that the boys whom war made their enemies were not born in hell. They could fight Germany, but they could not hate the Germans. They were in a fever to get the war over as quickly as they could, of course, and once a fight started, they went into it with high hopes of making that fight the deciding one. They were always the first to volunteer for dangerous service, always the first to crawl out into No Man's Land and do what they could for the wounded and the dying." The Major touched the empty sleeve of his coat. "Two of them brought me in the night I got this. One by one, their bravery led them to their deaths; none of them came home with us. But there is many a German and many an American, private and officer, who was saved from a painful, lonely death out there under the stars by those splendid young heroes. Citations and decorations, for them, were just something to send home to their mothers. They realized that they had a duty not only to their country, but to God, and that their duty to God meant charity to their neighbor, whether he wore the khaki of the United States or the grey of Germany. How well they fulfilled that duty is shown by their military records, and, even better, by the respect and gratitude that still linger in the hearts of the officers and enlisted men who knew them. In a joking way some of the officers used to call them the Gleaners. They were christened 'The Gleaners' one night when they slipped out into No Man's Land after a day of terrible fighting and crawled back to our lines carrying a few badly wounded soldiers whom the hospital corps and Red Cross men had evidently failed to find. They brought me in like that one night, two of them creeping slowly across the field, in and out of shell holes, with me lying unconscious across their backs." The Major's eyes glistened, and in sympathy with him, the eyes of not a few of the boys blinked suspiciously.

"Boys," he continued, "I'm sure that not one of those young fellows would ever do a mean or dishonorable thing, and if you think that your club can honorably carry the name we gave them, I'd be glad to entrust it to you, a sacred trust because of the sacred memories we have of our buddies who bore it in France."

For a moment after the Major finished the boys sat silent and still. Then one of them arose and asked quietly "Major, you mean that you want us to have the same name as those soldiers who died in the war?"

The Major slowly nodded. "I want you not only to take their name, but to honor their memory by being worthy of their name. Some of you, I am told, have begun to slip. You know what I mean; playing truant from school, dodging duty; perhaps a bit of petty stealing now and then; or going out looking for trouble as you did yesterday; making friends of young crooks who think they're hard-boiled, but who would be among the slacker crowd if a new war broke out tomorrow. Tonight, I'd like you to bury all that with your old name, and go out of here after the meeting, carrying in your hearts some of the respect I have for my buddies, the Gleaners, and ready to act from now on as you think they would act if they were in your places. Will you do that?"

As Major Williams was speaking, he noticed a blush here, a pair of downcast eyes there. Guilty consciences. Now, at his question, a loud shout, "Yes, sir," greeted him.

"All right, fellows. A boy can show his devotion to his country's flag by observing her laws in peace time just as well as he can by defending that flag in time of war. Now, before I go I want you to do something in honor of the Gleaners, the boys who are sleeping 'over there.' I want you to stand and repeat with me the oath of allegiance to their flag and yours."

The boys leaped to their feet and heartily joined the Major in the pledge.

"All right, Gleaners," exclaimed the Major with a radiant smile. "I'm going to send you a flag before the next meeting. I must be going now. Get busy on some plans. We must have a baseball team for the summer, and we must get ready for camp. I'll leave you to yourselves now to talk over the death of the Dodgers and the birth of the Gleaners. Goodnight."

Major Williams was hardly out of the basement when Jim Neville slipped off his jacket, calling out "Who's got a knife? I want to get this D off right away." Other boys quickly followed his example and stripped the once prized emblem from their jackets. Dixon, who had not entered whole-heartedly into the spirit of the meeting, now angered the boys by declaring in a sarcastic tone, "Well, I suppose we all have to be goody-goody boys from now on." Before he could be answered, the door opened, and in walked Small.

"Well, where were you?" asked one of the boys with a sneer.

"Outside. Waiting for that guy to get going. What did he want?" asked Small.

"Oh, we got a new club now," answered Dixon, in a tone that was meant to offend the rest of the boys. "Now we are the Gleaners. The Dodgers were too rough. Now we must all be good boys and say our prayers and see what Santa Claus will bring us."

"What do you mean?" asked Small, showing genuine interest.

Charlie Russell arose and in a few words told Small what had taken place and why the new name was chosen. Then he added with spirit, "And now, if you two guys don't want to line up with the rest of us, you can get out and stay out. Dixie there didn't have a word to say to Major Williams's face, and if he has anything to say now that he's gone, he can keep it to himself."

Another boy jumped up and cried out to Dixon and Small, "Yes, and you will give back those two bikes you stole from school the other day, or we'll get them and give them back for you."

"Oh, yeh?" returned Dixon, sneeringly. "What about Nick Perin's glove that you swiped the other day?"

"That goes back tomorrow," answered the boy. "Nick will find it hanging under his coat in the dressing-room, just where it was."

Dixon and Small looked around them. They read the same story in the face of every boy; they had turned to the right.

The tense silence was broken by Russell's demand. "Do you guys intend to go along with us or not? We won't have any more jawing. Say Yes or No."

"No," answered Dixon, and the answer was repeated by Small.

"Then get out before we throw you out!" yelled Russell angrily, as the two boys started for the door.

As they flung open the door, they almost bumped into one of the loafers from the nearby corner. They brushed past him without speaking. The newcomer was about twenty-five years old, known to the boys only as "Lefty," and, as far as any one of them knew, had never earned an honest dollar. He had more than once enlisted the aid of one or more of the Dodgers in some thievery or in disposing of stolen property. The sullen departure of Dixon and Small and the silence of the boys watching them go told Lefty that he had walked in on the end of a quarrel. He looked around at the boys, but nobody spoke to him. "What's wrong with youse guys now?" he asked.

"Aw, we broke up the Dodgers," replied Russell, "and started a new club. Those fellows didn't want to come in on the new one, that's all."

"That's nothing," said Lefty with a laugh. "Now, let's get down to business. Who wants to make a nice piece of easy money tomorrow?"

Nobody answered. Lefty looked around in surprise. "What about you, Mike?" he asked.

"No," came the answer.

"Well, Shorty?" Lefty asked of another boy.

"No," came the answer again.

"You may as well know, Lefty," said Russell, "that we're through with all that line. We got into a mess of trouble yesterday and Major Williams squared it for us. Now he's running the club. He won't stand for anything crooked."

"Major Williams?" repeated Lefty. "Who's he?"

"He's a friend of Captain Meadows," replied Russell. Lefty's eyes opened wide at the name of the police captain. "He picked out a new name for us, too," added Russell. "Now we are the Gleaners."

"The Gleaners?" repeated Lefty. "Why that name?"

"That's a name he and some other officers used to have for a swell crowd of young soldiers who were killed in the World War."

"Oh, he's been feeding you that line?" asked Lefty with a sneer. "That's the bunk. This country ain't worth fighting for. It's only for the rich guys. The Gleaners, huh?" Lefty laughed mockingly. "Killed in the war, huh? Well, they was just a bunch of saps that didn't know."

Instantly every one of the Gleaners was on his feet, eyes blazing with anger. "Listen, Lefty," Russell almost screamed with rage. "That's enough from you, you lousy bum. Get going." He walked toward Lefty menacingly. "Get out of here and stay out of here! Get out! Get out before we throw you out. There's enough of us here to do it, and we'll take you apart if we ever hear you say anything like that again."

Lefty's fist shot out at Russell's head, but before it could reach its mark, somebody grabbed his arm, and instantly the Gleaners were all over him. There was nothing ladylike in the Gleaners; they were tough; they relied more on physical force than on persuasive argument; and Lefty had not only angered them by laughing at their new ideals, but he had wantonly insulted the memory of their new and sacred heroes. A short, noisy scuffle, shot through with words ugly and profane, and Lefty's head, arms and legs were in the punishing grips of all the Gleaners that could reach him. Lefty struggled vainly to free himself. He cursed the Gleaners viciously until one of the boys angrily slapped his hand across Lefty's mouth and firmly kept it there.

The Gleaners roughly carried Lefty out of the rear door of the basement and more roughly dropped him to the pavement in the alley. "Now beat it," ordered Russell. Lefty arose to find a group of determined young wildcats in front of him, all eager to resume the battle, and, knowing that any further conflict would be even more painful to him than his forcible ejection from the club quarters, he blurted out, "I'll get youse guys for this," and turned and walked down the alley.

The boys laughed. "Well, Major Williams," said Russell, "that was for your Gleaners." The boys were smiling proudly. "Let's go in and finish the meeting," said Russell. "That guy is all washed up."

At this moment, Major Williams was arranging with Father Walsh to send his new protégés to Camp St. Mary. He would have been more than delighted if he could have seen how the boys of whom he was speaking were manhandling one of the neighborhood's budding Communists.

CHAPTER VIII

Red Thinks It Over

WHEN Red Devlin reached his home he was quite composed again. He did the usual errands and chores, but the buoyant cheerfulness that usually betokened Red's clear conscience and happy disposition was plainly lacking, and Red's mother soon saw that something was worrying her boy. Mrs. Devlin assumed that Red's depressed spirits were probably due to the teasing he received from his schoolmates when they saw his bruised face; she decided not to question him, but to let this gloomy mood pass away as others always had. "Thank God," she said to herself as she went about her work in the kitchen, "the boy has too sunny a disposition to let little clouds of trouble darken it very long."

After Red's work was done, he took the evening newspaper and went into the parlor to await supper. But he did not read. He was ashamed of the scene he had created in the classroom, and the words of the newspaper swam in a mist before his eyes. How could he face his classmates in the morning? He had cried; had acted like a baby. Down in his heart he knew that he had not fooled them by that display of temper. He was sorry he had brought shame to the class, and he knew that they knew it. But instead of being a man and squaring himself with them and with Father Walsh, he had told them angrily to mind their own business. Red frowned. "Their own business"; how eagerly that crowd took up his battle with the Dodgers. He well knew that he had been the cause of all their trouble and their bruises. They had taken up his battle. They always stuck up for each other like that. And now, he had put an end to all that had made his school life so pleasant. He had told his very best friends to mind their own business; he had broken with them. And Lieutenant Carroll. Red's face clouded in anger when he thought of the Lieutenant and the letter. So that was Carroll's way of "getting even." "And he called me a double-crosser," Red said to himself. "I suppose he'll tell Pa now, too." He remembered how proud the Lieutenant said his father was of him. "That young red-head of mine." For an instant Red thought of running away from home, getting away from the whole business, from his classmates, from Father Walsh, from everybody. He quickly put that thought aside; he had tried that once, about two years ago. How they all laughed at him that night when he came home crying; even his mother. She was weeping when he came into the house, but she started to laugh when, sobbing with loneliness, be ran past his father and buried his head in her shoulder. He had run all the way from the park. He had planned to sleep there, under a tree, but sleep didn't come; only tears came, till he could stand it no longer.

Red was suddenly awakened from his unhappy reverie by the sound of his father's voice in the kitchen. Arthur would be with him; they always came home from work together. Red arose to greet them; it would not do for him to let them suspect that there was anything wrong. Mother might silently try to guess what the trouble was, but his dad and brother would ask.

"Hello, Dad. Hello, Art," said Red, with forced cheerfulness, as they entered the living-room.

"Hello, son," returned his father. "Were you at the Engine House today?"

Red's heart sank into his shoes. "No, sir," he answered.

"I've got some news for you," said Mr. Devlin. He didn't notice the startled look that crossed Red's face. "I'll see you at supper; I want to wash up a bit."

Supper was ready, and in a few moments Mr. Devlin and Arthur joined the rest of the family at the table. Red tried hard to conceal his anxiety about the news that his father had for him. Could Lieutenant Carroll have reported him already?

"Well, Frank," began Mr. Devlin. "Did you hear about your friend, Bo Wickers?" Red breathed more easily; evidently this was the "news."

"No, sir," Red answered quickly. Mr. Devlin laughed.

"The poor fellow is in trouble again. He and a pal of his, both intoxicated just enough to over-estimate their physical prowess, dropped into the Engine House and started a quarrel with the Captain. When the firemen threw them out, Wickers picked up a brick and threw it through the wind-shield of the fire engine. Of course, the Captain bad both of them arrested. Then, later in the day, Wickers's brother-in-law, who seems to be a political power on the north side, came in to see if the matter couldn't be hushed up. He agreed to pay for a new wind-shield, and asked the Captain not to push the case against Bo.

"I met the Captain as I was on my way home. You know, mother, one of the Captain's boys turned out to be somewhat of a ne'er-do-well himself. The poor fellow could readily sympathize with Bo's parents, so he agreed to drop the case. Fortunately for the family, Wickers is not the fellow's right name. The Captain didn't tell me what the right family name is; he's too much of a gentleman for that."

"The poor boy," said Mrs. Devlin quietly. "I'm sorry for his mother." Red kept silent, his head bent over his plate. Then he heard his mother say wistfully, "The black sheep of the family." Involuntarily she glanced at her three boys. Arthur caught his mother's glance and laughed at her unspoken fears.

"Why, I don't break wind-shields, Mother," he said gaily, "and with that head of hair Red has, he couldn't possibly be a black sheep." He turned to Robert. "Bob, it's up to you! Are you going to be a black sheep?"

Bobbie's blue eyes snapped as he replied with spirit, No, I'm going to be a squad!"

"A squad, Bobbie?" asked his father. "A squad of what?"

"A squad," repeated Bobbie, impatiently. "Just a squad. Don't you know what a squad is?" he asked, somewhat nettled. "Didn't you ever hear of a squad car chasing criminals? Pete Smith's father is a squad. He's got a great big Cadillac. That's the kind of squad I'm going to be. A copper with a big, fast auto. That's me."

Amid the laughter of the family, Mrs. Devlin explained to Bobbie the difference between one policeman and a squad of policemen. Bobbie saw and laughed with the others at his mistake. "Then Pete's father is only part of a squad. Wait till I tell him. He said his father was a squad, and that only the coppers who were squads had Cadillacs."

Supper time passed pleasantly. Only Red's mother noticed that he was unusually quiet, evidently preoccupied with some unpleasant thoughts. He was not eating with his usual zest.

"Don't you feel well, Frank?" asked Mrs. Devlin, as the family left the table.

"I'm all right," answered Red quietly.

"How about the lawn, Frank?" called out his father from the front room.

"Yes, sir," answered Red. "Right away." Red was, indeed, glad to take up a task that would permit him to be alone for a while. He went slowly about the work of attaching the lawn hose, turning on the water, and, generally impatient to get the lawn watered, now remained at the task until his father and Arthur had gone out for the evening. When he went into the house, his mother and sister were busy in the kitchen; Bobby was out somewhere playing.

Red did not care to go out. He went into the front room and sat moodily looking out the window. No school for him tomorrow, he decided. He did feel unwell, though he knew that there was nothing wrong with him physically. Tomorrow morning he would admit to his mother that he did not feel well. Then he could stay home. He wouldn't have to face the fellows then till Wednesday, and then, he thought with some satisfaction, only long enough for the graduation exercises.

Twilight was passing into night as Red sat there gazing out into space and brooding over his misfortunes. Suddenly he sat erect and peered through the gathering gloom. Steve Nolan was coming down the opposite side of the street, looking over toward Red's home. Steve crossed the street diagonally and, standing in front of Red's home, whistled for Red. Red drew back from behind the curtained window into the darkness of the room. Why should Steve call him after what had happened today? Red was almost in a panic. What could he say to Steve? Why was Steve calling him? Steve whistled again, and Red hastened to the front porch.

"Hello, Steve," said Red, quietly.

Steve climbed up a few steps and sat down. Red went down and sat a few feet from him.

"Red, I came over to square myself," said Steve.

"Square yourself? Why?" asked Red in genuine surprise.

"Father Walsh knows that you were with White and Stone in that alley affair, and it's my fault," bluntly explained Steve. "I didn't mean to mention your name, but it slipped out when I got sore at White and said, while Father was listening, that they got 'Red and the rest of us' into trouble and didn't have guts enough to square things."

Red blushed guiltily.

"You see, Red," continued Steve, "after you went home, we had it out with those two. Then we sent for Father Walsh. We made those guys come clean with the story then and there. I'm sorry I mentioned your name, Red. On the square, I didn't mean to."

Red felt a lump rising in his throat and made haste to say, "Why, Steve, you didn't need to square yourself with me. Father Walsh saw me going home. I...I guess he knew what had happened upstairs. I was—was acting like a baby."

"Forget it, Red," exclaimed Steve. "The fellows all know you. They know how you felt. They didn't blame you."

Red silently bent forward and for a moment idly traced figures on the step with his finger. Then without raising his head, he said, "I told them to mind their own business, Steve. I'm sorry I said that."

"Well, forget it," said Steve. "Or, if you feel like it tomorrow, tell them so. They know it anyhow. And

listen, Red, Lieutenant Carroll didn't write that letter to
Father. We asked him tonight, Jack and I. Lieutenant
said he told you about seeing you in the alley, but didn't
say a word to Father Walsh or to anybody else."

While Steve was speaking, Red's anger at the
Lieutenant flared anew. "He's a…" he began hotly.
Then he suddenly stopped. The Lieutenant wouldn't
lie about it. "Did he say that?" he asked quietly.

"He surely did," declared Steve. "So that's out. He
had nothing to do with it."

"Well, I wonder who did," said Red.

"What difference does it make, Red?" asked Steve.
"It's all over…"

Red interrupted him. "It's not all over, Steve. I've
got to square myself with the fellows, and with Father
Walsh."

"Well, if you feel that way about it, I'd get it over
before the bell rings if I were you," said Steve, rising.
"I'm going home now. I'll see you in the morning.
So long."

"So long, Steve," answered Red. He arose and
watched Steve until he turned in at the side passageway
of his home. Then he sat down on the steps again. His
heart was lighter now, and a new resolution was forming
in his mind. He would not only square himself at
school, but he would tell Dad the whole story tonight.
He looked down the street again towards Steve's home.
"Steve came to square himself with me. Gosh!" he
murmured. "Steve is just like that. No beating around

the bush. He always says just what he thinks. No wonder all the fellows are keen for him."

Red began to wonder how he would explain things to his dad. Soon he heard his mother call through the open window. "Frank, it's getting late. Almost time for bed." He entered the house and went out to the kitchen for a drink of water. Then he returned to the sitting room where his mother was reading.

"Ma, may I wait up for Dad?" he asked.

"Certainly, son," answered his mother smiling, "if you promise to get up the first time you are called in the morning."

"O.K., Ma," Red agreed, and his mother noticed that her boy's cheerfulness was returning. Mrs. Devlin had seen Steve on the front steps with Red and guessed that something had passed between the two boys that made Red's troubles lighter. She was curious to know why Red wanted to see his dad, but decided to wait. Mr. Devlin, she knew, would give her the whole story later. Red knew that too, so he just smiled at his mother and went back to his place on the front steps. He began rehearsing what he would say to his father.

It was not long before he saw his father and Arthur coming down the street. Arthur! He had forgotten about him. Well, Art was a square fellow. He'd tell them both about it. Many a time before when he was in a tight fix with his father, Arthur helped him out of it. He felt he could rely on Arthur's help again tonight if things didn't go well.

Red arose to greet them.

"Well, what are you doing up so late, young fellow?" asked his dad kindly.

"Mother said I could wait up for you. Are you in a hurry? I'd like to talk to you—and Art for a minute."

Mr. Devlin sat down on the top step, and Arthur took his place on the porch railing. Mr. Devlin took Red's hand and swung him in place alongside of him.

"Now, what's on your mind, son?" he asked.

"Last Friday," began Red, "after our ball game, I started home with two fellows from our class. They're not like the other fellows, Dad. They're ..well, I guess you'd call them bad company. We started through an alley, and they began to razz me because I wouldn't smoke with them. Well, Dad, I...I was yellow, and lit a cigarette. Then we came to a crap game. I know I should have kept on going, but I didn't. I stayed with them; but, Dad, I didn't get into the game, except to make one bet on another fellow's luck. Somebody saw us then and reported us to Father Walsh. He got a letter saying that we were smoking, shooting dice, and using gutter talk. Now, Dad, I was there; I was smoking..."

"Smoking? or trying to?" interrupted Arthur with a laugh that was meant to cheer Red up, and to show his father that he knew Red didn't smoke.

"But Dad," continued Red firmly, "I wasn't in on the crap game, and I wasn't in on any gutter talk."

Mr. Devlin threw his arm across Red's shoulders. "I know you weren't, son," he said. "What did Father Walsh do about it?"

Red's eyes began to blink. "He just read the letter and then said he thought he could trust us, but some of us double-crossed him. He felt pretty bad about it. Then he left the room."

"Doesn't Father Walsh know you were in on it, Red?" asked his dad. "Doesn't he know who the boys were?"

"Yes, sir," answered Red. "You see, after he left, things began to happen. Everybody was sore."

"Didn't you admit you were one of them?" asked his dad.

Red hesitated. "I know now, Dad, I should have done that, but…well, when the fellows asked me, I went up in the air…and…well, I acted like a kid, I guess, and lost my temper. I said some mean things to the fellows and ran out of the room."

"Then what, Red?" asked his Dad.

"Steve Nolan told me the rest a little while ago," Red answered. "Then the fellows sent for Father and made the other two tell him they were there."

Arthur laughed. "I'll bet Steve Nolan had a hand in that," he exclaimed.

"But, Frank, doesn't Father know that you were one of them?" asked Mr. Devlin, somewhat anxiously.

"Yes, sir," answered Red. "One of the fellows mentioned my name by accident, but Father must have known when he saw me running down the corridor… acting like a baby. I was so sore I was crying, I guess."

What were you sore about?" asked Mr. Devlin, rather surprised.

"At everything, I guess," said Red impatiently. "Mostly at myself. I was yellow…clean through." Red sighed. "Guess I'll always be yellow," he added.

"You weren't yellow tonight, Red," declared Arthur. He knew that what Red had done was no easy task.

"Yes, I was, till Steve came over," said Red quietly. "You see, Steve was the one who let my name slip out, and he came over to tell me about it, and, as he said, 'to square himself for it.' Steve is a swell fellow."

"Are your classmates sore at you?" asked Mr. Devlin.

"Steve said they were not. I'll find out for myself tomorrow," answered Red.

"You're going to see Father Walsh yourself, too, aren't you, Red?" asked Arthur.

"The first thing in the morning," declared Red firmly.

Mr. Devlin arose and pulled Red up with him.

"Well, that's that, son," he said. "I'm glad you told me about it yourself, of course. I know that you'll be wiser next time. Square things up at school, and then forget it."

Mr. Devlin passed into the house. Red followed him; but his big brother suddenly threw his arm around Red's neck in a strangle hold, and a cheery whisper of congratulation came to Red's ear, "Nice going, Red."

Red struggled free, and, looking up at his big brother with a smile that explained everything, said, "Nice going, Art." But even in his present happiness, Red recalled the tone of disappointment and rebuke his classmate had put into those same words a few hours ago.

Early the next morning, Red was standing before Father Walsh telling him painfully the same story he had told his father. But he added, "I'm sorry, too, Father, that I kept on going when you called me back yesterday. But I just couldn't talk to you or anybody then, Father. I'd just start bawling again."

"Well, Frank," said Father Walsh, wearily, "for the life of me, I can't see why you care what fellows like Stone and White think about you. That's your whole trouble, Red; you're afraid to be laughed at. You've got to get over that, and the sooner the better. Now, get over to school and help check the athletic equipment. I saw some of the boys bringing theirs back."

"O.K., Father," said Red, "and thank you."

"By the way," added Father Walsh, "tell the boys that the campers' schedule has been prepared, and your crowd will go to camp six weeks from now for a two weeks' stay. And also tell them this: the Dodgers are through. Those fellows have a new club now, under Major Williams. They are the Gleaners now. And I want no trouble between your crowd and theirs. You may all be in camp together six weeks from now."

"O.K., Father," said Red lightly. "I'll tell them."

Red was so delighted with the prospect of another stay at St. Mary's Camp that, as he ran down the front steps of the rectory and into a group of his classmates, he forgot entirely to speak about yesterday's trouble, but excitedly gave them the message from Father Walsh. By the time Red realized that he had not apologized to his friends for his conduct in the classroom, there was so much gay chatter about the camp and the new club of the ex-Dodgers, he decided not to bring the matter up, at least, for the present.

CHAPTER IX

A Stormy Meeting

EARLY Tuesday morning, Charlie Russell appeared at the office of Major Williams. The Major welcomed him cordially and listened attentively to Charlie's lively narrative of the events that followed the Major's departure from the meeting of the Gleaners. Charlie was somewhat disappointed that Major Williams did not share the satisfaction of the boys over the withdrawal of Dixon and Small, but he rejoiced when the Major laughed heartily over the abrupt expulsion of Lefty. He asked Charlie a few questions about Lefty's appearance and his favorite haunts; then, with a few words of encouragement, he dismissed the president of the Gleaners, promising to be with them again at their next meeting.

Major Williams wanted to make sure that Lefty would not molest any of the Gleaners; so, as soon as Charlie left his office, he called Captain Meadows on the telephone and told him the whole story. Then at his request, Captain Meadows had Lefty brought into the station.

"Sit down there for a little while. Somebody wants to see you," said Captain Meadows to Lefty. A telephone message to Major Williams brought him to the station; he was immediately ushered into Captain Meadows's office. A few moments later, Lefty was called into the Captain's office, where in no uncertain terms he was warned by both the Police Captain and Major Williams that any attempt to avenge the treatment he had received at the hands of the Gleaners would bring to him immediate and prolonged regret "with no questions asked."

Later that afternoon, lest Lefty ignore that warning and count upon the influence of crooked but powerful local politicians to keep him out of trouble with the police, Major Williams called to his office two or three husky, iron-fisted members of the National Guard from the neighboring armory, where the Major was a general favorite. One of the visitors was the middleweight boxing champion of his regiment. The Major explained the situation to his friends and suggested that they interest themselves, at least temporarily, in the welfare of the Gleaners. The civilian soldiers joyfully and immediately accepted their appointment as the unofficial guardians of the Major's new friends, for the Major's wish was their will.

That very evening the group of hoodlums to which Lefty belonged was loafing as usual on a street corner not far from Charlie Russell's home. An automobile quickly slid to a stop at the curb; the man sitting next to the driver stepped out of the car and briskly announced, "My name is Lawson. I'm looking for Lefty Carvel."

An automobile quickly slid to a stop at the curb; the man sitting next to the driver stepped out of the car and briskly announced, "My name is Lawson. I'm looking for Lefty Carvel."

Instinctively all eyes turned to Lefty. Before Lefty could speak the stranger continued. "We're from the Armory," he said, "and we heard that you might get tough and try to hit back at that crowd of boys Major Williams has interested himself in. We thought it was only fair to run over here and tell you that it will be just too bad if you or any of your gang lay a finger on those kids. Understand?" Nobody answered. "Well," continued Lawson, slowly, "what we want to make plain is this. No matter what big fellow lays a finger on one of them, if they think you," and he pointed his finger directly at Lefty, "or any of your gang was behind it, we're coming over here to get *you*. See?" Here Lawson waved his finger back and forth to include the whole crowd.

There was a rumble of protest from Lefty's friends; Lawson looked entirely too serious and capable. Instantly out of the car tumbled Lawson's companions. To the startled group of hoodlums each of them seemed bigger and tougher than the other. The civilian soldiers were smiling, but said nothing. "We're taking a good look at all of you now," Lawson went on, "so we'll know you in case we have to find you. Now, you take a good look at us, and if your feelings are hurt by this little visit, come over to the Armory tomorrow night. We'll have a lot of boxing there tomorrow, and if any of you are looking for a fight, any one of us will be more than glad to accommodate you. Do you all understand?" Nobody answered; the frightened hoodlums sheepishly turned their eyes away from the speaker. "Lefty," exclaimed

Lawson sharply, "do you think you and your friends understand?"

"Aw, we weren't going to bother the kids," sullenly replied Lefty.

"Well, just don't change your minds; that's all," declared Lawson firmly, as he and his friends turned back to their car and drove away. And the Gleaners never found out why Lefty and his crowd seemed deliberately to avoid them.

As the days went on, the seemingly magical influence of Major Williams over the Gleaners wrought in most of the wayward lads a change that definitely turned them from the downward path. Even Dixon and Small, through the personal efforts of the Major, seconded by a timely word from Captain Meadows, came back into the club. The Major was well pleased with the good spirit of the boys, and found in Charlie Russell, a year or two older than most of the others, a dependable lieutenant in his efforts to transform the truant, lawless Dodgers into a group of decent, ambitious, law-abiding boys. The Gleaners had learned, from some of their adult friends and teachers, the outstanding war record of Major Williams; they were proud of him and proud of his genuine interest in them. It was not long until the Major managed to have each of them call at his office for a private chat about their school record and their plans for the future.

The Major knew that the boys were dissatisfied with their old quarters in the dim and cramped quarters of the basement of the Russell home, and the Major himself was anxious to get the boys out of the poor environment in which he had found them. Therefore, without a word to any of the Gleaners but Charlie Russell, he had been busy in preparing and equipping a clubroom in a vacant store not too far from their homes, and nearer to St. Mary's.

A few weeks later, when the new quarters were ready, Major Williams called a special meeting of the Gleaners in their usual meeting place. Then, to the great surprise of the boys, he announced the opening of the new quarters and immediately led the way to the club's new home.

The boys were delighted with what they found waiting them: a boxing ring, a punching bag, a billiard table, a wrestling mat, and a few pieces of gymnasium apparatus occupied the space in the rear half of the store; while up in the front were a few tables and a sufficient number of chairs to accommodate more than twice the number of Gleaners already in the club. A back room had been transformed into a shower room, and a row of shiny, metal lockers ran along the wall. Major Williams' face shone with pleasure as he watched the boys scurrying back and forth noisily examining and approving the equipment of their club-room.

The meeting soon turned into a house-warming. Captain Meadows and a few of the policemen from the station dropped in to congratulate the boys on their improved conduct. Their appearance startled the boys for an instant. Troubled, questioning glances furtively flashed from face to face. Were the police looking for any of them? Captain Meadows and the Patrolmen noticed their fears and laughed heartily.

"Nothing wrong, boys," he announced cheerfully. "Just dropped in to wish you good luck in your new home. Aren't we welcome?" Relief was plainly evident on the faces of the Gleaners as a hearty "Yes" was their glad answer.

A little later, in walked Father Walsh and a few of the boys from St. Mary's: Red, Steve, Bill and Jack. The boys were not surprised to see Father Walsh; they knew that he and Major Williams were good friends. They were, however, greatly surprised to see some of the recent enemy. Since the fight at the ball game, the two groups of boys had maintained a cool aloofness. There was no trouble between them, but there was no cordiality either. To please Major Williams, the Gleaners avoided contact with the boys from St. Mary's, and to please Father Walsh, the boys from St. Mary's acted the same way toward the Gleaners. Though both groups of boys had baseball teams, it was generally understood that the teams did not care to play each other. The St. Mary boys saw some of the Gleaners at Mass on Sundays, but that was all. Rumors had reached both groups that they were all going to Camp St. Mary for the same period, but neither Father Walsh nor Major Williams would satisfy their boys' curiosity when asked about the camp registration. Lieutenant

Carroll, at the fire engine house, was a member of St. Mary's Camp Committee and well acquainted with the plans for the coming camp season, but when the boys from St. Mary's asked him about the camp schedule, he smilingly referred them to Father Walsh.

Some of the boys from St. Mary's looked forward to the presence of the Gleaners at camp with them as an opportunity to "settle accounts once and for all" with them. Others realized that if both groups lived in camp together Father Walsh and Major Williams would insist that the boys "bury the hatchet" and share the burdens and pleasures of camp life as friends.

Red Devlin was in no mood for friendliness when he stepped into the Gleaners' clubroom. Poor Red had just undergone another somewhat humiliating experience.

Red had not gone near the fire station since the Sunday before his graduation. The breach between him and Lieutenant Carroll was still open. Steve Nolan and the rest of his friends knew that something was wrong between Red and the fireman, and assumed that it was because Red still believed that Lieutenant Carroll had written that letter to Father Walsh. Red let them think so. That was easier than telling them the truth. Nearly all of them had been warned or scolded by the big fireman at one time or another, and they would have laughed at Red for "keeping a grouch" over a little thing like a scolding.

On the way to the Gleaners, Father Walsh stopped the car in front of the Engine House. Red was sitting next to the priest. "See if Lieutenant Carroll is there, Frank," said Father Walsh. Red blushed in confusion, and the boys in the rear seat grinned at his discomfiture. But Father Walsh's word was law; so Red opened the car door and went into the fire engine house. The boys thought they saw a sly smile on the Priest's face as he watched Red's going.

"Is Lieutenant Carroll on duty today?" Red asked one of the firemen.

"Upstairs," answered the man, with a twinkle in his eye.

Red was embarrassed. The boys were not allowed upstairs; if the Lieutenant was upstairs when they came to see him, they merely shouted for him and waited till he came down. Red hesitated a moment. He couldn't bring himself to call out for the Lieutenant like that now.

"Will you…" he began, but stopped abruptly. He could hardly expect the fireman to be his messenger. "Father Walsh wants to see the Lieutenant," he said hesitatingly. "He's out in his car."

"Is he?" asked the fireman, and, leaving Red, he walked out to speak to Father Walsh. A feeling of abandonment seized Red. He looked around. No one else was in sight. "They must all be upstairs," thought Red peevishly. There was nothing else to do but yell; so Red yelled loudly, "Lieutenant Carroll."

"Yes," came back the Lieutenant's answer, in a tone that showed no surprise. Red raised his voice again and solemnly announced, "Father Walsh wants to see you. He's out in his car."

Lieutenant Carroll started down the steps, and Red, without another word to him, turned and went back to his place in the car.

"He's coming," he said to Father Walsh. Red didn't notice the grins on the faces of his friends in the rear seat.

Father Walsh stepped out of the car and met the Lieutenant at the door of the fire station. They chatted a few moments; then Father Walsh returned to the car and resumed the drive to the Gleaners. Red's friends noticed that his cheerfulness had left him and that, on the way to the Gleaners, he took no further part in the happy discussion of the visit to the club and the new relation that evidently was to be formed with their former enemies. The boys ignored Red's moody silence, however, for they did not sympathize with him in his attitude toward Lieutenant Carroll.

When Father Walsh and the boys entered the Gleaners' clubroom, Steve Nolan emitted a prolonged whistle of surprise and admiration at what he saw. All around him, sparkling in their newness, were the things to delight the heart of any normal, active boy.

Major Williams raised his hand for silence and announced: "Boys, here are some friends of yours who are going to share Camp St. Mary with you next week. Only for Father Walsh we would have had a hard time finding a good camp. He has invited you to Camp St. Mary." A spontaneous cheer from the Gleaners showed their appreciation of Father Walsh's invitation.

"Now, with him tonight," continued the Major, filing, "have come to see your new headquarters a few boys whom you know." Some of the Gleaners were eyeing the quartet with cold disapproval. Charlie Russell started to applaud, but seeing that only a few joined him, and those only half-heartedly, he stopped and bent to fix an already tightened shoe-string. "I invited them over tonight, so that we could bury the hatchet," continued the Major. "Even Germany and the allied nations are friends now. Our war here is over, too."

The boys from St. Mary's saw from the faces of the Gleaners around them that the Major's suggestion was not entirely agreeable to all. The smiles left their faces, too. "Say, Father...," Steve whispered. "We don't..."

"Wait a minute," interrupted Father Walsh, in a low tone.

"What about a speech of welcome, Mr. President?" asked Major Williams of Charlie Russell.

Russell looked around him, blushing with confusion. He didn't know just what to say. Major Williams had not told even Russell that some of St. Mary's boys were coming this evening. The Major was curious to see just what would happen when Father Walsh and the boys walked in.

"Well," began Russell, "I guess they're welcome."

"Like the measles," he heard somebody say in an undertone.

"As you say, Major," continued Russell, "the war is over." Then what Russell thought was a happy idea came to him. "Only for these fellows, I guess we wouldn't have this club," he said gaily.

Immediate an angry denial was voiced by the Gleaners, but Russell added, "Yes. We got into a fight with their crowd. Some of us got pinched, and Captain Meadows turned us over to Major Williams." Captain Meadows and Major Williams laughed aloud.

"That's right, boys," exclaimed Captain Meadows.

"Nothing doing," declared Dixon, sullenly.

"If we got it from them," exclaimed another of the Gleaners, "they can have it right back."

Suddenly Steve Nolan pushed his way through a knot of Gleaners, reached Russell's side, and turned to face the club.

"Listen, you fellows," he began angrily. "Father Walsh and Major Williams want the crowd from St. Mary's and your crowd to be friends. Some of you say 'Nix.' That's lousy," spat out Steve, his face showing plainly his disgust. "After all Major Williams has done for you, you can at least do as much for him as we are willing to do for Father Walsh." Steve's face paled in his earnestness, and his dark eyes snapped. "You fellows who were in on that scrap got what was coming to you. You were in the wrong." He pointed his finger straight at one of the three who caused the trouble at the ballgame, and who now was very emphatic in expressing his displeasure with the turn of events. "That loud guy there tried to start a scrap with me;" he pointed to Small—"and you slapped the little kid we sent to you. Would your gang stand for that if we did it?" Steve didn't expect any answer; he kept on excitedly. "We didn't know we were coming here tonight until a little while ago. And when Father Walsh told us, nobody raised a squawk. We don't hold grudges." Father Walsh, Major Williams, and the policemen were smiling, their eyes shining with admiration of Steve's spirited speech; but he didn't see them. He turned to Russell. "You're their President," he said. "There's nobody here that walloped each other as you and I did. You said the war's over. That goes for me, too." Steve extended his hand to Russell; the president of the Gleaners grasped it and shook it cordially. Somebody began to applaud, and in an instant most of those present followed heartily. A few of the Gleaners, however, including Dixon and Small, stood motionless. The rest of the crowd paid no attention to them. Even Red was laughing again. Plain speaking had cleared the atmosphere.

"Well, show them what you have here, boys," called out Major Williams. "Father Walsh and I have some business to talk over." He turned to the policemen. "You'll excuse us, gentlemen?"

"Certainly, Major. We must be on our way, too," answered Captain Meadows. The Captain caught Steve's eye and beckoned to him. Steve came to him blushing. "That was fine, son," said Captain Meadows, as he slapped his big hand down on Steve's shoulder. "That was just what was needed."

"Thanks," murmured Steve, with some embarrassment, as the Captain and policemen left the club.

As Steve walked back to the boys with whom he had been standing, he heard a whispered insult from Dixon. Steve whirled on the young tough and said in a low tone, "Aw, grow up, you poor sap." Then, with a look on his face that Dixon could not misunderstand, he added slowly, "We'll all be in camp together. Do your stuff there."

The rest of the evening was spent in talking "camp" and examining the gymnasium equipment of the club. At Red's urging, Steve gave the boys an exhibition of his skill with the punching bag. Charlie Russell looked on for a moment or two and then, rubbing his jaw, laughingly exclaimed, "That explains a lot. No wonder that guy packs such a wallop."

Then Red turned to Dixon. "What does that remind you of?" he asked, tauntingly. Dixon, angered by the laughter that greeted this barbed question, thumbed his nose at Red in reply. Red's smile left his face, but before he could say or do anything, Father Walsh called out, "Come, boys. Let's go. It's time to start back."

On the way home, Father Walsh complimented Steve on his courage and on his speech. "Those boys are not such a bad lot," he added. "They got off to a wrong start, that's all. Being in camp with us will do them a lot of good." And the boys in the car knew that what Father Walsh had just said was intended as a gentle warning that there was to be no quarreling at camp. They made no comment.

Steve and Red left the car at the corner near their homes. As they walked down the street, Red asked Steve, "Did you see that guy Dixon thumb his nose at me?"

Steve laughed. "Yes," he replied. "He and one or two more of them are still sore, I guess. He made a nasty remark to me, too. I told him that we'd all be in camp together."

"Oh, they won't try anything up there," said Red. "Boy, it's only a few days more and we'll be on our way."

The boys parted at Steve's home, happy in the anticipation of good times in store for them at camp.

Poor Red. If only he could but know that before camp was over he was to face the greatest trial of his life, he would not have been so happy.

CHAPTER X

"Yellow?"

THE following Monday morning, the 9:30 train steamed out of Central Station, carrying three special cars filled with happy, noisy boys on their way to Camp St. Mary. The two weeks to which they had long looked forward had now begun. Father Walsh and Major Williams accompanied the boys today, but in charge of each of the three cars were two or three young men, students of the diocesan seminary, who spent their summers at the camp as councillors. Red Devlin and his friends felt like veterans. They were "old timers"; for the last three or four summers, they had spent some time at the camp. When the excitement of departure had died down, Bill Harte suggested to Steve and Red a trip through the cars to see "who's going to be up there this season, besides the Gleaners." Jack Clemens had another idea. He wanted to get a look at the councillors, for he knew from past experience that the councillors would be a big factor in their life at camp. The campers of the two previous periods had enthusiastically assured the boys that the councillors this year were "the berries."

"Let's get talking to some of them," insisted Jack. "We'll see for ourselves." They started through the car to find Father Walsh. He'd have the list of cabins and councillors. They came upon him talking to two of the seminarians, Bert Conroy and Dan Cooney.

"Here, you fellows," said Father Walsh to the boys. He introduced the boys to the councillors. Then he said, "Bert will have charge of your cabin, boys, and Dan Cooney will take charge of one of the Gleaners' cabins with Bill Murray in charge of the other. He's in the next car talking to Major Williams. Now, I expect you fellows, who are old timers in camp, not only to give good examples to the other boys but to do all you can to see that the Gleaners enjoy their stay with us." Father Walsh nodded to the boys significantly.

They laughed. "O.K., Father," they answered cheerfully. The priest left the boys chatting with the councillors and moved on through the car. In a few moments the boys passed into the car that carried the Gleaners. All but Dixon, Small, and two other boys sitting opposite them returned the greeting of Red and his crowd. It was clear that these fellows did not share the fine spirit of friendliness that marked the trainload of campers that morning.

Most of the campers were roaming noisily back and forth through the cars. It was very evident that they were out for a good time.

"It will be a great two weeks," exclaimed Jack Clemens. "There are a lot of live wires with us."

"And the councillors are swell fellows, too," added Bill Harte.

Soon some of the boys were opening the lunches they had brought with them for the ride. Their enjoyment seemed to create an appetite in the rest of the boys, and in a short time all the campers were following their example.

Though the camp was only about six hours' ride from the city, the trip to the boys seemed endless. For a full half-hour before the train arrived at the camp, the boys were impatiently consulting their watches and craning their necks through open windows to see landmarks that told them they would soon be at the camp's station.

After a mile's walk from the station, the new boys got their first glimpse of Camp St. Mary. They saw fourteen big log cabins built in a huge crescent at the edge of a clearing, the "campus" of Camp St. Mary. At the right of the campus stretched out a wide, sandy beach that ended at the inviting waters of the cool Lake St. Mary. The boys' eyes sparkled at the long pier and the diving float anchored not far from the end of the pier.

The long column of boys wound its way to the director's cottage. There the boys received their assignments to cabins, and soon each cabin group, in charge of a councillor, was joyously scampering across the campus to take possession of its new home. To refresh the boys after their long, dusty trip, the councillors announced a short dip before supper; and soon the lake was alive with merry, splashing campers, all under the watchful eyes of half a dozen councillors who had qualified as Red Cross Life Savers to prepare for their work at camp.

In the meantime, Father Walsh and Father Sexton, also an assistant at St. Mary's parish, who had been acting as camp director for the earlier groups, took Major Williams on a tour of the camp buildings; the chapel, the mess hall, the recreation hall, the handicraft shelter, and tool house; then, to the shower house and, at the edge of the lake, the new boat house. As the three men approached the pier, Father Sexton raised his hand, and a shrill blast of a whistle through a megaphone at the lips of a councillor perched high on the lookout tower at the edge of the pier told the boys that the swim was over. The lads were hardly in their cabins when the bugle sounded the mess call. After a hearty supper, the entire camp trouped into the chapel for a short visit to the Most Blessed Sacrament, then across to the recreation hall for a talk from Father Walsh, who was to take Father Sexton's place during this camp period.

"Now, boys," said Father Walsh, "we have only a few rules here, but they must be obeyed. The first and most important rule is short: 'Be gentlemen.' The camp is run for your pleasure, but you are not the only one in the camp. Obedience to the rules of the camp works like oil in a machine: it keeps the camp running smoothly. When the camp runs smoothly, everybody has a lot of fun. You'll find the daily program and the rules tacked up on the wall in your cabin. Go back with your councillors and read them now. Then see that your things are all unpacked and put in their proper places." Father Walsh paused a moment with his finger uplifted. "Remember this," he said significantly, "there's only one councillor in each cabin. He is in charge of the cabin and in charge of the campers who live in that cabin. Dismissed."

The boys who had been in camp greeted Father Walsh's warning with good-natured laughter. They knew what that hint meant. "Keep your family troubles at home," called out several of them, and Father Walsh laughed. They were repeating another of his "famous sayings." Father Walsh held the councillors strictly responsible for the conduct of their campers when they were in the cabins, and the boys knew, from experience, that their leader's word was law and his decisions binding. The petty squabbles that were bound to arise, Father Walsh humorously called "family troubles." He discouraged appeals to him in such cases by the warning the boys had just repeated, "Keep your family troubles at home."

As the boys rushed pell mell from the recreation hall, somebody accidentally stumbled against Red Devlin, throwing Red to one side and against the boy next to him as they passed through the door. Red instinctively grabbed the boy's arm to keep himself from falling.

"Beg pardon," murmured Red goodnaturedly, but the boy to whom Red's apology was addressed shook Red's hand off his arm and answered with a vile epithet. Red looked up in amazement and anger. The boy to whom he had apologized was one of the two he saw with Dixon and Small on the train. Without a word, Red crashed his fist into the face of his insulter, but before he could strike out again, Bert Cooney jumped between the boys. He grabbed the Gleaner's shoulder, whirled him around, and gave him a violent push.

"To your cabin," he snapped sharply. Then he turned to Red, "Nice going, Devlin. He had it coming. I heard what he said to you. Now forget it, and get over to the cabin."

It was all over in less than a minute, but several of the boys saw and heard it all. Red blushed, as he heard on all sides the same compliment, "Nice going, Red." His anger gave way to a smile.

Bert Cooney came into the cabin with the last of the group, smiling. "Boy, Red," he exclaimed, "you certainly gave that fellow a surprise. Do you always hit like that?" Red grinned, and the other boys laughed aloud. "Why, he's a head taller than you, Red," continued Bert. "He'll get you later."

"Go get him now, then," said Red, still grinning.

"He'll get you in the football game tomorrow. He's in Cabin Six, and a team from Cabin Six and Seven, the Gleaners' cabins, is scheduled to play a team from our cabins, Nine and Ten, tomorrow."

"Are Dixon and Small playing?" asked Steve Nolan, quickly.

Bert consulted the slip he had in his hand. "Yes, they're in Cabin Seven."

Steve crossed the room and dramatically extended his hand to Red. The two boys shook hands while Steve said, with mock solemnity, "Well, goodbye, Red. Take care of yourself."

Bert Cooney looked on with amazement. "What's this all about?" he asked.

"Well," said Steve, "as long as you are our councillor we'll tell you." Then while the boys were setting their cabin to order, Steve and Red, assisted now and then by the other boys of Cabin Nine, told Bert the story of the Gleaners and of the unfriendliness of four of them. "The rest of them seem to be all right now," said Steve, and just between you and us, we're out to 'take' the four hard guys before camp is over." Steve noted the frown that darkened the councillor's face. "But," he added quickly, "we'll give you our word of honor that we won't start trouble or do anything that's unfair."

"Well," said Bert, lightly, "that's fair enough. I'm glad you told me about it, too. Now let's get back to the 'rec' hall. There's a movie tonight. After the movie, we go to chapel for night prayers, and then back to our bunks for a good night's rest."

It seemed to the boys of Cabin Nine that they had scarcely fallen asleep when the boom of the miniature cannon at the base of the flag staff near the director's cottage rudely awakened them to hear the bugler sounding *Reveille.*

Red was on his feet instantly. "C'mon, Bill," he called to Harte, still stretching and yawning in the cot across from his. "We're serving Mass this week. I forgot to tell you." Bill jumped. That summons meant a more particular washing and dressing than the other campers would bother themselves with.

"Why didn't you say so?" demanded Bill, as both boys skipped out to the basin rack at the rear of their cabin.

"Go easy on that water, you guys," yelled Steve. "I'm on the bucket brigade till Wednesday. Then you fellows get it."

"Listen to him," exclaimed Red, "yelling about the water already." Nevertheless, the two servers were careful not to pour into their basins more water than they needed. In a few days they would be charged with the duty of supplying their outdoor washroom with water, and willful waste now would bring certain retaliation when their turn came to lug buckets of water from the camp pumps to the cabin.

A few minutes after the rising signal, the boys were streaming from their cabins, in various stages of dress, to the center of the campus, for a brief and more or less vigorous performance of setting-up exercises. After Mass, at which most of the campers received Holy Communion, a noisy breakfast followed. Then back to their cabins hastened the boys to get things ready for "inspection." An award of merits, the accumulation of which brought privileges to the honor cabins, made even careless boys meticulous housekeepers while at camp.

The mornings at Camp St. Mary were given over principally to instruction in the various branches of camp activity: athletics, woodcraft, handicraft, swimming, etc. For the new campers the swimming class was the most important, for until a non-swimmer had demonstrated his ability to swim fifty feet, he was condemned to wear, from morning till night, a little lead sinker dangling from a red ribbon, and to be commonly referred to as a "sinker."

Red and Steve, who had long ago earned their Junior Life Guard emblem, were detailed to assist the councillors in charge of water activities in teaching a score of such youngsters "to swim off the sinker." Today they would rather have reported to the football coach, Bill Murray, an ex-collegiate All-American, for football practice with the rest of the boys who were to play this afternoon. As they were on their way to the lake, ready for work, they passed close to some of the Gleaners, who were carelessly tossing a football around as they waited for Bill Murray, who was, incidentally, their councillor. The Gleaners noticed that Red and Steve were in swimming suits.

"Yellow?" called Dixon, with a sneer. Red instantly slipped out of his bathrobe and started toward Dixon, but Steve roughly grabbed him by the arm.

"Nix, Red, don't let him get your goat," admonished Steve.

Red frowned, but yielding to Steve, picked up his bathrobe and continued on his way. The two boys then heard, with not a little satisfaction, loud and angry voices; some of the Gleaners with Dixon were unmistakably condemning his uncalled-for remark to Red.

"They're telling him," said Steve, with a laugh. "Most of them are going to be all right."

"Listen, Steve," said Red, earnestly. "You'll probably be quarter-back this afternoon. If I'm in the back-field, give me the ball to take through that guy's place every now and then."

That afternoon Steve was quarterback, and Red was playing left-half with the team from Cabins Nine and Ten against the team of Gleaners from Cabin Six and Seven. There was not much science in the game. The boys were too young and inexperienced for that. But there was a lot of enthusiasm and desperate effort. There was more polish and smoother teamplay in the work of the boys from St. Mary's, for they had played together, under competent coaching, not only in previous camp seasons, but during the parochial school football season. The Gleaners, on the other hand, had a few players who seemed to make up in weight and strength what they lacked in skill. Major Williams and Father Walsh followed the game from the side-lines; the coaching was entirely in the hands of Bill Murray for the Gleaners and Bert Cooney for the boys from St. Mary's.

"I've been trying to talk sportsmanship into that outfit," said Major Williams, "and I'm anxious to see how they act in a game where there is a lot of room for unfair tactics."

"Well," cautioned Father Walsh, smiling, "don't be too critical of what you see. I don't suppose they have much knowledge of the rules." Then he added with a laugh, "And if Steve Nolan finds any particular player on the opposition who is inclined to be dirty or unfair, he'll send some pretty tough plays over him time after time."

"Good," exclaimed the Major. "Now let's see."

Father Walsh's prediction came true. Despite the warnings and the vigilance of the councillor-officials, who without argument penalized every violation of the rules, and the pleading of Charlie Russell in the back-field and of Jim Cox, the scrappy quarterback of the Gleaners, Dixon and Small, in the line, frequently ignored the rules, explained to them by the councillors, against illegitimate use of the hands and unnecessary roughness. Twice in the early part of the first quarter, some of the St. Mary boys came out of a scrimmage heap, wondering which of the opposition had deliberately kicked or punched them as they lay on the ground hugging the ball. That the blow was repeated two or three times was good reason for them to believe that it was deliberate unfairness and no accident. In a "time out" period, they mentioned their suspicions.

"It's Dixon or Small," declared Red. "Let's all keep an eye on them and catch them at it."

St. Mary's had the ball on the Gleaners' forty-yard line, third down, six yards to go. Steve called for a play, Red to take the ball through left tackle, where, in the opposing line, Dixon and Small were huddled, tackle and guard. Red grabbed the ball and like a shot tore up to the line. Where an instant ago there crouched a double line of football players, now appeared an opening two feet wide. Devine and Malach, in St. Mary's line, put every ounce of strength into a lunge that knocked Dixon and Small sprawling. Charlie Russell took Red in a tackle from behind, and the referee announced, "First down—ten yards to go." Red came back to his place, laughing at Dixon and Small.

"Yellow?" he called to them, in a tone of derision

"Try it again," Small barked angrily. Even the Gleaners were smiling.

"O.K.," exclaimed Red—but Red wasn't quarterback. Steve's voice cracked out, a signal for a forward pass. Most of the Gleaners expected Steve to take up Small's challenge, and before Jim Cox, their alert quarter, could warn them that the signal called by Steve was a new one, the whole team seemed to rush to the spot in the line where they expected Red to charge through. They were amazed to see Red take the ball and, running back a few steps, throw a long forward pass to St. Mary's totally unprotected end, who gathered in the ball and galloped the length of the field for a touchdown with only Jim Cox in pursuit.

That they were so easily fooled made the Gleaners angry, not with St. Mary's, but with themselves. Only Dixon and Small felt a keener desire to avenge themselves on Red or any of his friends. The other Gleaners appreciated the quick-thinking and strategy of Steve's decision. Jim Cox was eloquent, however, in condemning his teammates for being so easily trapped.

St. Mary's made the point after touchdown, and kicked off to the Gleaners. Cox caught the kick and started down the field like a deer. One, two, three St. Mary's boys were either taken out by his quickly formed interference or sidestepped or dodged by the goal-bound ball carrier. He reached St. Mary's twenty-five yard line before Bill Harte brought him down.

In the next play, Russell tried a plunge through the line, but was stopped dead. Then a dash around left end gave the Gleaners five yards. In a huddle again, they planned a forward pass. Maybe it would work like Red's. As Russell made the suggestion, he unconsciously moved his hand; just a slight forward snap of the hand at the wrist, but Steve Nolan's watchful eye saw it.

"A pass," Steve whispered. "Everybody on your toes."

As the play started, Russell saw too late that St. Mary's was expecting a pass. Panic-stricken, he hurried the throw, but instead of the ball falling into the arms of the Gleaner for whom it was intended, it was grabbed out of the air by Red Devlin. The boys who had gone down in the line scrimmage scrambled to their feet and raced to stop or to protect Red in his flight to the Gleaners' goal. Ten yards from a score, he was dragged down from behind, and felt the thud of other players piling upon him and his captor. Before the heap was untangled, Red's face was banged into the ground twice. He turned to catch Small just jumping back from the heap.

In a trice he was on his feet and in a huddle with the team, demanding that he be given the ball for the next play.

"Now, Mal," he said to Malach, "get out of his way. Let him come through. I'm going to go over him or through him, and I don't mean maybe. If he can take me, he's welcome."

The team grinned and agreed. They quickly returned to their places.

At the signal, Red took the ball, tucked it firmly in the crook of his right elbow, and, knees flashing high, made straight for Small. Small, easily slipping past the obedient Malach, reached out awkwardly to grab Red. Bang! Red's left arm extended stiffly caught Small full in the face. Then before he could recover from that shock, Red's knee caught him almost under the chin. Small's head snapped back, and Red went over him and kept going until Russell, from the secondary defense, brought him down. Small was still lying on the ground where he fell, bruised and stunned. Now he slowly arose, helped to his feet by one of his teammates, and looked around sheepishly. Red was grinning at him. Then he remembered what had happened, as Jim

Cox exclaimed sharply, "Looks like Red caught you roughing him a few moments ago. Want to quit?"

Russell looked over to the sidelines and then back to Small. "You'd better quit, fellow," he said. "You can't stop him when he comes through like that."

Small rubbed his head. "I got a headache," he said weakly.

Just then another Gleaner came tearing across the field. He reported to the referee, who called "Small out." Without a word Small walked off the field, and play was resumed.

The boys from St. Mary's mixed line plunges, end runs, and passes so fast that the Gleaners were forced back farther and farther until they were on their own three yard line. There St. Mary's lost the ball on a fumble that was recovered by Charlie Russell. Then for a while the Gleaners, by powerful drives through the lines, made steady headway against Red's lighter team. Two offside penalties incurred by the over-eager St. Mary's team contributed ten yards to the hard-fighting Gleaners.

On St. Mary's thirty-five yard line Charlie Russell took the ball from center and shot a short pass to Ben Nevers, who had come into the game to replace the starting left half-back. Nevers, far out to one side, caught the ball, turned to run, but was stopped in his tracks by fleet-footed Bill Harte, in a tackle that sent both boys sliding along the grass, and so jarred Nevers that the ball bounced out of his hands. Before it hit the ground, Jim Cox, coming up fast, grabbed it out of the air, but tripped and fell over the sprawling Nevers and Harte. Cox held the ball, however, and the referee declared it down on St. Mary's thirty-three yard line.

Before the next play got underway, the timekeeper's gun declared the half over. The official Camp St. Mary score-book read "Cabins Nine and Ten, 7; Cabins Six and Seven, 0;" but to the boys who were in the game it was "St. Mary's, 7; Gleaners, 0."

When the boys, flushed and perspiring from their autumn game in the summer's heat, reached the sidelines, Father Walsh announced: "That's enough for today; it's pretty warm. Everybody down for a swim."

CHAPTER XI

Disturbing Rumors

WHEN the boys reached the pier, they saw one of the councillors who had been watching the football game talking to Small. The councillor turned away as the boys approached, but they heard him say to Small, "Well, it won't get you anywhere, kid. What you did to him wasn't football; it was just meanness. What he gave you in return was just straight, hard football, and you couldn't take it."

At the end of the pier a few of the Gleaners were waiting for the councillor on the look-out tower to blow the whistle for "All in." No one was permitted to enter the water until that signal was given, and that signal would not be given until all the councillors appointed to water activities were in their places in the boats and on the diving platform.

As the Gleaners saw Red and his cabin-mates coming down toward them, they broke into a cheer. Red and his crowd answered it by jovially shaking their clasped hands over their heads. When they reached the Gleaners, Jim Cox spoke up, "Nice going, you guys. You can sure play that old football."

"Huh, they won the parochial school championship last year," chirped up a youngster from St. Mary's.

Major Williams and Father Walsh on the pier noticed with pleasure the greeting the St. Mary boys received from the Gleaners. "It is evident, Father" remarked the Major, "that most of my crowd want to be friends with your lads."

Just then the "All in" whistle blew, and in a twinkling of an eye, the pier was almost empty and the water was full of splashing, yelling swimmers, bobbing up and down like apples in a tub. Then on the diving platform some of the boys reappeared one by one, and a few of the better swimmers scampered up the ladder to the high dive. Red, a splendid swimmer, reached there first and, with a loud "Whooppee!" shot out into the air and down in a graceful swan dive. After him went, as fast as safe landing permitted, the rest of the Junior Life Guards and some of the Gleaners.

Soon the Junior Life Guards were challenging their friends to "drown" them. They were anxious to try their skill in "breaking holds," the technique of which they had learned as a part of the requirements for the rank of Junior Life Guard.

Red was treading water and calling to Jim Cox, poised on the platform for a dive. Suddenly he felt someone's arms tightly encircle him around the neck from behind him. Charlie Russell was accepting Red's challenge to "drown him." Quick as a flash, Red grabbed Russell's lower hand and twisted it down and in towards his body. With his other hand, he grabbed Charlie's elbow, and, going under the water, pushed up hard on the arm he now held firmly, and ducked under it as he raised it. Coming up out of the water free from Russell's grip, he continued to twist Russell's hand until he had the boy's arm in a hammer-lock. Russell was amazed to see how easily Red had not only broken his hold but had fastened one on him that he couldn't break. He felt Red's hand slip under his chin and found himself tipped flat on the surface of the water. Then Red finished his work off by pushing Russell's head under water, releasing him suddenly, and swimming for the platform. Russell came up spluttering and instantly started after Red. Red saw him coming and jumped in again. That was just what Red wanted, a goodnatured tussle in the water, with a lot of tough holds to break. The boys on the platform watched the struggle eagerly; to most of the Gleaners it was just a water wrestling match, but to St. Mary's campers it was a contest of strength versus strength and skill, for Red, they saw, was merely applying with a good measure of success, the lessons they had learned in breaking holds and applying "carries" to save a panic-stricken swimmer in danger of drowning.

Soon the St. Mary campers found themselves explaining and demonstrating Red's work to their friends on the platform. In a little while other pairs took to the water for a better lesson. Time passed quickly and the "All out" whistle blew all too soon for the happy crowd.

On the way back to the cabins, Tiny Laurel, the smallest of the Gleaners, said to Small and his three friends, who had kept aloof from the sport in the water, "Why don't youse guys snap out of it? They're a swell bunch, and, boy, do they know their stuff!" The four said nothing, so Tiny paid no further attention to them.

Following the after supper game period that evening, the campers gathered around a camp fire for songs and stunts and a story, perhaps, from Major Williams, who, Father Walsh had told some of the boys, was a master at that art.

Major Williams did tell them a story; in fact, several stories, including a weird ghost story or two, that made all the boys instinctively move closer to each other as they sat there in the deepening darkness. He told them ghost stories of Indians who lived "right where Camp St. Mary now stands. Perhaps, if you dig down just where you are sitting now, you'll hit an Indian's grave." The Major's cigar had gone out. He glanced at it, scratched a match and carefully watched it till it burned brightly. The boys sat and watched him silently. Then he lit his cigar again and continued. "Yes, boys," he said solemnly. "There are spirits that roam through the world unseen by man." A piercing, mournful howl came from the dense woods that lined the athletic field, and some of the boys turned with startled eyes in the direction of the sound. "Don't mind that. Perhaps it's only an owl, or a loon on the lake beyond the woods," said the Major. His tone, however, was not at all convincing. He went on.

"We see each other, human beings that we can touch, who play and eat and work as we do, but..." Again, that weird howl from out of the dark, but this time it seemed closer. The Major paused a moment and glanced in the direction of the eerie sound. Then he said, "But there are other mysterious beings around us, whom we cannot see, we cannot touch, who neither play nor work nor eat as we do." The boys were scarcely paying attention to the Major now; they were keenly listening for that mournful howl. A wild shriek, much closer, brought them all to their feet; they turned to see Bill Murray come running lazily out of the darkness into the dim light of the fire. As soon as he knew the boys saw him, he laughed and, putting his hand to his mouth, repeated tone for tone, the cries he had sent forth a few moments ago. Then, before the boys could say a word, he dashed forward and joined them.

"Good evening, fellows," he said, laughing. Then to the Major, "Pardon me, Major, you seem to have been speaking. Did it do it all right?" Then the boys understood. It was part of Major's story. They burst out laughing and denied that they had been at all disturbed or frightened. Major Williams raised his hand.

"We were talking about real spirits that hover right around us here in camp." Some of the boys grinned; Major Williams had fooled them once, but there would be no second time. "Now, I mean it," said the Major earnestly, "and, boys, before you turn in tonight say a prayer to the spirit whom God has appointed to look after you, your Guardian Angel."

The boys instantly broke out in laughter and applause at the way in which the Major had held their attention to tell them again a truth they seemed always to have known. Then Father Walsh took the Major's place. "Well," he said, with a broad smile, "you were fooled that time. Every one of you. I was watching you."

"Hey, Father," called one of the campers, "how did that councillor know when to scare us? He couldn't hear the Major from where he was."

Father Walsh laughed. "Ask the Major," he answered. They did. "Well boys," explained the Major, "perhaps you noticed me light my cigar, and wondered why I was so slow about it. That burning match was my signal to Bill Murray, who had slipped away from you without being noticed."

"We'll get you, Bill," threatened a crowd of young campers, as they clambered all over the councillor.

"All right, boys," called Father Walsh. "To the chapel now, and then to bed."

Red Devlin and the campers of Cabin Nine were getting ready for bed when Bert Cooney, their councillor, walked in. All the boys were talking, in hushed tones, about ghosts and tales of Indian cemeteries hidden in the woods. The room was dimly lighted by a single, tiny electric bulb.

"Who wants to go for a hike through the woods?" he asked.

"O.K.," instantly answered Red, reaching for the shoe he had just dropped.

"There's a rumor going about that a crazy man escaped from the asylum down the river a few miles, and is hiding in the woods up here. Did any of you fellows hear any shots last night?"

"No," answered the boys, their eyes like saucers in surprise at Bert's announcement.

"Well," he continued, "they say he has a gun; but don't let it get on your nerves. And don't say anything to the little kids about it. I don't think that we're in any danger."

"Aw, that's some more of your kidding," declared one of the campers.

"Well, you know as much about it now as I do," declared Bert. "Forget it and go to bed."

Steve picked his flashlight up off the floor and slipped it under his pillow. Red was lacing his shoe. "C'mon, Jack and the rest of you," he said, "let's take a hike."

Silence. None of the boys seemed eager to accept that invitation. "C'mon," Red urged.

"Nix. I'm going to sleep. I'm tired," answered Jack.

"Let's you and I go, Bert," said Red.

"On second thought, Red," said Bert, "perhaps it would be just as well if we didn't go. If anything happened, you know..." he suggested, doubtfully.

"You mean that wild man stuff?" demanded Red, disdainfully.

"Why, yes," answered Bert. "It may not be more than a rumor. Maybe the councillors are kidding, and all that, but..."

"Oh, c'mon," urged Red impatiently. "We're both in the state of grace. We received Holy Communion this morning. You're not 'chicken,' are you?" he asked, with a laugh.

"Hey, Bert," called Steve. "Don't listen to that guy. He's plain goofy. He'd go out there alone if you'd let him."

"Bert," called Bill Harte, "take him out and drown him. He wanted Russell and Cox to do that today."

"You take him out and try to drown him, then," challenged Red, with a grin. "A guy that can't tackle a fellow without sliding all over the football field," he added with pretended scorn.

Steve, now in bed, sat up and raised a hand. "All in favor of Red's drowning, say 'aye.'" A hearty and unanimous "AYE" answered him.

"Shh. We'll have Father Walsh over here," cautioned the councillor. "Taps will blow in a few minutes."

"Oh, Red," said Bill Harte in a loud whisper, "be a good fellow. You sneak out now and drown yourself."

The boys chuckled. "And break Irene's heart," added Jack mischievously.

Instantly, Red's grin left his face as his cheeks crimsoned. A sudden hush came over the cabin. Jack had gone a little too far. Red was offended. Instantly Jack sprang out of his bed and crossed over to Red, his hand extended.

"I'm sorry, Red. Honest," he said sincerely. "I take it back."

Red grinned again and shook Jack's hand. "O.K., Jack," he said, in a cheerless tone.

Bert Cooney, surprised, looked on in silence. Then anxious to restore the cheerfulness that reigned a moment ago, he ignored what had happened and said, "Say, fellows, I've got some more news."

"About what?" asked Steve, quickly.

"Some of the other councillors want to trade cabins with me. One of them even offered a tennis racket to boot."

"Why?" asked Red.

"Well, so far I've had a snap. They haven't. Some of them have had to gallop all over the place to keep track of their campers. They say that you fellows evidently can take care of yourselves."

Cabin Nine smiled. They appreciated that compliment.

"They were in today looking over our cabin, and didn't find a single thing out of its place. Everything was as neat as a pin," continued Bert.

"That must have been before Red came in," said Steve, quietly.

"Yeh?" demanded Red. "Say, Bert, are you going to listen to these guys, or are we going for that hike?"

Just then taps sounded and the light, controlled by a switch in the director's office, was turned off.

"No. Let's turn in, Red," answered Bert. "But listen, fellows. About that madman in the woods.

Don't spread that rumor too much tomorrow. It might frighten some of the little kids."

"Like Steve," quickly added Red. The campers of Cabin Nine were still thinking of the wild man when slumber overtook them.

Before noon the next day every boy in camp knew of the supposed wild man in the woods. The rumor had gained in definite detail as it passed from group to group. Some of the boys could even describe him. Several of them had wondered at the shots they had heard during the night, they said, but didn't want to say anything about it. During the afternoon, three of the young campers who had been along the shore of the lake came running back to camp with the startling news that they had seen him "on the other side. No hat on, and a big black beard. He stared at us, too."

Red Devlin alone seemed to be the only camper who was at all anxious to test the truth of the rumors. He coaxed almost all of the available councillors, one by one, to accompany him and "a few more guys" on a trip through the woods. The smaller boys looked at Red in frank admiration, as they listened to him pleading for a hike. Unable to get a councillor to go with him, he asked that he be allowed to go alone.

"No, Red," said Bert Cooney, "I can't allow you to do that. Father Walsh would have to give you that permission, and he and Major Williams have gone out of the camp and won't be back until this evening."

The day passed happily. Even tales of wild men in the neighboring woods couldn't keep the boys away from baseball, football, tennis and the lake. The woodcraft shelter took part of Red's time today. He decided to build a bird house. "One of those tricky ones, without any nails in it," he announced. "You make it all with twigs and a knife."

Mr. Joseph, the village carpenter, who came to the camp each day and took charge of the handicraft and woodcraft activities, gave Red a few preliminary instructions and left him to himself.

Shortly before supper, Father Walsh and Major Williams returned. They were immediately surrounded by excited boys, all talking at once, trying to tell the director and his guest all about the wild man in the woods.

"Well," exclaimed the priest, laughing. "Is that so?" Then he and the Major disappeared into the cottage.

Soon the senior councillor came to Father Walsh. "What's all this about?" asked the priest, smiling. "I hear that you have a wild man in the woods."

"Well, Father," answered the councillor, with a laugh, "nobody really said so. A few of us just dropped a hint, mentioned a rumor, and the boys themselves did the rest. Why, some of them claim to have seen and heard him."

"What's the idea?" asked the priest.

"We are planning a ghost-hunt for tonight. You remember what Father Sexton said about the keen fun it was a few weeks ago," explained the councillor. "We thought, as long as most of these boys are pretty big fellows, to give them a new thrill out of the ghost hunt. They'll be told, of course, that the ghost will be a fake, a councillor in white oil cloth, with a flash light to light himself up every now and then out there in the dark; but the idea of a possible wild man loose in the woods might add a little zest to the hunt."

"What about the little fellows? There are a dozen or so that might be badly scared," cautioned Father Walsh, frowning.

"We will let them in on the secret. In fact, one of their own councillors is going to play the wild man. They'll bring up the rear, enjoying the hoax played on the big fellows."

"By George," exclaimed the Major, who had been listening. "I'm going on that hunt myself. It should be great fun."

"We were going to ask you to come," said the councillor. "We thought that, perhaps you could help us keep the little fellows from being scared."

"Certainly," agreed the Major. "I think I'll have a talk with some of them now. We'll fix those big fellows. What's the plan?"

"After dark," explained the councillor, "Jim Saunders slips out into the woods. Whether he's seen or not makes no difference; the boys will know that he's out there. A few of us will know pretty well where he will 'flit,' for he's a ghost, you know, and has to 'flit.' With the aid of his flash light and the oil-cloth, he'll appear and disappear, on the ground, in the trees—he'll use a pole to hoist the costume for that—almost anywhere. The game is to catch him. Flashlights are forbidden, except to the leaders. The boys go in groups of eight, holding a rope that not only slows them up in the chase, but keeps them together. Unless the ghost is caught within an hour or so, he slips back into camp and fires the rising cannon. If he's caught, he has to take the group that catches him into town and stand a treat for them."

"Good," exclaimed Major Williams.

"Now, it's up to you and Father Walsh," continued the councillor, "to assure the boys that the rumor of the wild man is totally untrue. Otherwise, we may not be able to get some of them out there, and those who'd stay behind might be badly scared. You see, the councillor who is going to play the part of the crazy man will shoot and yell for all he's worth when the hunt is well underway."

Darkness could not come quickly enough for the boys. Major Williams told them that he wouldn't miss the hunt for anything, wild man or no wild man. That settled it. Not a camper showed any inclination to remain in the camp. Major Williams' little friends went around whispering and chuckling; they were the only campers who knew that a "wild man" was due to put in his appearance while the boys were trying to catch the "ghost."

CHAPTER XII

The Ghost Hunt

NATURE seemed to conspire with the councillors of Camp St. Mary that night. No stars, no moon; only inky blankness, with a soft breeze swishing through the trees, foretelling a storm. The entire camp was gathered into groups, under the strong light that flooded the campus from the top of the tower at the end of the recreation hall. Each group of eight boys shared a rope that was to keep them together and, as Bert Cooney jestingly remarked, "tangle them up." A councillor was at the end of each group. The campers were to do the hunting and lead the way. Assembled on the campus the boys were now impatiently waiting for the light to be switched off, the signal that the hunt was on. "All ready," called the senior councillor, and off went the light, leaving Camp St. Mary pitch dark.

A shout went up. "There he is," yelled the boys, and away went the pursuers across the campus. At the direction of the senior councillor the groups spread out fan-like as they neared the woods. "He's liable to appear again anywhere, you know," he explained. He swept the woods with a powerful flashlight. Of course the ghost was nowhere to be seen.

"All right, fellows," called the councillor. "From now on each group is on its own. Keep a tight hold of the rope. Good luck to you. Remember that the campers and not the councillors are to do the hunting."

A low rumble of distant thunder came softly. "We'll be back before it rains," remarked Bert Cooney to his group.

Peering into the blackness and gingerly feeling their way through bushes and trees, the campers behind Red spied the weird sheen of the ghost slowly moving about 150 feet ahead of them.

"There he is," called one of the boys.

"Where?" came excitedly from other groups. It was so dark the boys could not see a foot ahead of them, as they moved cautiously along. From somewhere behind them, they heard a councillor playfully scolding and urging his campers onward.

"Somebody is chicken," laughed Steve. They were skirting the edge of the woods now, fumbling and stumbling along, and keeping a watchful eye for the next appearance of the ghost. A constant chatter of loud talking came from all sides.

"Hey, shut up," called out Jack. "He can't see you, and if you keep quiet, he won't know where you are either. You're like a bunch of scared kids in a dark basement, talking out loud to make believe you're brave."

Jack's warning seemed sensible, and the loud talk became guarded whispers. The sighing of the wind through the branches overhead covered the slight noise the boys made. At least, they hoped it did. Soon, in what seemed to be a clearing, the eerie figure appeared again. Those who saw it gasped and hastened forward into the darkness. In their eagerness, they tripped time and again over unseen fallen tree trunks or got tangled in underbrush. As they plodded along in the darkness, trying their best not to make any noise, the occasional momentary flash from a leader's light showed them nothing but trees and bushes, and the darkness that followed the light seemed each time to be deeper and more impenetrable. After a time, they saw towards the crest of a hill in front of them, the dim flash of the ghost's light, a plain signal; then the ghost turned into their faces the beam of a far more powerful light, and laughed at them. They started toward the light, but found that climbing the hill in the dark was slow and tedious work. "Wish he'd show that light down here again," murmured one of the boys. The noise of crackling twigs and the shuffle of slow moving feet told Red's group that another group of searchers was nearing them. Red began in a mournful voice to chant the weird camp song:

> "Your eyes fall in, and your teeth fall out;
> The worms crawl over your nose and mouth."

The boy behind Red giggled, but the chant was interrupted by a pleading voice from a youngster in the rear, "Nix, Red, please," he pleaded, jokingly, "it's bad enough now."

"Hang on to the rope," cautioned Red."

"Heck, I'm scared to let go," frankly admitted the boy.

Again the thunder rolled; this time it was much closer. "Now I lay me," began Steve, in a whisper, feigning fright, and the boys with him chuckled.

The ghost suddenly appeared again for an instant and was gone. This time he was far off to the right. "That ghost is crazy," declared one of the boys. "He's hopping all over the place."

Just then, not very far off to their right, the boys heard a mournful wail, and, following the cry, they say, the ghost ascending up, up, up, into space. It seemed to hesitate a moment, then vanish as quickly as it appeared. The silence of the night was suddenly shattered by a scream. The boys froze in their steps. Bang! Bang! Two shots in quick succession reverberated through the woods. Sharp echoes came clearly from across the lake.

"The wild man!" gasped Jack. Loud exclamations of surprise and fright came from all sides.

"Applesauce," growled Red. "It's some wise guy. Pipe down."

Suddenly another shot rang out. "If there's a crazy man out there, he's shooting at the ghost," exclaimed Steve. Deathlike stillness reigned throughout the woods as the echoes of the shot died away.

"Maybe some guy is shooting at Rogers; he's the ghost," gasped one of the boys. Then Red went into action. "Hey, Rogers!" he shouted. "Rogers, Oh

Rogers!" The boys waited for a reply. "He doesn't answer," exclaimed Red, thoroughly excited. "Hey, Bert, give me the light. I'm going up there. Where's Bert?" demanded Red, peering into the darkness around him. "Get Bert, tell him to come after me," exclaimed Red, as he dropped the rope and plunged off alone into the inky blackness.

"Red," called Bert, as he turned the rays of his flashlight on the departing boy. "Red! Come back."

Red turned, and Bert switched off the light. "Let's have that light, Bert," he demanded. "Rogers may be hit."

"Wait a minute," said Bert, as with the other boys he started toward Red.

Then farther to the right, in what seemed to be a clearing, the boys again saw the ghost. This time it seemed to be dancing. Rogers had heard Red's call and took this means of showing him that he was unhurt. Then he shot the beams of his strong flashlight at Red's party, and laughed loudly. He was standing in a broad path that ran straight the whole distance between him and the searchers, but Red and his party, not having discovered the path, were almost crawling through the underbrush that skirted it. They leaped out into the road and tore down toward the ghost. Rogers kept the light on them until they had run up the path about twenty-five feet; then he suddenly switched it off and left them in utter darkness. They ran on, and, in a few moments, they again heard the ghost laughing at them, this time behind them. Rogers was striving hard to get them interested in the ghost hunt again. "He fooled us. We ran past him," exclaimed Bert.

Just then the wild man shrieked again, now from deep in the woods off to their left, and again his gun split the silence of the night. This time Red thought he saw the flash from the gun-fire. "Let's sneak up closer and get a look at him," he suggested. "The ghost is safe."

"No, Red," said Bert quickly. "He's got a gun. Let him alone."

"Aw, he can't see us in the dark," insisted Red. "You've got a flashlight. We'll sneak up, and you get behind a tree and turn your light where you think he is."

"Nothing doing," said Steve, firmly. "Let's get out of here. That guy is crazy, no fooling. He'd kill you, maybe."

The boys could hear the subdued voices of campers and councillors all around them. Some of the boys were rebelling against hunting any longer for the ghost. They were afraid of the wild man; they wanted to go back.

Suddenly a sharp rumble of thunder was followed by flashes of lightning that danced in the sky and illuminated the woods as clearly as the noonday sun. With its disappearance came darkness that took the boys' breath away. They could not even dimly see the boy trudging along nearest to them. But the wild man had seen them, and now he came toward them crashing noisily through the underbrush and screaming in a most insane and terrifying manner.

"Lie down," whispered Red. "If he comes close enough we'll tackle him. There are enough of us here to handle him if we get the jump on him. Steve, you hang on to the rope. Keep quiet.

Tense expectancy gripped the boys as, flat on the ground, they awaited the approach of the wild man. A little distance from them, they heard some campers call "There's the ghost." Instinctively they turned their heads in the direction of the sound, but could see nothing. Then the noise of the wild man's approach suddenly stopped.

"Take me back; take me back," one boy some distance from Red's group began to whimper. "I want to go back."

Indistinct voices and noises gradually growing fainter and fainter told Red's group that the scared boy and his companions were moving away. Bang! The report of the wild man's gun scarcely fifty feet away was followed by a shrill scream from some young camper off in the woods, now thoroughly scared.

Red's lips tightened. He had begun to suspect from his councillor's reluctance to have anything to do with the wild man, that Bert knew the wild man was another councillor. Now, "Joke or no joke," he angrily exclaimed, "that's going too far. He's picking on the little kids."

A strong light appeared through the woods in the region whence came the scream, and Major Williams's voice boomed out, "It's all right, sonny. I'm coming. Don't be scared."

"Here we are, Major," called the boy's councillor, as he turned on his flash-light. Red and his friends heard voices ringing with hearty welcome; more than the scared boy were glad to see the Major. Then the light went out.

They could hear Major Williams talking low and rapidly, and the smothered laugh of the boys that followed whatever Major Williams said aroused Red's suspicions to the point of practical certainty. "Say, Bert," he demanded, "is this thing a fake?"

"Shh—" commanded Bert, "he'll hear you."

Then came through the night a blood-curdling yell from the wild man, and the crackling of branches told the boys, still lying on the ground, that he was coming again straight toward them. Instantly, Red began to squirm forward. Suddenly the man stopped—and Red stopped breathing. He was sure that the fellow was not six feet in front of him. Should he jump at him? Was there a tree in the way? Red could hear the thumping of his heart. Then a flash of lightning whipped across the sky, and Red saw the man, standing with his back turned, his gun raised over his head. Bang! went the gun, and Red sprang to his feet and, bending low, dashed at the man, his arms outstretched to tackle him. Red struck the man at the knees, wrapped his arms around the fellow's legs, lunged forward fiercely. With a cry of genuine surprise, the wild man went down. In an instant Red's pack was upon him. "The rope, the rope," called Red, as his mates piled on top of the prostrate but wildly struggling "wild man."

Bert Cooney, bent double with laughter, turned the light on the struggling mass of arms and legs. The boys had caught and were holding helpless on the ground Tom Kalas, the councillor-wild man, who, blinded by the rays of Bert's light, was vainly endeavoring to free himself from his captors.

"Let him up," cried Bert. "It's Tom Kalas."

"Nice going, Bert," gasped Tom angrily, as the boys suddenly released him at Bert's command. "You put them wise, didn't you?"

"No, Tom," laughingly declared Bert. "On the square. I couldn't keep them back. Blame Red."

With the exception of Red, the campers were now laughing. They were glad that it was only a joke. Jack was holding Tom's gun.

"Some wild man," exclaimed Red, sarcastically, as he reached out to help Tom to his feet. "You scared one of the little kids, anyhow, if that was your game."

"You had us going, too," said Steve. "Own up to it, Red. You were as scared as I was."

"Hereafter," declared Tom Kalas, "I'm only going to play Santa Claus when you fellows are around." He was brushing himself off and rubbing his bruises. "You've got me all bent up," he said ruefully.

Bert was still laughing; what a story for the school next year!

"Let's get that ghost, now," exclaimed Jack. "He'll be back in camp soon if we don't."

Bert snapped off the light. The lightning shimmered in the western sky again, and by its light, the councillors and the boys got their bearings.

"The path is just in front of us," said Bert. "The last appearance of the ghost showed that he was slowly moving toward the camp."

Red thought of the scared young camper. He made a megaphone of his hands and yelled into the night: "Cabin Nine speaking. Wild man captured by Cabin Nine. Gives his name as Tom Kalas, councillor at Camp St. Mary, Cabin Four. Identified by Councillor Cooney, now leading wild man home. Much tamer now."

"Yea!" rose a long, hearty cheer from searching parties within the range of Red's voice. Then from the silent woods came the mockingly weird voice of the ghost, "Cabin Nine not so hot. Ghost ran right past them."

At the sound of the voice, Red, forgetting the rope, started swiftly but cautiously toward it. Bert didn't notice his leaving, and Red had gone about forty or fifty feet before he realized that, contrary to orders, he had left his group. He stopped and turned. Inky blackness was all around him. He started back. He had gone only a few feet when he heard his pals' voices. He listened, startled. They seemed to come from far to his left. He started that way, but an almost impenetrable wall of heavy bushes, higher than his head, confronted him. Within fifty feet of his group, he was lost in the dark. Then he heard Bert call, "Oh, Red!"

Red was just about to answer when he heard low voices and the noise of bodies moving slowly through the brush to his right that told him another group was cautiously approaching. Curious to identify the boys, he listened. "I'll bet that Redhead was in on that," came a voice that Red recognized as Charlie Russell's. Then back again to his right, he heard Bert's voice, but could not understand what he said. Bert turned on his flashlight and slowly moved it in a circle. Charlie Russell's group evidently saw it, for the noise of their approach suddenly ceased. Red grinned and began to give his best imitation of a growl, followed by the well known signal of his friends, the call of the wood pee-wee.

"What's that?" gasped one of the boys with Russell. Then Red heard the call softly answered by Steve or one of his group. He growled again and added, for good measure, an angry snarl.

"Let's get out of here," gasped one of the startled Gleaners.

Red grinned. He dropped to his knees and started toward the voice, growling ferociously. Bill Murray, accompanying the group of Gleaners, snapped on his light, but Red was still concealed by the intervening undergrowth. The light went out. Then Red heard the pee-wee call again, and, straightening up, answered it. It evidently meant nothing to the frightened Gleaners and their puzzled councillor, but it gave direction to the boys from St. Mary's, who closer now, heard the growl and the voices of the Gleaners. Bert's flash went on, and Steve quickly covered it with his hand.

"Red's kidding some Gleaners," he whispered to Bert, joyously.

Then came the voice of Bill Murray, who, with the Gleaners in his charge, had seen the instantaneous flash of Bert's light, before Steve could cover it. "If you're human, speak!" commanded Murray. Red was laughing so hard that he had difficulty composing himself for another wild snarl, as he made a sudden rush a few feet forward through the brush toward the Gleaners, and then dropped to the ground.

"It's coming," cried a voice in suppressed terror. "It's over here." Red recognized the voice as Small's.

"Climb a tree," urged Murray, who by this time had decided that some of the other boys were responsible for both the light and the animal noises, and willingly entered into the fun. Then Red heard a smothered snicker not far behind him, and realized that his group knew what was going on. The noise of a hurried scramble told him and the boys from his cabin that the Gleaners were seeking means to escape. He began a loud hissing.

"What's that? Listen!" exclaimed Russell, startled. Obligingly Red repeated the hissing, as he backed away toward his partners. A soft pee-wee call, as softly answered, told him they were not far behind him. Soon he was with them, the entire party smothering with suppressed laughter.

"The tough guys," whispered Red. "Scared stiff. Let's mooch off and leave them here. That'll be their initiation into the woods."

"Boy," exclaimed Jack, "I still remember the first time I went through here at night. It's no place for a city fellow."

"It's time to start back anyhow," Bert said softly. "There's a road back here a ways. Don't make a sound. We'll get away if Murray doesn't use his flash-light and I don't think he will. It's too good a joke on the Gleaners; he won't spoil it."

The boys, moving as silently as possible, hardly reached the road when the "boom" of the camp cannon told them that the ghost hunt was over and the ghost safe home. Then from near and far in the dark woods came loud bursts of whistles carried by the councillors, followed by happy calls back and forth that came closer and closer as the groups still in the woods made their way, with the help of their leaders' flash-lights, to the camp, now brightly illuminated by the tower flood lights.

When Cabin Nine reached the campus, the campers already back were gathered around the uncaught ghost, exchanging tales of amusing incidents of the hunt. Not a few of the campers were examining the damage that their scramble through the dark woods had done to their clothes, their arms, and their bare legs. Taps would find some of them daubed with mercurochrome till they looked like Indians in war paint. Of course, most of them denied that they were at all frightened by the shots and cries of the wild man, who, plainly embarrassed by his capture, was now coming across the lighted campus with Red's group. He was greeted by the campers with playful hoots and jeers of derision.

By the time Bill Murray and his group of Gleaners appeared everybody knew of the hoax Red had played. The Gleaners broke away from Murray and came into camp on the run, their faces lighted up with excitement. But when scores of waiting boys broke out into a variety of growls and hisses, they suddenly realized that somebody had fooled and frightened them, and that now the whole camp knew the story.

"Wait a minute," exclaimed Charlie Russell. "We're in for it. Somebody pulled a fast one on us. Let's make the best of it."

The half-hearted denials of fright made by some of the Gleaners were met by sharper accusations. Others frankly admitted that they were scared. "And how!" Charlie Russell added emphatically.

The threatening storm had not yet broken, and the boys were clamoring for a "midnight dip," although it was not much past nine o'clock. A midnight dip meant any swim period after dark.

"O.K.," agreed Father Walsh, "but you'll have to hurry. That storm will soon be upon us. Turn on the beach lights," he called to the councillors. The boys hurried into their cabins, changed to their swimming togs, and ran down to the brightly lighted beach. Fifteen minutes later, the megaphone sounded "All out."

Before the boys reached their cabins the rain was upon them. "Night prayers in your cabins tonight," called the Senior Councillor, as they scampered through the storm. The sharp peals of thunder and the angry flashes of lightning that seemed to center around the immediate vicinity of the camp caused Father Walsh, sitting on the porch with Major Williams, to remark, with a smile, "Well, they'll all say their night prayers tonight."

CHAPTER XIII

Red's Greatest Trial

EACH day at camp brought a more friendly feeling between most of the Gleaners and the boys from St. Mary's. There was, for boys of good will, too much fun for fighting. Cabin Nine was keeping its promise to Bert Cooney; they did not look for trouble nor take unfair advantage of the four Gleaners who, under Dixon, seemed to be the only members of their club who nursed the old grudge. Major Williams took keen pleasure in watching the rest of his boys enter into the games and contests at camp with a noticeable improvement in their sportsmanship.

"Father," he remarked to Father Walsh, one afternoon as he watched the boys coming up from the lake talking and laughing together after a canoe-tilting contest and a swim, "this stay at camp is going to help my lads more than anything else I can think of."

"Except Major Williams's influence," said Father Walsh, smiling. "I'm afraid that when the boys go back to the city and to that splendid clubroom, my crowd will all want to be Gleaners. Especially now, since they all seem to have learned the story behind that name."

Major Williams laughed. "I'm a bit disturbed over Dixon and his three cronies, though," he said.

"Oh, they'll come through all right," said Father Walsh. "They are beginning to realize now that they are out of step with the rest of the camp. Their sulky attitude is keeping them out of a lot of fun, you know. They'll break soon. Watch and see."

"Well, Father," said Major Williams, "so far I haven't said a word to them. Do you think I should?"

"Not yet. A few of the councillors have talked to them. Let's wait a while," answered Father Walsh.

Just then, Earl Snow, one of the four under discussion, came, almost flying, through the door of Cabin Six, and behind him came the boys who had thrown him out. They stood on the porch of the cabin, laughing heartily at Snow, who, still in his bathing suit, his face flushed and eyes blazing, was trying to remove from across his mouth a wide strip of adhesive tape. The process was evidently a delicate and painful one, and was being keenly enjoyed by the other boys on the porch.

"Now, for heaven's sake, Father," exclaimed Major Williams, "what's the matter with him?"

Father Walsh looked intently across the campus. "Well, it can't be anything serious. Those other boys are laughing about it," he said.

"Well, I'm going to take a closer look," said the Major, as he started toward Cabin Six. The boys saw him coming, and leaving Snow gingerly picking at the tape that gagged him, they re-entered the cabin. As soon as the Major reached Snow, he firmly grasped a loose corner of the strip of tape in his fingers. "Hold still," he commanded, and with a single quick jerk, removed the tape from Snow's mouth. A sudden sharp sting brought tears to Snow's eyes, as he spat out a mouthful of creamy lather. Leaving the boy coughing and spitting, he entered the cabin. One of the boys was putting the cap back on the councillor's tube of shaving cream.

"What's all the excitement?" he asked sternly. "Why the gag and the soap?"

"Make Snow tell you, Major, please," answered one of the boys. "If we say anything, it might sound like tattling." The Major, with a twinkle in his eye, turned to the door. He had already guessed the truth. "Snow," he called. There was no answer, and Snow was nowhere to be seen.

"He's behind the cabin, Major," answered a youngster standing nearby. "I guess he's sick or something," he added significantly.

Major Williams smiled. Then turning back to the boys of Cabin Six, who were now looking through the rear window and door and laughing at Snow's distress, he said quietly, "O.K., boys," and went out to Snow.

"Well, Snow," he asked, "What's wrong?"

"I'm going home," blurted out Snow.

"Why?" asked Major Williams blandly. By this time Dixon, Small and Kane, the fourth of the troublesome quartet, with a few other boys, had gathered in a group, within earshot of the conversation. Having been busy

in their own cabin, changing their clothes after the
swim, most of them missed the excitement in front
of Cabin Six. Major Williams, seeing the group of
onlookers, raised his voice and asked, "Why did those
boys put soap in your mouth and then tape it up?"

At this question, all the boys, even Dixon and his
friends, broke out into a merry laugh. They understood.
Snow started toward the door of his cabin. Major
Williams grasped his arm. "Listen, Snow," he said, "you
had it coming to you, didn't you?" Snow didn't answer.

"We warned him half a dozen times, Major," called
a voice from the cabin window.

At this point, Bill Murray walked up to the group.
By the time he reached Snow and the Major, he had
learned from one of the boys what had happened.
"Can't take it, Snow, can you?" asked Murray. Then
he turned to the Major. "The Gleaners have declared
war on indecent speech, Major," he explained. "Both
cabins. A good squeeze of soap and a piece of tape
across the offender's mouth is the penalty. The boys
chose that themselves, and it looks as though Snow got
caught. That's all."

"Aw, did I mean it?" angrily demanded Snow of Bill
Murray.

"Didn't mean it?" asked the Major, smiling. "Well,
that's good."

" 'Didn't mean it' doesn't go in Cabin Six, Major,"
called one of the boys, laughing. "Anybody can say that
when he's caught."

By this time the boys of Cabin Six, having finished changing their clothes, came out of the cabin. "He shouldn't be sore, Major," declared one of them. "He agreed to the penalty. If one of us said it, and he was around, he'd be glad to pile on and tape us up."

"Major," said Jim Cox, "Snow is in Cabin Seven, and his own cabin bought a big, new tube of soap yesterday afternoon. One of them even had it with him at the ball game this morning; he had the tape and everything, all ready, just laying for the first one of us to make a slip."

"Yes, and we nearly got you!" exclaimed one of Snow's cabin-mates.

"When?" demanded Cox, indignantly.

"When you got tagged out sliding home. That's when," came the answer.

Cox feigned surprise. He was about to make a vigorous denial, but a general laugh from the Gleaners made him look around and realize that it would be useless. "Well, I caught myself, didn't I?" he demanded. Major Williams patted him on the shoulder. Then he turned to Snow.

"Now, Snow," he said, "change your clothes and forget it. Keep your ears open, and, if you can, get back at them; that's all."

The storm was over. Major Williams walked back to the director's cottage with a light heart.

"They're coming around, Father," he said to Father Walsh, waiting on the porch. Then he told the story.

"I'll bet Bill Murray is behind that," he said quietly when Major Williams had finished.

Father Walsh turned to see Steve Nolan coming across the campus. "Father, do you know where Red is?" Steve asked. "We haven't seen him since the rest period after lunch."

"Yes," answered Father "Walsh. "I had to send him into the city on an errand. He just had time to dress and catch the train. I sent him in to get some films for my movie camera. He'll be back before you are up tomorrow morning."

Steve walked back to the Cabin.

"Devlin knows a lot about cameras and films," Father Walsh explained to the Major. "He's my right hand man in taking care of my movie camera at home and at camp."

"That lad is pretty well liked by the boys, isn't he?" remarked the Major.

"Yes," answered Father Walsh, "but he's very sensitive, and that gets him into trouble once in a while. He can't stand ridicule." Father Walsh walked up and down the porch thoughtfully. "It's his only weakness," he continued. "He's a regular daredevil, apart from that," he added with a laugh. "See that flag pole out there?" Major Williams nodded, smiling. "Well, last summer," said Father Walsh, "I heard a lot of yelling outside the cottage one afternoon, and came out on the porch just in time to see Red on his way to the top of that pole. The little monkey was more than half-way up. He had his legs around the pole and was pulling himself up hand over hand on the ropes. I yelled at him to get down, and when I tried to scold him for his foolishness, he calmly informed me that before he started, he had hung on the ropes to make sure they would hold him. It seems that one of his friends saw him, and dared him to climb the pole; so up he went."

"Why, if he ever fell, he'd be killed," exclaimed the Major, shaking his head.

Suddenly the Major straightened in his chair and peered intently across the campus. "Look," he exclaimed, "some lad is hurt." Father Walsh turned and saw one of the campers carrying a smaller lad to the doctor's cabin.

"That's Small carrying him, isn't it?" asked Father Walsh.

"Yes, that's Small," answered the Major. "The lad can't be hurt very much; they're both laughing."

"Say, Major," exclaimed Father Walsh joyfully. "That lad is young Fields. Does that mean anything to you?"

"Fields?" repeated the Major. "Why, no. Who is he?"

Father Walsh laughed. "Why, that's the boy Small slapped that famous Sunday afternoon. Don't you remember? That slap occasioned the miniature riot between your crowd and mine."

"By jove," exclaimed the Major, rising from his chair. "That's right. They must have squared things up."

Major Williams's surmise was correct. Sonny Fields had been playing on the swinging rings in the minim's Playground, and falling, had twisted his ankle. Small, stretched out on the grass nearby, had seen the accident, and when Fields got up, and, trying to walk, tumbled over again, Small ran over, picked the boy up, and started to the doctor's cabin for first-aid. He had the boy in his arms before he recognized him. The game youngster was biting his lip to keep back the tears. Small blushed with shame at the recollection of his disgraceful blow that Sunday afternoon.

"I sprained my ankle, I guess," said Sonny, weakly. "I can't stand on it." Then he saw who was carrying him. "Hello, Small," he said, grinning in spite of the pain. "Take me to Doc's office, please. Will you?"

"Sure," answered Small, gruffly.

"Are you sore at Red?" asked Sonny.

"Huh?" asked Small, pretending not to have heard the question distinctly.

"Red's a good guy," said the youngster.

"He's sore at me," said Small, evasively. Sonny Fields moved his ankle, and a spasm of sharp pain flashed across his face. He gritted his teeth. Then, he said slowly, "Aw, Red don't stay sore at anybody."

"Say, kid," said Small, quietly, as he trudged along, nobody within hearing distance, "I'm sorry I socked you that day." The long delayed apology was made.

"Well," said Sonny, with a smile, "then you knocked me down, and now you picked me up. That squares it, doesn't it?" They both laughed.

Dr. Allen was in his office, and Small gently set Sonny Fields down on a chair and watched while the doctor examined and skillfully bandaged the ankle. "Not a bad sprain," said the doctor. "We'll tape it up a bit, and then you stay off of it for a while." In a few moments he dismissed his patient. "You take care of him," he said to Small.

"You can't walk," said Small to Sonny; "so you'd better climb up on my back." He turned his back to the boy and squatted before the chair. Sonny put his arms around Small's neck, and Small tucked the lad's legs in the crook of his elbows and straightened up.

"Bringing home the wounded," said the doctor, smiling at the pair. Then like a flash there came to Small's mind a thought that lit his face with keen pleasure.

"Well," he said, as he left the doctor's office with his burden, "I'm one of the Gleaners, you know."

As the two passed Cabin Nine, Steve Nolan and Bill Harte came out on the porch to await the call to supper. Their eyes opened wide with surprise as they saw Small and Fields.

"Hello, Steve," called Sonny. "Hello, Bill, I'm wounded. I sprained it." He pointed to the bandaged ankle.

"Nice going, Small," called Steve, pleasantly. Small blushed and grinned. "He sprained his ankle," he explained, disregarding Sonny's explanation. For a full minute the two boys from Cabin Nine watched the "horse and rider" in silence. Then Bill said slowly, "Can you beat that?"

"Red won't believe it," said Steve, smiling.

Small, after supper, appeared at Father Walsh's cottage with Sonny Fields on his back and another young camper beside him. "Father," asked Fields, "may we go out in a boat, just rowing?"

Father Walsh had noted with pleasure the solicitude Small had shown for Sonny before and after supper. "Got a councillor?" he asked, for it was a strict rule at Camp St. Mary that no campers go out in a boat without a councillor.

"I'm taking out a boat with a few lads, Father,"* said Bill Murray, standing near. "I'll stay near them." Bill winked at the director, and furtively nodded his head. He wanted to give Small the responsibility of his own boat.

"O.K.," agreed the director. "You're his councillor."

When Father Walsh and the Major walked down to the pier a little later, they saw Small and his young charges enjoying themselves immensely. Small seemed like a new boy. In the laughing, chattering boy at the oars was no trace of the sullen, somewhat discontented camper of the last few days.

"Well, I guess that takes care of Small," said Father Walsh. "He's in right with the camp now, and he'll have more fun."

"Yes," answered the Major, thoughtfully. "He has found happiness in just being a good fellow."

They returned to the campus to see that everything was in readiness for the evening campfire.

By this time, Red Devlin had reached the city, fulfilled his errand there, and was now standing before the locked door of his home. Nobody answered the bell, and Red had no key. There was a light in the front room, but Red knew that that was merely a floor lamp, kept burning evenings even when nobody was at home.

"Hey, Red," called the boy next door. "They're all gone away. They drove away right after supper."

"Where?" asked Red. "Do you know?"

"Bobbie said that they were going for a ride out into the country," the boy answered.

"Well, tell them tomorrow that I was sent in from Camp on an errand, but had to go back on the night train. Tell them everything at camp is fine," said Red.

"I'll tell them, Frank," called the boy's mother, who had overheard Red's message.

"Thanks," exclaimed Red, doffing his cap. "I had to come in for some films for Father's camera." He held the package up to his neighbor's view. "I guess I'll just knock around a while until it's time for the train."

Red had not gone far when he was hailed by three boys in a small car.

"Hey there, Red," called one of them. "Want a lift?"

The car swung over to the curb and stopped. Red recognized two of the boys, Ken Hobart and Barry Willis. Both of them had just finished their first year in high school. He didn't know the driver.

"I thought you were at camp with the rest of the gang," said Ken.

I was. I'm going back on the night train," answered Red. "Father Walsh sent me in for some stuff."

Hop in," invited Barry Willis, opening the door. "We'll take a spin. You got lots of time before the train goes." Red got into the car.

"What time does the train go?" asked the boy at the wheel, who was introduced to Red as Bonnie Porter.

"11:10," answered Red. Then turning to Ken Hobart, he asked, ""Why didn't you fellows come up to camp this year? This is about the first season you missed, isn't it?"

"Too tame," answered Hobart, with a laugh.

"Do they still put you to bed at 9:30?" asked Willis. Red frowned. He had not seen much of these boys during the school year; during previous summers they were both happy, active campers. Now they seemed to have changed.

"Everything is just as it was before," answered Red, a trifle nettled.

"Heck, we're just starting out at 9:30," boasted Hobart, "The last show doesn't start till 10:30."

"Still have movies in camp?" asked Willis, grinning. "Mickey Mouse and that stuff?"

"The camp movies are all right," declared Red, displeased at the attitude of his friends.

"The one we saw last night was all right, hey, fellows?" called Bonnie, over his shoulder. The three boys broke into a laugh. "And how!" declared Hobart. Then began an excited story of the picture, the three boys talking at once to Red. It was the story of a debasing portrayal of filth that they had seen in a cheap theatre on the darkened fringe of the business district, a theatre that seemed to operate successfully in spite of the law, and that drew its patrons from the scum of the city, the lowest of the men and boys.

Red was startled to hear Willis and Hobart's account of the picture. He sincerely liked these boys; only last summer they seemed to be as fine and clean as any boy at the camp. And now they were describing for Red, with evident pleasure, the indecent scenes in the picture. His amazement prevented him from doing anything but stare at the boys, and they, thinking that the intent look on Red's face was due to his interest in what they were saying, continued hilariously in their sinful recital. The car approached a stop light showing red, and the boys, noticing other cars around them, cautiously lowered their voices. "They know it's wrong," flashed through Red's mind. When the green light flashed, the car started again.

"What's there tonight?" called out Bonnie, swinging the car to the left and passing the cars in front of him.

"The same one," answered Hobart. "There's a new one coming tomorrow, though. The usher said last night's was tame to what's coming."

"Didn't you fellows sign that pledge in the Legion of Decency?" asked Red, bluntly.

"Aw, grow up!" exclaimed Willis, with a laugh. Then Red said, "We had better be getting to the station." He wanted to change the course of the conversation; he was even now worried about what he had listened to. Guiltily he reflected that he had half-heartedly joined in the laughter of the boys, once or twice.

"Don't worry. We'll get you there in time," said Bonnie.

His amazement prevented him from doing anything but stare at the boys, and they, thinking that the intent look on Red's face was due to his interest in what they were saying, continued hilariously in their sinful recital.

"Say, Red," exclaimed Hobart, grinning. "Why not tell the kids at camp that story? That would make a good camp fire story."

"Why don't you come out and tell it?" countered Red.

"Here's one you can tell them," called Bonnie. A quick frown of displeasure crossed Red's face. The story, as Red expected, was unclean, but it had an unexpected and comical ending that made all the listeners, including Red, laugh at it. Red's laugh died suddenly. Was he taking pleasure in a dirty joke? He was confused. He did not want to hear it, but he laughed at it. While Red was feverishly trying to untangle the twists of his conscience, another story followed, less comical but dirtier. This time Red, whispering a prayer, leaned back in his seat, bit his lip, and said nothing. He forcibly fastened his mind on Cabin Nine and his friends there to help banish the sinful picture the story painted in his imagination.

Barry Willis, in the front seat, looked over his shoulder. He saw Red and laughed. "That one knocked Red out," he exclaimed. Bonnie, who had told the story, laughed aloud. Hobart glanced at Red beside him and exclaimed, "Why, we're just giving him a few good ones to take back to camp. I hear Major Williams is out there with a crowd he picked up. How are they getting along, Red?" he asked

"Great," said Red, enthusiastically, glad to have an end to the story telling. "There are some dandy fellows in that outfit. One of them..."

But Willis interrupted, "I'll bet the Major has some keen stories," he exclaimed, with a smile. "Those soldiers always have."

"He certainly has," exclaimed Red, before he realized the insinuation in Willis's last remark.

"Yes?" asked Hobart, anxiously. "Does he tell them to you? Tell us some of them."

Red saw that he was misunderstood. "I mean war stories, not...dirty stories," he said somewhat weakly, trying not to offend the boys in the car.

"You mean bedtime stories," called Bonnie, with a sneer. Hobart and Willis laughed. "All about Big Mr. Bear and Little Mr. Rabbit," continued Bonnie.

Red was embarrassed and growing angry. "You still go for bedtime stories, Red?" asked Willis with a grin.

Before Red could answer, Hobart said, with a disdainful wave of his hand, "Oh, grow up, Red. Don't be a baby all your life. Get over that sissy stuff."

"Oh, Red's all right," added Willis. "He's got a lot to learn, that's all."

Red laughed, a weak, embarrassed laugh. Then Bonnie said, "Red is like the fellow who..." and off he went into a coarse, though humorous, story. That story awakened, away back in Red's memory, the recollection of a story that had not meant much to him when he heard it, and had passed from his mind. Now it returned. Red smiled. It was, indeed, funny, and not very coarse. Should he tell it? It would fit in perfectly with the one Bonnie had just told.

"Did you get the point, Red?" asked Willis, with a patronizing air. The other boys awaited Red's answer.

"Sure," he said, petulantly. "That's like..." and then he began the story. He had hardly started when he faltered. He had never in his life told a bad joke or story. Was he fooling himself about this one? Now that he had started it, to stop, he feared, would be to expose himself to the ridicule of the boys listening to him eagerly. But... He suddenly stopped. "I ... I forget now just how the last part goes," he lied weakly. Bonnie, listening intently, instantly picked up the threads of the broken story, and, to Red's surprise and confusion, improvised a conclusion far coarser than the one Red had in mind.

"That's a peach, Red," exclaimed Willis. "Do you know any more?"

A crushing sense of guilt and shame came over Red. His mouth and tongue went dry, the light of fear shone in his eyes, his face paled, and he felt faint. His companions were still laughing and commenting on the story when Bonnie stopped the car in front of the depot. Red got out mechanically, and, with a solemn, unsmiling, "thanks for the ride, fellows," turned and entered the station. He was positively wretched with remorse as he waited for the train. Soon he was lying back in a luxurious reclining chair, speeding back to camp. The car porter dimmed the lights, but there was no sleep for Red. He tried and tried to analyze his conduct during the auto ride in the light of all that he had learned in his catechism classes. "A grievous matter, sufficient reflection, and full consent of the will," he recalled. He well knew that definition, but never before did he have seriously to apply it to his own conduct. He did not deceive himself about the seriousness of the matter; dirty talk, dirty stories. Red had no doubts about that. "Did I realize?" he began to himself. He stopped suddenly. The question made him feel like a hypocrite. Of course, he realized! Consent? Red felt his cheeks burn with shame and humiliation. He remembered that he whispered an aspiration a couple of times, but...he couldn't decide. He was afraid he might be deceiving himself. He covered his face with his hands, and a piteous, "Oh, God," was all the prayer the miserable boy could say.

He thought of Ken Hobart and Barry Willis. What could have come over them? When did they begin to change? Who was Bonnie Porter? Was it he who had led them astray? That picture! Red saw before him the gleeful faces of his two friends, and in his ears rang snatches of their rotten story. He shook his head vigorously as instinctively he recoiled from the hideous recollection of what he had heard. "Oh, why didn't I get away from them...or tell them to shut up?" he asked himself despairingly. "Now..." Red's brow wrinkled in perplexity..."looks like...my first mortal sin." The thing he had so often prayed would not come into his life. The thing he had feared, he thought, more than anything else in the world. He took some slight consolation from the fact that even tonight no foul word had passed his lips. "Bonnie made up that part," he reflected, "but...oh, why did I have to meet them?" If only his folks had been home.

Red glanced through the open window. The speed of the train was emphasized by the swift appearance and disappearance of shadowy objects along the tracks in the dim light that streamed from the car. Suddenly an express train, racing in the opposite direction, roared past Red's car. It had come and gone in an instant. The appalling thought of a possible wreck broke in Red's mind. Sudden death...No time even to say a prayer...An act of perfect contrition...Red composed himself to say that prayer now. Father Walsh's words in the classroom came back to him: "Just one beat of a guilty heart between life and an eternity in hell... They deliberately chose the state in which sudden death found them...They have no one to blame but themselves...."

"Oh, my God," began Red. He finished the prayer and took out his rosary. Let sudden death find him saying his beads.

And thus, afraid to go to sleep, Red passed the hours until the train stopped at the camp station. Leaving the train, Red looked around him. It was not yet dawn. Everything was hidden in silent darkness. He watched the twinkle of the lantern light on the rear of the departing train until it swung around a curve and was gone. Then he turned and started slowly toward the camp. He knew of a shortcut to the camp, but it was through the heaviest woods. He had planned to take that path, but…"conscience doth make cowards of us all." He chose the longer but more open road. "Thursday morning," he said almost aloud, "tomorrow's the First Friday." Then almost joyfully he said, "There'll be confessions this afternoon." But suddenly his heart sank within him. In his mind, he saw himself kneeling at the confessional of the camp chapel, just at the side of the window. How often he had knelt there, lighthearted and free from serious sin. Even in his dejection, he recalled a head being poked in through the window occasionally "to see how many were there," by campers who waited till the last minute to get ready. Father Walsh would hear confessions this afternoon. His head bent in gloom, he plodded on. What would Father Walsh think of him now? Then came before him the picture of Father Walsh that day in the parlor, after the alley episode. He again heard Father's warning, "that's your whole trouble, Red; you're afraid to be laughed at." Tears came to his eyes. Tonight, he knew, that was the cause of it all. How he hated to admit that, even to himself. Father Walsh and the boys were right. "I guess I just can't take it."

Red was tired and weary when he reached the camp. He quietly set the package of films down on the porch of the director's cottage, and slowly walked across the campus to his cabin. Dawn was just breaking.

CHAPTER XIV

Conscience

RED tiptoed into the cabin. His councillor and cabin-mates were sleeping soundly. He cautiously felt his way through the dark room to his bunk, quietly got ready for bed, knelt to say his prayers, and slipped into bed. He could hear the deep breathing of the sleepers around him. He recalled that Ken Hobart and Barry Willis occupied this very cabin last year. "They're a lot different now, though," he said to himself. Then he added sorrowfully, "And so am I...I can't receive Holy Communion this morning." A lump rose in his throat; he buried his face in the pillow and, broken-hearted, cried himself to sleep.

Father Walsh had given orders to let Red sleep until breakfast. "He'll be pretty tired after his trip," he said. Accordingly, when the cannon boomed the signal for rising, instead of the usual noisy hustle and bustle in Cabin Nine, there reigned a courteous quiet as Red's friends arose and prepared for the day. Red stirred at the noisy greeting of the cannon, partially awakened, but, dead tired, fell fast asleep again.

After Mass, Steve came into the cabin in a lively bound.

"Hey, Red," he called, shaking the sleeper, "come on. Breakfast." Red's eyes opened slowly. Steve was laughing at him. "Come on. Make it snappy, pancakes this morning."

Red sat up in bed. "Hello, Steve," he said drearily. "What time is it?" The sun was shining brightly.

"Time to eat," answered Steve. "Get up now. See you later," he added, as he scampered out of the cabin.

Red slowly got out of bed. He could hear merry voices all over the campus. He sat on the edge of his bed and covered his face with his hands. A surge of loneliness came over him. The happiness of Camp St. Mary was not his. He felt unworthy to associate with the rest of his friends. "They received Holy Communion this morning," he murmured. "I'm not fit to talk to them."

"Hey, Red," came a chorus of voices from the campus.

He stepped to the door and waved to the boys. He didn't have the heart to call out to them. Then he quickly dressed, said his prayers, washed and went to breakfast. The boys at his table noticed that he was unusually quiet. "What's eating you, Red?" asked Bill Harte. "You look as though you lost your last friend." Red smiled weakly and forced himself to take part in the conversation around him.

On the way out of the mess hall, Father Walsh stopped him and said, "Well, Frank, I see you got everything all right. How was the trip?"

Pretty good, Father," answered Red. "My folks were out riding. I didn't see them; I was afraid to wait for them for fear I'd miss the train back."

"You had supper on the train, didn't you?" asked the priest. Red nodded. "Well," said Father Walsh, "I can take some pictures of you fellows now."

As Father Walsh started for his cottage, some of Red's friends, on their way to the cabin, called to him. "Hurry, Red," called Steve, "we've got a ball game on this morning."

Red frowned, but quickened his steps to join his cabin-mates. "Who's playing?" he asked listlessly. He was in no mood for a ball game.

"Two teams made up of campers and councillors," answered Steve. "You're on our team. Bert Cooney is playing with us, too. Jack and Bill here are playing against us today."

"Sorry, boys," exclaimed Bill Harte, with feigned seriousness, "but we're going to trim you, too."

The cabin was ready for inspection in a few minutes. The boys impatiently awaited the visit of the senior councillor. Steve glanced out the door. "Here comes Father Walsh," he said. The boys quickly joined Steve at the door. A visit from Father Walsh so early in the day was unusual. The boys silently noticed the serious look on the priest's face as he entered the cabin.

"Boys, I have some sad news," he said. "I have just received a call from the Rectory. One of the altar-boys who was coming to camp next session was suddenly killed by an automobile while he was on his way to serve the 6:30 Mass this morning."

"Who, Father?" the boys asked quickly.

"Danny Evans," answered Father Walsh. "He was in the seventh grade."

"We knew him, Father," said Bill Harte quietly. "He was coming to camp with us, but some of the fellows in his room got him to switch sessions so he would be with them. He was a swell kid."

"He certainly was," answered Father Walsh. "If there was a boy at St. Mary's who had no reason to fear sudden death, it was Danny. A daily communicant since he made his First Communion."

The cabin swam before Red's eyes. Sudden death! He seated himself on the edge of the bed. He heard Steve's voice as though it came from far away. "He never missed an appointment to serve Mass, either," Steve was saying. Red, unnoticed by the others, buried his face in his hands. He knew Danny Evans well; he had often served Holy Mass with him. He didn't feel sorry for Danny; he envied him. He raised his head as Father Walsh remarked, "The Eternal Priest has called His acolyte." The boys recognized the line; it was from a poem composed by a priest-friend of Father Walsh and tacked up in the sacristy. It was called "His Last Dream," and beautifully portrayed the death of an altar boy.

"He sleeps and, smiling, dreams:
                    On bended knee
He gazes on the Cross; the waxen lights
Seem pentecostal tongues; like clouds that flee
The wind, the smoke of incense trails. Now, rites

Of Holy Mass his fancy keep in thrall:
The priest is Christ; the altar is the Mount
Of Calvary; beyond the Tabernacle wall
Is Love imprisoned—of grace the Living Fount.

The prison opens! From a throne aglow
With light supernal, Christ the King, His face
Benignly sweet, descends, and, bending low,
The dreamer gathers unto His embrace!

He smiles, but dreams no more. His soul takes flight:
The Eternal Priest has called His acolyte."

"That's right," exclaimed Steve Nolan, rather enthusiastically. "On his way to serve Mass."

"It's a break for Danny," said Jack Clemens, "but it's pretty tough for his folks."

"We'll all offer Holy Mass for him tomorrow morning. Tell the other boys, and I'll make an announcement at dinner," said Father Walsh, as he left the cabin.

"Boy!" exclaimed Steve, with feeling. "You can never tell when your turn is coming, or how it's coming, can you?"

"Well," said Bill, "I wouldn't mind getting it that way if I was like Danny. Just a sudden flash and it's all over. A swell kid like him has nothing to fear."

Red slipped out of the cabin while Bill was talking and started across the campus toward the chapel. He wanted to be alone. Many times, as a light-hearted altar boy at St. Mary's, he had read that poem and imagined himself dying the peaceful, happy death of that altar boy as he dreamed he was serving Holy Mass. But now everything was changed, and the thought of death filled him with terror and dismay.

The camp was breaking up for the fun of the day. Boys on all sides were shouting and laughing as preparations for the various activities were under way. But, walking slowly across the campus, Red felt himself out of it all and very lonely. With bowed head he made his way to the chapel to pray—for the grace to make a good confession and start all over again. He didn't see the two boys sitting on the chapel steps until he was almost upon them. Then Sonny Fields's voice brought him back to the camp.

"Hello, Red," he said cheerily. Red looked up and saw Fields and Small. Both were smiling. Fields laughed at the look of surprise that came to Red's face. "We're friends, Red," explained the boy. "I sprained my ankle yesterday and Small took me to the doc. Then he carried me around, 'cause I couldn't walk on the bad ankle."

Red was in no mood to continue unpleasant relations with anybody. He wished later that he had not been so solemn, but at Sonny's words, he put out his hand to Small, smiled weakly, and said, "Nice going, Small." Then he passed on into the chapel.

"Red's going to make a visit," explained Sonny to Small. "He went to the city last night for Father; he had a sleep-over this morning and didn't get to Mass."

Red was still kneeling in prayer when his teammates, impatient to begin the big ball game, began to call loudly for him. He glanced through the open window and saw them waiting just outside the cabin. He had no heart now for a baseball game. He may just as well tell them, he thought, as he arose and left the chapel.

"I don't feel like playing today," he said. "I'm all in." Then turning to Bert Cooney, he said, "Bert, I'd like to lie down for a while. I didn't get much sleep last night. May I?"

"Certainly, Red," agreed Bert. "Go ahead. We'll get somebody to take your place, and we'll call you in time for dinner."

Red said nothing more, but walked into the cabin. He heard the boys moving toward the ball field. He knew that they would have no trouble getting somebody to play in his place. Wistfully, he crossed to the window and watched them until they disappeared around the corner of the cabin nearest to the field. Then he threw himself across the bed disconsolately.

Some time later, Father Walsh and Major Williams strolled across the field to the game. They noticed that Red's usual place at third base was filled by another camper, and that Red was nowhere to be seen.

"Didn't Devlin want to play?" asked Father Walsh of one of the boys.

"No, Father," the boy answered. "He said that he wanted to rest a while. He got permission to stay in the cabin till dinner."

The two men watched several innings of the game; then Major Williams said, "Let's take a look at Red."

They found Red still lying, wide awake, across the bed. He arose as the priest and Major Williams entered the cabin. "Tired, Red?" asked Father Walsh, kindly.

"No, Father, not now," Red answered quietly.

"A bit played out from the trip last night, Red?" asked Major Williams.

Red nodded glumly. "Did you see any of your friends in town?" asked Father Walsh.

"Yes, Father," replied Red, "Ken Hobart and Barry Willis."

"It's too bad they didn't come up with us this year," said Father Walsh.

"Yes, Father," exclaimed Red, somewhat eagerly. Then Red's face flushed and he got a bit panicky. He didn't want to talk about Ken and Barry. He asked quickly: "Is the game over, Father?"

"It's almost over. Your team is winning," answered Father Walsh.

"Does Red know about Danny Evans?" asked Major Williams.

"Yes," answered Father Walsh, as he laid his hand on Red's shoulder. "Red and Danny used to be partners serving Mass. They were both very faithful."

"That should be a very happy memory for you, Red," said Major Williams earnestly. "From what Father told me of Danny, he must have received a happy welcome from Our Lord. He'll be sort of a guardian angel for you fellows now, Red. His going should certainly make his partner feel closer to God. For myself, I haven't felt closer to Him in a long time than I do out here. To see you fellows going up to the Communion railing morning after morning, and putting the same earnestness into your prayers as you do into your games is certainly inspiring."

As the Major spoke, Red's eyes began to blink. He couldn't keep back the tears, tears of shame and humiliation, but the Major and Father Walsh assumed that the thought of Danny's death had deeply moved Red for the moment; so Father Walsh said kindly, "Now, dry up those tears, Red, and get over to the field. Danny wouldn't change places with any of us today, I am sure. I only hope that all you fellows will be as ready to go as Danny was." With that the two men left the cabin.

Red, with a heavy heart, went out to the basin-rack to bathe his face. How could he go to confession to Father Walsh this evening? Maybe he could find some excuse and ask Father to let him go home this afternoon; then he wouldn't have to go to Father Walsh. Red was thoroughly ashamed to tell Father Walsh what happened last night. Perhaps Father Walsh would let him go home to attend Danny's funeral—but that wasn't to take place until Saturday morning. As Red left the cabin for the ball-field, he saw, to his dismay, Father Walsh and Major Williams drive away. What if he didn't come back before the afternoon train had left! There would be nobody in camp who could give him permission to go home.

He took his time going to the ball-field. The game was almost over anyway. He watched the last inning from behind the back-stop. Then, forcing himself to appear cheerful, he walked back with the teams to the cabins. It was now almost time for a swim.

"How about a diving contest today, Bert?" asked Steve, as with bath robes around them and swimming suits and towels in their hands, he and some of the other boys who had been in the game were making their way to the shower-house. Red, in his bathing suit, kept on toward the lake."

"I'll see," said Bert. "Wait till we get down to the pier."

Red waited on the pier until his friends joined him. Then at the signal, "All in," the usual merry splashing as the boys dove into the water made the "sinkers" in the shallow water increasingly anxious to "swim off the sinker." Red started, as usual, straight for the diving platform. Then panic seized him. Suppose he drowned! Cramps…heart failure…sudden death. Father Walsh gone. To die without absolution! He stopped swimming suddenly and stood up in the shallow water. The diving board never seemed so far away. He saw his friends climb up the ladder. One of them, looking back, saw Red.

"Hey, Red," he called. "C'mon out. What's the matter? Chicken?" Red looked longingly toward the diving platform but made no move to swim out there. A youngster on the pier heard the friendly taunt and shouted, "Aw, Red's chicken! Red's chicken! He's afraid to swim out to the high dive."

"I'll chicken you," exclaimed Red, with a forced grin, glad to have an excuse to go back to the pier. As soon as Red climbed up on the pier, the teasing youngster dove off, swam out a little way, and stood up. From what he thought was a temporarily safe place, he renewed his teasing. All the junior campers liked Red, and a chase through the shallow water with him after them never brought them more harm than a moderate ducking. It was worth that. So, following the example of the lad in the water, several of the younger boys took up the cry, "Red's chicken." Red dove after them, but before the chase was well underway, the shrill whistle of a councillor on the pier brought all the swimmers to silence. "All Juniors to the right of the pier for swimming and life-saving instructions," came the announcement. Red was immediately left all alone.

"Hey, Red," called Steve imperiously. "C'mon out. The diving contest is on. You've got to do the jack-knife and the swan for our cabin." Red didn't know what to say or to do. By this time he was back on the pier. The boys had seen him go after the little fellows with what seemed to be his usual zest. He couldn't say that he didn't feel well after that. Well, he wouldn't have them think that he was afraid; so, quickly blessing himself, he dove in again. Before he was half-way to the high dive, however, his imagination and his conscience got the best of him. He turned and swam back to the pier. Charlie Russell was in mid-air doing a fairly good swan dive. "Cabin Nine," shouted Bert Cooney. Red's cabin-mates, who had been giving their attention to Russell, looked around, expecting to find Red climbing up to the platform. They saw, with surprise, that he was again standing on the pier.

"Hey, Red," Steve called impatiently. "C'mon. These guys are ahead of us." Red ignored the call. A rowboat came alongside the pier. "Hop in, Red," said the councillor at the oars. "I'll row you over." Red flushed. Evidently, at least, the councillor actually thought he was "chicken."

"I'm not going over," declared Red, angrily. "I don't want to dive." The waiting boys heard him.

"Aw, we'll do without him," exclaimed Steve. "Jack, you do the swan."

"Well, come on out in the boat then anyhow, Red," invited the councillor, with a smile. "You don't have to get peeved." Red frowned, then quickly smiled back at the councillor, hesitated a moment, and slid down into the boat. The poor fellow tried hard to keep up his end of the conversation about camp affairs and such, but was in decided ill-humor because he knew he had displeased his friends on the diving platform by refusing to take part in the contest. He was glad when the whistle blew "All out." The boat and the divers reached the pier together. Red's cabin-mates just glanced at him. They had lost the contest to the Gleaners. Red's diving would, unquestionably, have won it for them.

Red caught the rebuke in Steve's tone as, jogging past Red, he said curtly, "Nice going, Red." Red bit his lip, but said nothing.

Happy boys in dripping bathing suits were gaily chatting and laughing as they gingerly picked their way up the road to the shower-house. Red noticed that even Snow and Small were pleasantly taking part in the fun; it was plain that they had caught the spirit of the camp. Red returned the greeting of a camper here and there as he walked along more slowly than the other boys. He wished with all his heart that he was once more one of his own happy crowd, now disappearing through the door of the shower-house up on the hill.

CHAPTER XV

The Impossible Happens

AS RED expected, none of the boys in the diving contest asked him why he refused to dive with them. He had displeased them by his refusal; now they were punishing him by ignoring it entirely. As the boys of Cabin Nine dressed after the swim to await the call to dinner, they left Red entirely out of their conversation. Red dressed quietly and walked out of the cabin.

Neither Father Walsh nor Major Williams appeared at dinner; there was no one now in camp who could give him permission to go home. He was secretly glad that the boys at his table did not notice that he had little appetite for food. He tried once or twice to appear cheerful; to pretend that he didn't notice how completely he was left out of the discussion of the diving contest. He realized that his companions were "giving him the silent treatment" to punish him for causing them to lose to the Gleaners. More than once he had participated in such a conspiracy of silence toward one of his group who had fallen into disfavor with the rest. Such discipline amounted to temporary ostracism, and it was generally very effective.

Dinner over, the senior councillor, sitting today at head table with the camp doctor, rang the bell and arose to outline the plans for the afternoon. Two of the camp baseball teams would play their game according to the camp schedule; there would be a volley-ball game; new material for bird-houses had been received and was now at the handicraft shelter; Mr. Joseph, the village carpenter, would be over this afternoon, and the boys who had been waiting to get started or to continue work on the bird-houses, must be ready to do so right after the rest period; Major Williams wanted a group of boys to take a stroll through the woods later on in the afternoon. That announcement was greeted with applause by a lot of the boys who knew that such strolls meant stories and interesting chats about the wild life in the woods—as they ate the Major's candy. The councillors in charge of the various activities were cautioned to see that all campers were back on the campus in time for confessions, five o'clock.

Then the senior councillor continued. "Cabins Six and Nine go horseback-riding today." They were to leave the camp in the truck at two o'clock, get their horses at the stable in town, and be back at the stable in time to meet the truck that would carry them home later in the afternoon.

At this announcement the boys at Red's table immediately began to register their claims for their favorite mounts. As some of the horses were less spirited than others, the more adventurous of the campers always wanted to avoid being assigned to ride the "nags." Red's cabin, it was generally conceded, had the best riders in the camp, and, of course, to them were usually assigned the horses more difficult to manage. Steve and Red could ride better than most councillors delegated to accompany them.

Red had gained fame the previous summer by chasing at top speed and catching a horse that, annoyed by the antics of an inexperienced rider on his back, got out of the boy's control and broke into a wild dash down the road toward the peace and quiet of his stable. Red was after him in an instant. The runaway horse, with his frightened rider clinging for dear life to the pommel of the saddle, seemed to catch the spirit of the chase as Red's horse came flying alongside of him and ran all the faster. Red, urging his mount to greater speed, caught up again with the runaway, and, without thought of danger to himself, leaned out of his saddle, secured a tight hold on the bridle of the horse dashing home at break-neck speed, and gradually brought him under control and to a stop. Since that event, the younger boys always seemed to feel safer if Red was riding with them.

Steve, not wishing to prolong the unpleasantness that the diving contest had created, called down the table to Red. "What horse are you going to ride, old Life-Saver down there? Firefly?" The boys at the table laughed; there were certain days when Firefly was judged by his owner too restive to be trusted to any boy. On those days one of the better riders among the councillors rode him or the horse stayed in his stall. Before Red could answer, the boys rose from their places at a signal from the senior councillor; grace was said, and in a trice the dining-room was empty.

When the truck rolled up to the director's cottage, the riders were eagerly awaiting it. "No little kids," exclaimed Bill Harte. That meant a fast ride now and then during the afternoon.

The councillor who was to take charge of the young equestrians walked up, and shaking his finger at Jim Cox, the Gleaners' peppery quarterback, said, half in jest and half in earnestness, "Now, Jim, you ride alongside of me this afternoon. Some day one of you fellows is coming back home with a broken neck. You'll have us bringing back a corpse." Instantly, the grin left Red's face. "Everybody here?" asked the councillor. He looked around.

"O.K.," exclaimed Steve. "Let's go. It's a dandy day for a ride."

Red had been chatting pleasantly with some of the boys while they awaited the councillors and the truck. Now, as the boys clambered into the truck, Red hesitated. How he enjoyed those occasional wild dashes sometimes grudgingly permitted when only good riders were on the trail! Now, the councillor's warning to Jim Cox made him wish that he were not going.

"Get in, Red." said one of the boys. "Let's be on our way."

Red frowned. "I don't think I'll go," he said. Then, pretending that either going or staying home was not of much importance to him, he added, "I think I'll do some more work on that bird-house of mine."

"Well of all the guys," sang out Steve, surprised at Red's sudden decision. "What's the matter now?"

"Why, I changed my mind, that's all," snapped Red. "Can't a fellow change his mind?"

No one on the truck even remotely imagined that lack of courage was Red's reason for withdrawing from the horse-back party. Steve and Red's closest friends were puzzled; then, recalling the diving contest, they became impatient.

"Well, let's go then," exclaimed one of them. "If he doesn't want to go, let him stay home, that's all."

"Coming, Red?" called one of the councillors.

"No," answered Red, bluntly, somewhat displeased that his friends were so frank in showing their disapproval of his conduct.

"We'll bring you back a little birdie for your bird-house," called Charlie Russell, as the truck pulled away. Red walked slowly toward the handicraft shelter, a disappointed boy. He had looked forward to that ride; he wanted to show the Gleaners, all of them, that he could be just as friendly as they. He wanted the thrill of the wind against his face and the satisfaction that came from ably controlling a galloping horse on a ride with boys whom he liked. He wondered if every boy in mortal sin was so sorely distressed as he. "Maybe they don't realize what mortal sin really means," was his solution. Then for the millionth time, the paralyzing thought came, "What will Father Walsh think of me when I tell him?" The afternoon train had gone, Red knew. Confessions began at five o'clock.

Red stopped in his tracks. Couldn't he disguise his voice? Some of the boys in camp had not been receiving Holy Communion. Maybe Father Walsh would think he was hearing the confession of one of those fellows. His conscience whispered, "would that be fair?" and Red angrily broke in two and flung from him a piece of willow branch that he had picked up a moment ago. Then he thought, "How could a priest remember everybody's voice?" He laughed mirthlessly. "Father Walsh couldn't know everybody's voice." He thoughtfully whispered a few words. "And whispers are all alike, anyhow," he said, almost aloud, satisfied with the experiment.

Red had done quite a bit of work on his bird-house. Now, from the carpenter in charge, Red received his unfinished bird-house and went to work. A lot of knife work was necessary, and Red was proving himself a good artisan. He paid no attention to the noisy young workers around him, and they paid none to him. The details of the task before him took his mind off the question of confession for a while. He even caught himself whistling softly as he met success with a difficult bit of fitting. He had not heard Father Walsh's car return to the camp, and was surprised when

Father Walsh and another priest, whom Red did not know, stepped into the handicraft shelter. The boys at work stood up and greeted the two priests. Red's eyes opened wide in glad surprise. Maybe this priest was going to help Father Walsh hear confessions this afternoon. That would simplify everything.

Father Walsh and his visitor returned the boys' greeting. Then Father Walsh introduced the elderly carpenter to his friend and in a few words explained to him the uses and advantages of the workshop. The priests stopped at Red's place at the long workbench. Father Walsh introduced Red to his visitor, Monsignor Mallon, the rector of the diocesan seminary. "This young fellow is one of our best campers, Monsignor," said Father Walsh. "I don't know but what you'll have him at the seminary with you some day." Red's face crimsoned.

"That's fine, Frank," exclaimed the Monsignor, as the two priests left to continue their tour of the camp.

Red watched them go with his new-born hope dying in his heart. Then he listlessly went back to work.

He had been having a fair measure of success in preparing the parts of the bird-house, but difficulties soon arose when he tried to assemble them into a sturdy dwelling for the feathered friends of the campers. Mr. Joseph had left the woodcraft shelter shortly after Father Walsh's visit. Now Red saw that he couldn't solve the puzzling problem of construction himself and he had no inclination to seek help from the other workers, most of them younger than himself and far less skilled.

He laid aside his unfinished task and strolled out toward the ball field. The teams were just coming back, so he turned toward his cabin. It was almost time for the horseback riders to be back in camp; if they were late, they would miss their swim. The baseball players and the boys of the volleyball teams were already appearing on the campus in their bathing suits. Red glanced at his wrist watch. It was time for swimming now. He decided not to go. He wished it were time for confessions. Would Monsignor Mallon help Father Walsh?

Soon Red heard the noise of the camp truck coming up the hill with its load of riders. In a few moments, Steve Nolan, Bill Harte, and the rest of the boys came noisily into the cabin.

"Boy, you missed a swell ride!" exclaimed Steve. Then, while the boys were dressing for their swim, they told Red of various amusing incidents of the afternoon's ride. Red listened, smiling; now and then he added some fitting comment to the hilarious description of the ride. Then Bill Harte, struggling with the belt of his bathing suit, asked: "How did you make out with the bird-house, Red?" Another boy asked: "Were you working on it all this time?"

"I worked till I got stuck," answered Red. "It's nearly finished, but it won't stay together."

"A wren house?" asked Steve. "A little bit of a thing?"

"No," answered Red. "A marten house, without any nails. You saw one of them. A kid made one up here last year."

"If you fellows keep at it," exclaimed Steve, with a laugh, "there'll be a separate house for every marten around here. I suppose you're not going for a swim, either."

"No," said Red. "You'll only have a short swim. Confessions today, you know."

"Well," called Bill, from the door, "let's go. There go the councillors."

Red stayed in the cabin. He wouldn't have to answer any questions there.

"Any mail?" he called after the departing boys.

"Yes," called back one of them. "Bert has your letter. He's down on the pier." Red decided to get his letter some other time.

As the campers were returning from the lake, Red strolled across the cabin and stood at the door. His heart sank. Major Williams and Father Walsh's priest-visitor were walking down to the pier. Red watched them with fading hopes. He saw them get into one of the boats with an out-board motor. "He won't be back," said Red aloud. He glanced at his watch; it was almost time for Father Walsh to go to the chapel. A few of the boys were waiting around the chapel door now. Just as Red's cabin-mates hurried into the cabin to dress, Red saw Father Walsh cross from his cottage to the chapel.

"Are they all going?" he heard Jack ask Steve, evidently continuing a conversation underway.

"That's what Bert says," answered Steve. "At least all of them who are Catholics. There are a few non-Catholic fellows in their crowd, you know."

"The Gleaners, Steve?" asked Red. "Are they going to confession?"

"Yes," answered Steve. "Some of them have been away from confession a pretty long time. They were talking about it on the truck."

"Where's Bert?" asked Red. "I want my letter."

"They're fixing one of the motors," answered Bill Harte. "He's down in the boat house with them."

In a few moments, Red and his friends were kneeling in the chapel. One by one they arose and took their places in the line near Father Walsh's confessional in the corner of the chapel. Some of the lads seemed to be more preoccupied with what they saw through the open windows near the confessional than with the sacred business of getting ready for confession. Occasionally Red glanced over his shoulder; some of the older fellows, of his own crowd and of the Gleaners, were in the line now. Red arose, genuflected, and took his place at the end of the line. Little by little the line shortened, bringing Red closer and closer to the moment he longed for, yet dreaded. Never before had the prospect of confession been for him an ordeal. Now he was becoming nervous, so nervous that he was beginning to tremble. It was soon his turn.

Utterly miserable, he began the preparatory formula in a whisper and, just as he was declaring the slight sins recalled at his examination of conscience, he heard Bert Conroy's voice outside, calling, "Where's Red Devlin? I got a letter for him." Red's heart froze within him, for the answer came through the windows clear and loud from a boy just leaving chapel. "He'll be right out. I just saw him go into the confessional." Father Walsh could not help hearing that answer, too, Red knew. Just a few minutes ago, kneeling in the chapel, he had rehearsed just what he was going to say, word for word. He knew that he should, even in confession, protect the reputation of Ken Hobart and Barry Willis. Now, panic-stricken at the realization that the boy who answered Bert's question had unwittingly revealed his identity to Father Walsh, scarcely knowing what he was doing, he mechanically repeated the closing formula. Then horror seized him. He felt faint. Realizing that Father Walsh was saying the words of absolution, with trembling lips he made an effort to say the act of contrition. Then, "God bless you," said Father Walsh in his usual tone dismissal. Red arose and started back to his place. The chapel swam around before his eyes. The words, *"a bad confession," "a bad confession,"* kept pounding in his brain; a thing that he had never, for even an instant, considered as remotely possible. He fell into the pew next to him and covered his face with his hands. It couldn't be! It couldn't be!

Somebody touched him on the shoulder and slipped a letter into his hand. Red didn't stir. He couldn't even look at anybody now. In the misery of terror and self-condemnation, shame and humiliation, Red couldn't even pray. The letter dropped on the seat before him. Instinctively he reached for it. He recognized his mother's handwriting on the envelope. He recalled how often she used to warn him never to be afraid to tell the worst he knew about himself to the priest who took Our Lord's place, anxious to pardon everything, no matter how bad it was. "Trust him with the truth, as you'd trust Our Lord," she used to say. The memory of her solemn words now only made him feel more wretched and guilty. Many a time that day he had looked forward to the peace that confession that afternoon would bring him. Now he had forfeited it all.

He heard Father Walsh step out of the confessional, whisper something to somebody in the rear of the chapel, and start back to his cottage. The thought of calling him back flashed through Red's head. He was afraid to do that. Some of the boys and councillors still in the chapel would guess that something was wrong; they knew he had just been to confession. One by one those around him arose and left. Red stayed in his place motionless. Soon the bugle blew "Retreat." Mechanically Red answered its call and stood with the rest of the campers at salute while the colors were being lowered. Then, in more or less orderly fashion, the boys entered the dining-room, and took their places at the tables.

"Well, how do you feel, Devine?" asked Steve cheerfully, as, grace said, the boys took their seats. Devine was one of the Gleaners who had not been to confession for more than two years.

"Great!" he exclaimed. "Boy, I feel like a new man." Then he burst out laughing. "You should have seen Snow, though. He danced around our cabin like a crazy man—crazy with joy. He expected a stiff bawling out."

"From Father Walsh?" asked Steve in a tone that showed how unfounded such a supposition was. The laughter from the boys from St. Mary's showed that they shared Steve's opinion. Only Red didn't laugh. He looked wistfully at Devine. The boy was surely happy. Happiness written all over him, thought Red. And how happy he'll be tomorrow, when he receives Our Lord in Holy Communion. Suddenly the thought struck Red: he couldn't receive! And the Mass would be for Danny! Tears came to his eyes. They mustn't see that. He blew his nose vigorously. With bowed head, he glanced at the boys around him. They were paying no attention to him. He tried to eat, but the food nearly choked him. That lump in his throat. After a time that seemed unending, supper was over and Father Walsh rang the bell for silence.

"Boys," he said, "we have a very distinguished visitor with us this evening, Monsignor Mallon, the Rector of our seminary, who is taking my place at St. Mary's while I'm out here with you and Father Sexton is away on a little vacation. With loud applause, campers and councillors gave their visitor a hearty welcome to Camp St. Mary. Then Father Walsh continued: "During the school year, Monsignor Mallon has charge of all these councillors of yours. They take orders then, instead of giving them." A good-natured yell of approval and loud clapping of hands greeted this news. "At camp fire tonight, boys, Monsignor Mallon is going to talk to you. I don't know what he's going to say, but I promise you it'll be well worth listening to."

CHAPTER XVI

The Camp Fire

URING the time between supper and camp fire, poor Red Devlin went about in a daze. He and some of his friends were assigned to gather wood for the camp fire. Red was glad that he had been one of those named for this task. It gave him an opportunity to get away from the happy, noisy crowd of boys that scattered over the camp premises, some playing football, others baseball, tennis, or engaging in whatever camp activity attracted them most. The "wood detail," working singly or in groups, went off searching the woods for dry logs or branches for the fire. No trees were felled without permission of the camp director. Just as long as a boy appeared at the camp fire site occasionally carrying an armful of wood, it was assumed that he was fulfilling his duty. When Red came in contact with the other campers, he put on a brave face, but his heart was as lead. Crossing the campus, he glanced occasionally toward Father Walsh's cottage. The two priests and Major Williams were sitting there. He wished he had the courage to go to Father Walsh and make a clean breast of the whole business. He saw Steve and Bill Harte walking toward the cabin. It was growing dark now, and the wood pile was big enough for any two camp fires. He bent his steps to following his friends.

Chatting about the events of the day and the plans for tomorrow, the boys washed up and then sat together on the steps of the cabin, waiting for the camp fire call. Groups of campers, returned from their games, were standing or lying idly around the campus. Red noticed that the Gleaners were mingling freely and good-naturedly with the boys from St. Mary's. Bert Cooney and a few of the councillors were building the fire. Satisfied that it had a good start, one of them blew the awaited bugle call; boys began moving to the camp fire from all directions.

A place of honor had been provided for Monsignor Mallon, who, walking with Father Walsh and Major Williams, also answered the summons.

The camp fire session opened with a few songs, in which all the boys but Red lustily joined; then followed some riddles proposed by Major Williams, who seemed to have an unending store of them and an unlimited supply of caramels, which he ceremoniously awarded to the camper who solved the riddle; then a few more or less funny stories told by the campers brave enough to face the ridicule of the crowd if the story didn't please them.

Father Walsh then glanced at his watch and stood up to present Monsignor Mallon to the campers. They greeted him with respectful applause.

"I'm not going to preach a sermon, boys," the Monsignor began, with a smile. "I'm going to tell you a story." At this the boys sat up showing greater interest. "I didn't read the story in any one book. I'm going to make it up as I go along. I can't help thinking that it must be true. I believe that, when I tell it to you, you'll agree with me that it must be true. It is a story about a boy. I couldn't help thinking of him when I visited your carpenter shop, your handicraft shelter, today, and saw a number of young carpenters doing, perhaps, the same kind of work that this boy used to do. They were taking rough timbers and with a few simple tools were fashioning various articles to be used at the camp here or to be taken home with them.

"Then, as I sat on the porch after supper, and watched you playing your games or bringing in fire wood, or just sitting in little groups talking and laughing, I thought of how this boy must have passed many a pleasant evening in much the same way with other boys about his own age who lived in his village.

"I closed my eyes and saw him with you here today, and he did not seem out of place. Then, with the speed that belongs only to thought, I saw him growing up with those boy friends of his year by year. They always seemed to be happier when he was in their group. He seemed to be the confidential friend of them all. You know what I mean, the one to whom they all told their troubles and their hopes. He seemed to know just the right thing to say to them. If they were downcast and blue, after talking with him a little while, their hearts seemed to grow lighter and their cares less trying. Everybody, big and little, just couldn't help loving him; mothers used to say to each other 'How happy his mother must be to have such a son.'

"Well the boy grew to manhood and became the village carpenter. Then boys used to take to him not only their broken toys and things to get him to help them fix them, but they often found themselves sitting alongside of him as he worked, laying before him their secret little worries and problems. And you know that even boys have little worries and problems that they are very backward about discussing, especially with somebody older than they. Boys soon learn from sad experience that sometimes, even when they are most serious, they are laughed at and made fun of. But this man never laughed at them or made fun of them; he listened to them with sympathy and talked to them with understanding and kindness that easily made him their favorite."

The campers were listening intently. Some of them were sure that they knew of whom Monsignor Mallon was speaking. He could see in their faces, lit up by the light of the camp fire, that they loved this man, too. Red bent his head and tears dropped from his eyes. "If he were only here now," he thought.

"Then one day," Monsignor continued, "this man slipped away from his home village. The place was not the same without him. They tried to take his place when the villagers came to his carpenter shop with some work they wanted done. Some of his young friends had grown quite skilled from watching him and helping him work. When they asked his mother where he was and when he would be back, she just smiled and told them that he had gone away on some important business and would be gone for some time. Then they began to do for her the little things that he used to do.

"Several weeks passed. Then surprising rumors began to come into the little village and to the ears of the boys. Word came that the friend they missed so much was gathering around him a few other men for some great work. Some of the men in the village, who had grown up with him, wished that he had told them about it before he went away. They would have gone with him; would have done anything for him. His mother just smiled and said, 'Wait and see.' Then one day they heard of a wonderful thing. Everybody seemed to be talking about it. In a town not far from their own, their friend appeared at a wedding and changed water into wine."

Now, even the faces of the youngest of the campers broke into a smile. "Our Lord," two or three of them said aloud. Monsignor Mallon smiled. "Now," he continued, "here comes the part of the story that will make you all as glad as the boy friends of Our Lord were when they first heard it."

"A boy like themselves lay dying in another little

town near them. His father hastened frantically to Our Lord to beg him to come and heal his son. Our Lord did it instantly, without even going down to the boy's home. It was His first miracle of healing, and He did it for a boy. The boys of Nazareth never forgot that. Although later on they heard cf other wonderful cures that their absent friend had performed, they were always proud that the first person to whom He did such a great favor was a boy like themselves, like yourselves. 'If we were sick, He'd do that for us,' they told everybody."

"And then, one day, when they were all gathered in the village temple for prayer, to their great surprise, they saw Him. They could scarcely believe their eyes. They motioned to one another, pointing to where He sat. But another and a greater surprise was in store for them. Soon their carpenter-friend stood up and, before all the people of the village, claimed that He was the Messiah, the great Leader all their nation had expected for centuries and centuries. Imagine the surprise of all who heard Him. His announcement shocked the villagers into silence; they listened to Him as He continued to speak. Then, recovering from their surprise, their wonder gave to sneers. 'Why, he is just a carpenter,' they said. Even the boys were puzzled. They had not expected anything like this. Then, before they realized what was going on, the grown-ups around Him turned on Him in anger and drove Him out of their village." Monsignor Mallon paused.

"What did the boys do?" asked one of the campers sitting near him.

"What would you do?" countered Monsignor Mallon. "At home they were afraid to defend Him. Outside they came together and talked freely; some of them repeated what the older people were saying; others staunchly claimed that Our Lord didn't get a fair chance. They believed Him; and, indeed, they didn't blame Him when as time went on they heard that He was spending a lot of His time in the neighboring town ruled over by the father of the boy whom He cured."

"And how His faithful young friends envied the boys of that town. Now they had Our Lord. And He was just as kind, they knew, to the boys of that town. The boys were right. Soon He was their favorite, too. Just being with Him made them want to be good and clean and manly as He was. When he spoke to them of God and heaven, they would go without their meals to listen to Him. He made them realize, as you fellows do, that sin is the most unmanly thing in the world." Poor Red felt his cheeks burn as they crimsoned with humiliation and shame.

"Sin," continued the Monsignor, "even secret sin, they came to feel could not be hidden from Him. He knew their best and worst secrets, they were sure. Why, the way He talked to some grown-ups who tried to cause trouble for Him showed, to the great surprise of those fellows, that He knew just what plans were in their minds and the meanness in their hearts.

Sometimes the knowledge of how easily He read their hearts made some of the boys unhappy, for their hearts were not right with God. They, like the boys of today, sometimes let serious evil take possession of their hearts." Monsignor Mallon glanced at his watch.

"Just let me draw a picture in your mind for you. Maybe it happened. It surely could have happened. I think you will agree with me about that," he said with a smile. "See Our Lord with a little group of boys just your age around Him. The day is just fading into the night. They are sitting on the grassy slope of a hill not far from their homes and Our Lord is talking to them. His cheeks are flushed, and His eyes burn bright with all the love of His Sacred Heart for the young, as he speaks to them so kindly, in simple language that they can all understand. As he speaks, they notice His glancing toward the nearby road now and then, as though He was expecting somebody. They look around. Sure enough! One of their friends, who now and then came with them to visit with Our Lord and who they thought was coming this evening, is missing. Some of them think that they see a look of disappointment cross Our Lord's face as His eyes turn back from the empty road to them."

"Well, this evening Our Lord shortens His visit with them, and, blessing them, turns to go. They walk with Him to the road. Then He kindly dismisses them and walks away in the opposite direction. Let us follow Him."

"He goes down the road a little way, then turns in at a lonely path that winds in through the trees and becomes quite hidden from the roadside. Not far down the path, sitting on a fallen log, his head buried in his hands, is a boy; it is the boy that was missing from the group that had just been visiting with Our Lord. He doesn't hear Our Lord's footsteps as He draws near him. He feels the touch of a hand on his shoulder and quickly glances up. He sees Our Lord looking down on him, oh so kindly and lovingly. Our Lord reads the shame and sorrow that fills the boy's heart and that kept him away from the little gathering of the rest of his young friends. The boy sees the sympathy and love that shine in the eyes of Our Lord, and throws himself at Our Lord's feet, sobbing. See Our Lord quickly kneel and gather the poor boy in His arms, as He whispers to Him words of understanding, of sympathy, and of forgiveness." Monsignor Mallon noticed that not a few eyes before him were blinking; here and there a boy furtively wiped away a tear. He glanced again at his watch.

"Boys," he said, "Our Lord loves each one of you just as much as He loved that lad. You heard today of the sudden death of one of your young friends. Now, that boy, if he was good, and Father Walsh told me what a mighty fine boy he was, has just gone home to meet Our Lord, has just gone from a happy boyhood to a happier eternity with the Greatest Friend boys will ever know. Only mortal sin, the most unmanly thing in the world, makes you unworthy of His love, unworthy of the friendship that He has for each one of you. Say a prayer at Mass tomorrow when you receive that Great Friend in Holy Communion, that you will always be brave enough to be true to Him; so that when death comes to you, it will not find you unworthy of Our Lord's embrace."

Monsignor Mallon turned and started toward the director's cottage. Somebody started to clap his hands, and surprised by the burst of applause and cheers that spontaneously followed, the Monsignor turned, smiled, and, with a wave of his hand, went his way.

Father Walsh raised his hand for silence and then said: "Now, boys, if I were you, I'd slip over to the chapel quietly for a special visit with Our Lord at night prayers, and then hurry into bed. Good night."

The boys scrambled to their feet and with a hearty, "Good night, Father; Good night, Monsignor; Good night, Major," started toward the chapel.

Red didn't go to the chapel. He felt too unworthy. He slipped through the dark across the campus, glad that the campus lights were not yet lit, and fell on his knees beside his cot, a most unhappy boy.

He was undressing when his friends came from the chapel talking quietly about Monsignor's talk. None of them seemed to notice Red's silence.

By the time taps sounded, all the boys of Cabin Nine were in bed, and, tired from the day's fun, were ready for sleep.

Red was restless; he could not sleep. As the noise of the cabins around him gradually died away, a feeling of utter loneliness came over him. He could not receive Holy Communion with the other fellows in the morning. He saw himself kneeling at his place watching them as they reverently approached the Communion railing in the camp chapel. Would they notice him if he was not among them? He could plead illness and stay in bed. He could break his fast. He could leave the chapel during the Mass. He could not stay in his place and have them wondering why he did not receive. He shuddered at the thought of receiving Holy Communion unworthily. He'd never do that. He tossed restlessly in his bunk. His companions' deep breathing told him that they were already fast asleep. "If I were only like them," he murmured sadly.

He thought of Monsignor Mallon's talk. He was one of the boys working in the handicraft shelter when the Monsignor visited it. How he wished he had lived at Nazareth in Our Lord's time, worked with Him in His workshop, knew Him personally, talked to Him. Scenes suggested by Monsignor Mallon's talk passed slowly through Red's imagination; he saw himself one of Our Lord's happy, young friends; then—that boy who was unworthy to come. How fine it was for Our Lord to slip away to him. Red wondered if it could have been true. He remembered a picture he saw of Our Lord, the Good Shepherd, coming back from the hills with a lamb across His shoulders. "Surely, it could be true," he decided. The sudden thought flashed into Red's mind. "What does He think of me?" Red was surprised to realize that in thinking of Our Lord and His young friends, he had almost forgotten his own present sorry plight. The shame of it all came to him again; he buried his face in his pillow and cried himself to sleep.

CHAPTER XVII

Courage

RED was dreaming.

He dreamed that Ken Hobart was working with him again in the camp handicraft shelter. They were crying to assemble the carefully carved parts of Red's bird-house.

"Well," said Ken, "it just doesn't seem to fit right, Red. Are you sure that you have this floor part notched right? It doesn't seem right to me."

"Sure, Ken, it's all right," said Red with emphasis. "Mr. Joseph was here yesterday and said it was well done. Some of this wall part or the cross-piece supports must be out of kilter."

"Let's get permission to go down and see Mr. Joseph," suggested Ken. "We'll be back in half an hour."

"That's not a bad idea, Ken," said Red. "Hand me that box. We'll put the pieces in it so we won't lose any of them."

Soon the boys were walking down the dusty road to Mr. Joseph's shop. The warning whistle of a passing train echoed across the silent camp; Red stirred, but did not awaken. In his dream, he and Ken were chatting about the events of the day. Then suddenly Ken Hobart seemed to fade away from Red's side and in his place appeared Bonnie, laughing, as he laughed in his car the evening before. Then in Bonnie's place, Ken appeared again, trying to fit together a few parts of the bird-house. "Here, let's have them. You'll break them the first thing you know," said Red to his friend. "There's Mr. Joseph just going into his shop."

The dreamer saw himself and Ken reach the gate that opened on a tree-lined path leading back a few rods to the shop. Then Ken Hobart again seemed mysteriously to disappear, leaving Red alone. Red dreamed that he walked down the path and into the shop. Mr. Joseph, clad in overalls, was already at work standing in front of a long work table that extended across one side of the building. Red saw that his entrance was unnoticed by the carpenter, busy at the task before him. Without speaking, Red took his place next to Mr. Joseph and stooped to take from the box, that he had laid on the floor, the parts of the bird-house.

"Well, son," Red heard the carpenter say, very low and kindly, "what's wrong?" Red, still stooping, froze motionless. That voice! That was not Mr. Joseph's voice. Then from the corner of his eye Red saw—not overalls, but a long, white robe. Slowly, without breathing, he turned his head and straightened up, and as he did he felt a hand rest gently on his shoulder. The boy's heart raced with a strange gladness—and expectation. To whose carpenter-shop had he come? He raised his eyes. The carpenter was Our Lord! Our Lord with His arms stretched out to him as he had seen them so often on the statue of the Sacred Heart in St. Mary's church. But the face! Displeasure? Disappointment? No. Only gentleness, understanding, sympathy, love. It was all so plain in those kindly features. Then, as deep shame overwhelmed Red and sent a burning flood of crimson to his cheeks, Our Lord's lips moved, and Red heard Him say, in tones of wondrous kindness, "I'm sorry." Red threw himself into Our Lord's arms' sobbing as though his heart would break—and suddenly awoke, tears streaming from his eyes. He leaped from his bed and looked wildly about him; then realized that he had been dreaming. Moonlight faintly streamed through the windows, dimly lighting that side of the cabin. Red's cabin-mates were still sleeping peacefully, but there was no peace in Red's soul; he never felt so wretched and unworthy. Now wide awake, he could still see in every detail the calm figure of Our Lord as he had seen Him in his dream. He fell to his knees beside his bed and buried his face in his hands. Tears of shame and sorrow trickled through his fingers.

As he prayed calmness and courage came to him. Suddenly he arose, slipped into his bath robe, and almost ran across the moon-lit campus to the director's cottage. He was fully resolved to awaken Father Walsh and go to confession immediately. He didn't know what time it was and didn't care. He was almost at the cottage when suddenly the beams of a flashlight from the Porch caught him, and he heard Father Walsh's voice, asking anxiously, "What's the matter, Red?" But Red couldn't answer. Father Walsh held the screen door open for the boy to enter. He saw that Red had been weeping and was in great distress. "Why, Red," he asked in surprise, "what's the matter? Are you ill?"

"Father," blurted out Red, "I want to go to confession."

In a few moments Red's confession was over. Taking care not to mention the names of his companions, he told Father Walsh everything that had happened from the time he met the boys to and including what happened at his confession that afternoon. He made a clean breast of everything that lay so heavily on his conscience. Then he told Father Walsh about his dream.

Soon Red, a new Red, arose from his knees. Father Walsh said kindly, "Now, sit down a few moments, Red. It's almost midnight, but I want to talk to you for a little while and I don't want to keep you on your knees." Father Walsh pulled a chair close to his own and Red sat down.

"Red," began Father Walsh, kindly, "you simply must try to get over your fear of being teased. It's childish. It has brought you nothing but trouble. The fellow with real courage, Red, is the fellow who does what he knows is right no matter what the other fellows think about it. You're not dumb. You have a head of your own, and a pretty capable one. Use it. When your friends tease you, go right back at them. They're friends of yours; they like you. Pay them back in their own coin. Be jolly about it, Red. Laugh it off. As long as you get angry with them, they'll continue to plague you. That's fun for them. They'll soon stop when they see you don't take their banter seriously, when they see that it doesn't annoy you. How many times have I told you that?" Red sighed, but made no answer.

"And," continued Father Walsh, "when you're with fellows who don't belong to your crowd, fellows who are not your style, be man enough to keep your conscience clear. If you're going to let the moral standards of every Tom, Dick, and Harry you meet mean more to you than your loyalty to Our Lord, you'll surely make a shipwreck of your life. It's easy to be good when you are surrounded by good fellows. It takes a man, Red—a real man—to buck up against bad company and come away clean. You're game enough in sports, Red. You're not a coward. Be just as game, just as courageous in resisting the temptations of bad companions."

Father Walsh saw the hard look of firm resolution that came into Red's face. Then he added, "Now, Red, from what I know of you and from what you told me about the way things happened last night, I believe that you did put up a very firm resistance to everything that you saw was mortal sin, but the fact that you were so nervous about it, so afraid of what the other fellows might think of you, that, when the whole affair was over, you just couldn't clear yourself before the bar of your own conscience." Red looked keenly into the face of Father Walsh, first surprised and puzzled, then, with deep consolation and gratitude, as the full meaning of Father Walsh's words came to him.

"And now, Red, just a last word. Whenever you go to confession, remember that no matter what you must tell, the priest is there to help you get straight again with your conscience and with God. That's why he became a priest, to be a friend when a fellow needs a friend. The whole business of confession and absolution, Red, is Our Lord's plan, and He knows what's best for all of us. Now, hustle back to bed; it's almost midnight. God bless you."

Red went back to his cabin with a light heart and a resolution more firm than he had ever made before. He would never again let the fear of anybody's ridicule bother him. "And, believe me," said Red almost aloud, "when it comes to choosing between offending some wise guy and offending Our Lord, there'll be no more 'being nervous' about it, and I don't mean maybe."

Red was the first of his cabin to be up and dressed, but he was the last to leave the chapel. On his way to breakfast, he fell in step with Bert Cooney.

"Bert, we lost that diving contest yesterday," he said. "How about another today? Challenge Cabin Six for us at breakfast, will you, Bert?"

Bert's challenge was eagerly accepted for the afternoon swim. Then Red heard a youngster, who had overheard the arrangements, cry out, "You'll lose again, Bert. Red's chicken. He's afraid to dive." Red was expecting some sally of that kind; so, true to his new resolution, instead of yielding instinctively to a frown of displeasure, he joined in the laughter around him. Father Walsh saw him and smiled.

While the boys of Cabin Nine were making their beds and setting their cabin in order, Bert Cooney was arranging the swimming meet with Dan Conroy, the councillor of Cabin Six. Before the boys' work was done, the two councillors came into their cabin with the news that not only had Cabin Nine's challenge been accepted, but that the winners were to receive the losers' dessert at supper.

Bill Harte and Steve looked at Red, busily arranging the pillow on his cot. They were still somewhat peeved over his default of yesterday. They did not know that he had asked Bert to challenge Cabin Six, and although they needed him to win, they would not ask him to take part in the contest.

"I suppose we'll have ice cream, too," said Jack Clemens, with a sigh. "Well, I don't care much for ice cream, anyhow," he added with a feigned tone of resignation. Red blushed; he realized that his friends were assuming that he would not join them, and were preparing for a repetition of yesterday's defeat.

"You won't lose your ice cream," he muttered, somewhat sulkily. Then, facing his chums, he exclaimed, "I had good reasons for not diving yesterday, and I asked Bert to challenge those Gleaners to another meet so I could get in on it. I'm sorry I couldn't go in with you yesterday. Now, that's that."

"Fine," exclaimed Steve. "Nice going, Red. We'll skin 'em alive today."

Just then Major Williams appeared at the door. "Come in, Major," called the boys, as one of them sprang to open the door for him.

The Major entered and sat on the edge of the bed.

"Fellows," he said, "it's possible that a few of my friends are coming down today to see your camp. Before we left town, they said they might come, but I haven't heard anything more from them. However, I'm going to take Father Walsh out for a ride this morning, and while we are away, I think it would be a good thing to see that everything is in apple-pie order around the camp. You know, just in case they come."

"O.K., Major," exclaimed the boys eagerly.

"Are they from St. Mary's?" asked Jack Clemens.

"There's only one of them from St. Mary's. That's Mr. Moore, the father of one of the girls who graduated this year."

"Irene Moore," exclaimed Jack. "That's Red's..."

"Nix," quickly cut in Steve.

Major Williams looked around and saw Red blushing to the roots of his hair. He smiled understandingly.

For an instant Red glared at Jack; then to the surprise of his friends, he turned to Major Williams, and with a jolly laugh, explained, "Oh, Mr. Moore gave me a baseball glove, and these hyenas are always kidding me that it was a present from Irene."

"Oh, yes," laughed the Major. "I heard all about that but had forgotten it. She's the girl one of my hoodlums tripped, isn't she? And you're the hero, are you not?"

"Yep," answered Red, smiling. "I'm the guy."

Red's friends looked on, amused and amazed. Was this Red Devlin? Was this really the lad, who when it came to teasing, "couldn't take it"?

"Good," exclaimed the Major, rising. "Now, I'll get Father Walsh and leave the camp to you fellows for a while. O.K., Bert?"

"Certainly," answered the councillor, as the Major left the cabin.

The boys could not withhold their surprise over Red's changed attitude. As soon as Major Williams left, Steve blurted out, "Well, for the love of Mike, Red, what has happened to you?"

"Aw, forget it," exclaimed Red. "I just made up my mind that it's goofy to get sore. That's all."

"Is this…ah…going to be…ah…permanent?" asked Jack, with feigned soberness.

Before Red could answer, Bill Harte, looking through an open window, exclaimed, "Say, Bert, what's the matter with this camp? It looks all right to me. What's the Major want us to do?"

"Well, I don't know, fellows," answered Bert. "I don't think that there is a lot to be done. I know that the councillors feel that the camp is kept in pretty neat condition. I'm sure Father Walsh does, too, or we'd hear from him." Bert hesitated a moment, and then added, "Just between us, Major Williams winked at me as he was leaving. I can't figure out what he meant by that either."

Had Major Williams cared to, he could have told Bert that he had received a confidential message from one of the newly reformed Gleaners that Dixon and a few more like him had decided that today was to see Dixon's effort to "get even" with Red. Unknown to most of the campers, Dixon had been "practicing boxing" as often as he could get one of his bosom friends to slip into the woods with him, and now he thought he was able to provoke Red into a fight and whip him. The Major just wanted Red's friend to be near him in case of trouble, that was all. And he wanted Father Walsh away from the camp, confident that if trouble started, it would be "Custer's Last Stand" for the discontented minority of Gleaners.

"Well, we'll have a look around anyhow," said Steve. "We said we would."

The boys continued to busy themselves with their interrupted morning duties until they saw Father Walsh and the Major start away. Then one by one they withdrew from their fellows and began a more or less haphazard round of the camp premises. Bert passed the word to the other councillors that his boys would be a bit late in entering into the scheduled camp activities.

Some minutes later, the boys from Cabin Nine, halfheartedly busy in various parts of the camp, were startled to hear from the campus their whistled signal, the pee-wee call. Quickly they bent their steps toward the campus to find Red and one or two other campers from St. Mary's surrounded by Dixon and a small group of Gleaners, standing near the Gleaners' cabins. Their angry voices told them that there was serious trouble brewing.

When Red left his cabin and started his round of the camp, he saw Dixon and a half a dozen campers sprawled out on the grass near Cabin Six, waiting for the signal that would start the day's activities. As he passed them, he was startled to hear Dixon call out to him, with a sneer, "Still yellow?"

Red stopped in his tracks and whirled around, his fists clenched and his face crimson.

"Going over to hang around Father Walsh, hey?" exclaimed Dixon, provokingly. "Well, he just went out of the camp."

Red started toward the group on the grass. "Stand up and ask that?" he demanded, his eyes blazing with angry resentment. Dixon, with insolent slowness, began to arise.

One of the Gleaners pulled him back to the ground. He had not been informed of the plan. "Cut, it, Dix," he cautioned. "Do you want to get in bad with the Major?"

"Aw, what do I care for the Major?" snapped Dixon, pulling himself free, and arising to face Red. "I'm sick of this dump anyway." The boy nearest him jumped to his feet and got between Dixon and Red; the others made no move.

"Nix—not here," the would-be peacemaker exclaimed. "Not while we're with you, anyhow. We'll all get into trouble. Go out in the woods somewhere."

Dixon pushed the boy aside, and just then one of the St. Mary boys gave the pee-wee call. "Aw, I'll tell him right here, and I'll fight him right here," Dixon declared, loud enough to attract the attention of the boys nearby. Then, turning to Red, he snapped, "I said you're yellow. What are you going to do about it?"

Boys were running toward the excitement from all directions. The boys of Dixon's group anxiously tried to turn them back. "G'wan. Scram. They won't fight," declared one of them.

Another was trying to drag Dixon away. He resisted wildly. "Let me go. Let me go," he demanded.

By this time a few of Red's cabin-mates were at the scene. "Dixon wants to fight Red," one of the smaller boys excitedly told them. "He's been practising and wants to fight him."

Dixon had succeeded in freeing himself from his captor. He bounded back where Red was standing in silent anger. "D'ya want to make anything out of it?" he demanded.

"I'll see you in the woods," declared Red with heat, although in his heart he did not want to fight.

"You'll see me right here and now," almost yelled Dixon. "You yellow quitter." At this insult, Red's self-control almost left him. He clenched his fists and started a step toward Dixon, but stopped suddenly.

"Slap him down, Red," impatiently snapped Bill Harte, amazed at Red's inaction. "He's been looking for it ever since we came out here."

Red looked at Bill appealingly. He was trying his best not to be provoked into fighting Dixon. Would Bill think he was afraid? In the few instants that passed since the sting of Dixon's first insult sent a wave of sudden rage through him, he was struggling to keep his resolution. Would thrashing Dixon here and now break his solemn promise to himself "not to get sore"? Dixon mistook Red's hesitation for cowardice, and he continued tauntingly, "I'll fix you so that even Irene won't know you!" A titter of laughter rippled through the crowd; several of them knew about Red's glove. Red was trembling with suppressed indignation and anger; he gathered himself as a furious tiger about to leap to mortal combat. Then, suddenly he turned on his heel and walked rapidly away—and not in the direction of the woods.

"Red," called Bill Harte in amazement; but Red kept going. He could not trust himself to face Dixon another instant, and he wanted so much not to break his solemn resolution. Dixon laughed aloud. "Told you he was yellow," he exclaimed with a wave of his hand at the departing boy.

Then Bert Cooney's voice was heard from the fringe of the crowd; though late in arriving, he had witnessed enough to understand what was taking place. "Dixon," he said, "I wouldn't want to be in your shoes now for anything. You know Red isn't yellow. He just didn't want to fight you, for some reason or other. But, you're not through with him yet, and don't forget it."

"Yeh?" returned Dixon, boastfully. "Well, where's he going now? There's no woods out that way."

The boys from St. Mary's watched Red's departure with puzzled faces. Never before had they seen Red back away from a fight. And yesterday, they recalled, he was afraid of the high dive.

The signal for morning camp activity broke up the group as the boys went scurrying to designated points.

Tears of anger and keen humiliation came to Red's eyes, as with bowed head and clenched fists he hastened away from the scene. He felt that he was thoroughly disgraced. "They'll think I'm afraid of him," he murmured. "They'll think I *am* yellow." He heard the camp signal, but ignored it. He couldn't face his fellow-campers now. The tears rolled down his cheeks as he passed through the circle of camp cottages and started off across the open field. He just wanted to be alone. He could plainly hear the cries and laughter of the boys gathering on the campus. He never dreamed it was going to be so hard to keep that resolution. But he kept it, and "now they think I'm yellow."

Suddenly he heard the rapid beat of footsteps coming faster and closer. Somebody was coming after him. He hastened his steps; he wanted no company now.

"Red," he heard. It was Steve's voice. The next instant Steve had him by the arm. "What's the idea,

Red?" Steve demanded, as he halted Red and swung him around. He saw the tears in Red's eyes. "What are you crying about? What's wrong? You're not afraid of Dixon, are you? I was down near the boat-house and missed the argument. Sonny Fields told me Dixon offered to fight you and you ran away. What's the matter?"

"I didn't want to fight him," said Red, somewhat surprised to find that he was able to speak rather calmly.

"Why?" demanded Steve, with the privilege of old friendship.

A quick frown that flashed across Red's face showed that he resented the tone of Steve's question. He made no answer. The storm of emotion had passed. Red was, indeed, quite calm now. Steve, however, was not to be silenced by a frown.

"Are you going to let him get away with that?" he asked in surprise.

"With what?" asked Red, weakly, trying to decide what to tell Steve.

"With what?" repeated Steve with spirit. "Why, he'll brag all over the camp and at home, too that you were yellow and afraid to fight him." '

"I'm not afraid to fight him," declared Red, glaring at Steve.

"O, heck, Red," exclaimed Steve, impatiently, "we know that, but what will the other fellows think?"

Red thought of his resolution. "I don't care what they think," was all he said.

"What ?" demanded Steve, his face and tone clearly showing his bewilderment. "You don't care what they think?"

"No," declared Red, trying hard to make his answer sound convincing.

Steve was silent an instant, puzzled. Then he asked, "What's come over you, Red? Yesterday you wouldn't dive or ride; today you let a guy like Dixon challenge you and get away with it."

"I'm diving today, Steve—and riding, too, if we go out," calmly answered Red. A shrill whistle from the campus. The boys glanced in that direction and saw the Senior Councillor beckoning them to return. Without comment, they began to walk back. For a few yards neither boy spoke. Then Red said hesitatingly, "Steve, I made a promise and a...a resolution not to let anybody...ah...ah...tease me into things." Steve recalled Red's similar remark in the cabin earlier that morning, as Red continued, "You saw me laugh it off in the cabin this morning."

"Yes," interrupted Steve, "but you knew we were only kidding; but Dixon—"

"Yes, I know," Red said quickly. "Dixon is different. He wanted to be mean. He had a few of his clique around him and thought it safe to go after me about being yellow when I didn't dive yesterday. You could have knocked me over with a feather. That guy. I told him to stand up and say what he had said. I was going to let him have it once and for all; but, before he got up I remembered my promise…and…then he thought I was yellow because I wouldn't fight." Red glanced at Steve. "Steve, I could hardly keep my hands off him, honest; I had to get away from him. But now I feel kind of glad that I kept my promise."

Steve had listened silently to Red's frank explanation, but now he asked impatiently, "But what promise, Red? When—"

"Let that ride, Steve," said Red quickly, with a wave of his hand. "I'll tell you about that some other time maybe."

"Yes, but now Dixon will be strutting all over the place. He'll think you're scared of him," insisted Steve. He couldn't get that conclusion out of his head.

"Steve," said Red, "I can't help that now. Every kid in the camp will probably think the same thing."

"Not the St. Mary crowd, Red," said Steve, lightly. "You know that." Then after a moment, he added, "But suppose some good reason turns up, Red. Will you fight Dixon then?" Steve was grinning; his mind, lightning fast, had been picturing several possible good reasons.

"And how!" exclaimed Red, smiling grimly.

"Well, let's get over to the field; there's a game on," said Steve. "And, Red, suppose you get Dixon off your mind for a while."

"O.K.," said Red. The gradual realization that he had faced the friendly teasing of his cabin-mates and the bitter taunts of an enemy, without losing his temper and breaking his resolution to conquer his sensitiveness, brought Red courage to face the campers with a firm resolution to say nothing. He would just await the first opportunity to disprove any suspicion that he was afraid of Dixon. And he was not to wait long.

CHAPTER XVIII

A Conspiracy

RED took his place in the line-up for a scheduled ball game in the camp league. He was somewhat surprised that there was no mention of the scene between himself and Dixon. There were few onlookers at the game, as most of the campers were busy in the routine activities of the camp. Red noticed, however, that Steve, Jack, and two or three of his crowd seemed now and then to band together for a chance moment of whispered remarks about something that was evidently amusing. He could not help wondering why they said nothing to him about it.

The seven-inning game ended a few minutes before the signal for swimming.

"Get your team ready for the diving contest, Steve," called Bert. "We're going to run that off right away."

Most of the Gleaners had spent their morning activity period out riding. They were now in their cabins, getting ready for a shower and a swim that would include the contest in diving. The Gleaners of Cabin Seven were quiet and serious. Dixon had not ridden with them, but he had, indeed, been the subject of most of the conversation while they rode in the truck to and from the stable. They were waiting for him to come into the cabin now.

"Here he comes," said Cox, quietly, as he saw the boy jauntily approaching the cabin. It was evident that he was highly pleased with himself and expected commendation from his fellows.

"Well," he called out boisterously as he kicked open the door, "how was the ride?" Nobody answered him. He looked around at his cabin-mates, silently changing from their ordinary clothes to a swimming suit or a bath robe. The unanimous and intended slight was not lost on him. "What's the matter?" he continued, gruffly. "Are you all dumb?"

Then Charlie Russell turned and exclaimed, "No, Dixon, you're the one that's dumb."

"Why? What's the…" he began, but Russell interrupted him angrily.

"Yes, you're dumb," he almost shouted. You think you're tough, but you're just dumb—plain dumb. Do you think that Red Devlin was afraid to fight you this morning ?"

"Well, he wouldn't fight!" exclaimed Dixon, puzzled at the attitude of the boys around him, sneering at him in silence.

"No? But he'll fight tonight…and you won't crawl out of it, either," declared Russell, grimly. "Dixon, either you put on the gloves with Red Devlin tonight or you get out of this cabin before taps. That's final. We don't know why Red didn't take you apart this morning, but we do know that he had a lot more guts than you did to stand up there and take your chin music the way he did." It was plain that Russell was angry enough to thrash Dixon then and there.

"He was yellow," cried Dixon.

"Aw, don't be silly, Dix," called out Snow from the rear of the cabin. "He didn't want to fight you, that's all."

Then Cox declared firmly, "And what Russell just said goes for us all. Either you apologize to Red in front of everybody or you fight him tonight in front of everybody. And if you don't want to go through with it, pack up now and get out of here." The speaker turned to the other boys. "Let's go down to the showers. We'll be late for the swim."

They left the surprised and subdued Dixon alone in the cabin. He began to wonder. Was it true that Red just didn't want to fight? It was awfully disheartening for him to realize that his cabin-mates had not the slightest doubt about it, nor about Red's ability to "take him apart." Dixon threw a shoe across the cabin in chagrin and disappointment. It was plain that he was not the hero he thought himself. A councillor appeared at the door. "Get down to the lake, Dixon," he said curtly, and turned away. Dixon slowly and thoughtfully changed into his swimming suit.

While Dixon was receiving his sentence from the Gleaners of Cabin Seven, two of their crowd from Cabin Six, with Steve and Jack, were quietly laying plans for his downfall. They were talking to Major Williams, who had just returned from his drive with Father Walsh, and with them was Jackie Barnett, a lively youngster whose eyes sparkled with excitement as he listened.

Steve and the others had given the Major a full account of what had taken place between Dixon and Red and Steve had loyally given Red's explanation for his refusal to fight. The Major smiled, but didn't tell the boys that earlier in the day he had received a hint from one of the Gleaners who seemed to be a supporter of Dixon, that Dixon had planned to challenge Red that morning, and that it was to have Red's friends nearby that he had asked them to have a "look around the grounds" while he took Father Walsh out of the camp. The Major wanted Dixon thrashed, and thrashed soundly, without any interference on the part of authority. He had won the Senior Councillor to his plan, too.

When the boys had outlined their trap for Dixon, the Major grinned.

"Well, what do you want me to do?" he asked. "Just keep Father Walsh up at the cottage during the swim period, please," begged Steve. "We'll take care of the councillors."

"Does Red know about this?" asked the Major.

"No, sir," answered Steve. "That's part of the plot; he probably wouldn't stand for it."

One of the other boys laughed. "He won't have to know about it," he said.

In a few moments the boys were on the pier; there
were a few moments of rapid scurrying here and there by
the conspirators; anxious boys were delegated to "take the
councillors out of the picture" when the time for action
arrived, for the cautious hand of authority must not be
allowed even probable interference with the plan.

The whistle blew, and the two teams dove off the
pier and raced to the diving platform. Most of the
other boys then dove into the lake, some to swim out to
the raft, others to play around in the shallow water near
the pier. A few more timid lads loitered on the pier
or were being taken out on the lake in boats manned
by councillors. Jackie Barnett was idly toying with the
anchor rope of a rowboat near the shore.

Soon Dixon came down the path to the lake. A few
of the boys on the diving platform saw him and nudged
each other. Jackie waited until Dixon was almost at the
pier; then he began his act. "Here's Dixon," he called
out, "the world's champion bull-dozer, the would-be
hard guy of the camp." Then grasping his nose between
his thumb and forefinger, he bellowed forth the most
derisive "Bah" he could execute.

The boys in the plot on the diving platform,
although they had seen Dixon's approach, seemed to
pay no attention to him; Charlie Russell and Steve
Nolan pretended to be very busy over a slip of paper in
Steve's hand, planning the meet. With all the noise of
scores of boys yelling and laughing in the water around
them, they could not hear Jackie's taunt clearly, but

they saw his gesture and Dixon's resentment of Jackie's conduct. Then Steve called out, "All right. Let's do the 'high dive and swim to the pier' for the best time. You're first, Red. Get going."

At this a few of the boys looked toward the pier and grinned. Red hurried up the ladder to the higher platform. He was in high spirits. He stepped to the platform and dove. It was a pretty dive, but that didn't interest the boys much, for with Red out of the way now, they were free to give their frank attention to what was taking place on the pier. The boys chatted impatiently as they watched Red come to the surface and break, in long, swift strokes, for the pier. Then on the pier they saw Jackie, to their great delight, fulfilling his role perfectly. He hurled jibe after jibe at Dixon, deadly in earnest, but pretending to be merely teasing him. The boys on the pier, most of them about Jackie's age, gleefully joined in what they thought was just some more of Jackie's playfulness. Dixon, already surly from the treatment he had just received from his cabin-mates, and nettled by Jackie's first greeting, grew more and more angry as he walked toward the end of the pier with Jackie a few feet behind him, berating him with scarcely a pause to catch his breath. He had seen Red dive and knew that he had not much time to complete his part of the conspiracy.

Half way to the end of the pier, Dixon whirled and almost shouted at Jackie, "Now shut up, I tell you. Any more from you and you'll get a clout in the ear."

"Sez you," retorted Jackie with a sneer, as undaunted, he walked closer to Dixon. Red, totally unaware that Jackie was acting a part in a hurriedly laid plot, climbed over the top of the ladder, a bit the worse for the exertion of his swim, just in time to see Dixon slap Jackie across the face. Instantly, Red went into action. The reasonable cause had presented itself.

With a yell, Red made for Dixon, grabbed him by the arm and swung him around fiercely. "Let that kid alone," he commanded.

Dixon, his anger heightened by the sudden appearance and sharp command of Red, hesitated a moment and then, with a curse, dropped the towel he was carrying and lashed out at Red. The fight was on. Red nimbly stepped inside the wild swing and sent a stiff right and left jab to Dixon's middle. Dixon gasped and tried to grab Red. Red felt Dixon's arms close about his wet body and quickly slid out of his opponent's clumsy embrace, sending a quick left hook to the bully's face as he went under his arms.

Dixon must have suddenly thought of his secret boxing practice, for he jumped away from Red and assumed a ring pose; then, with much bobbing and weaving, that he assumed was the proper ring technique, he came toward Red again. The poor fellow looked so ludicrous, Red laughed aloud, feinted with his right, and, as Dixon, deceived, instantly shifted his guard, Red sent a ripping left uppercut straight through Dixon's loose guard and caught him flush on the chin. Red was surprised to realize that instead of being furiously angry at the fellow in front of him, as he usually was when fighting, he was now quite calm, even somewhat amused. He found himself actually hoping that Dixon would not quit too soon. Dixon, on the other hand, infuriated by the suggestion of a smile that played tantalizingly about Red's lips, started a right swing at Red's head, but before the swing was half way to its mark, Red's left fist shot out like a flash, straight into Dixon's face. Dixon had chosen to "box" Red, to apply the skill he thought he had recently acquired, but now he was getting a taste of Red's real skill.

By this time most of the boys were swimming or rowing to the pier, and Red's young friends were doing all they could to interfere "accidentally," of course, with the progress of their councillors, now hastening to reach the pier and stop the fight. Many of the boys had reached the shallow water and were richly enjoying the thrashing that Red was administering to Dixon in a most business-like manner. They keenly enjoyed Dixon's grotesque antics that he thought were clever boxing moves. Even boys of Dixon's own crowd were taunting him. "Give it to him, Dix," they called laughing. "He hasn't touched you yet. You can lick him, Dix; like you said you could this morning."

Just then Dixon staggered back under a lightning-like jab from Red, but recovering his balance, came in again with little crow-like jumps, his idea of crafty foot-work. The spectators roared with laughter. Red grinned, and, catching Dixon in the middle of one of those queer little hops, lunged forward like a streak of greased lightning, and sent a quick shower of telling punches to Dixon's face and body. Dixon felt a trickle of blood from his bruised nose, and, forgetting or abandoning all he thought he knew about the science of defense, he suddenly buried his head in his folded arms and backed away. He had not yet succeeded in landing a single blow on the boy whom he had insulted and challenged earlier in the day, and on his own face and chest were the plain marks of Red's superior strength and skill, large red splotches.

Red glanced at a figure climbing up the ladder from the water to the pier. He saw that it was a councillor and knew that the fight was going to be stopped. The smile instantly left his face, and his eyes flashed contempt, as again he stepped in toward Dixon. "This is for Jackie," he said sharply, and, feinting with his left to bring down Dixon's guard, he slapped the fellow fiercely across the face with his open right hand, just as he had seen Dixon slap Jackie. "And this is for the camp," he barked as he put every ounce of strength he had in a blow that caught Dixon off his balance and knocked him off the pier into the water. Above the riotous tumult of the jubilant boys, the councillor's whistle blew. Silence—or, at least, an honest effort to become silent—greeted the blast of the whistle. That was one of the strict rules of the camp, governing water activities, and the boys were well trained in obeying it.

"All right, fellows," called the councillor. "Back to your diving, you fellows," he announced to Red's friends. "The rest of you get back to your swimming, or up to the showers. Everybody away from the pier."

The fight was over. Red was unmistakably the victor. With much laughter, yelling and splashing, the campers cheerfully obeyed the councillor's command. Red looked for Jackie and was surprised to see him and Major Williams smiling from the shore end of the pier. Major Williams waved his hand toward the diving platform.

"They want you out there, Red," he called. They did. Red's friends, swimming to the diving platform, were trying to make themselves heard above the bedlam of happy swimmers as they yelled, "Hey, Red, c'mon." Red dove and swam out to join them. Dixon sullenly trudged through the water and up the hill to his cabin. Major Williams waited a few moments and then turned and followed him.

"Nice going, Red," called the boys, now on the platform, as Red climbed up the ladder.

"Did you see that guy hit Jackie?" demanded Red.

A loud peal of laughter greeted this question. "Yeh, the sap," answered Steve, as soon as he could calm himself.

"What did he hit him for?" asked Red. "I didn't see how it started."

None of the boys, now in high glee over the success of their plot, tried to answer. They had, before Red reached the pier, quickly decided to explain nothing to Red; at least, for a while.

"You've got to fight him again, Red," said Cox.

"Why?" demanded Red, in surprise. "Well, a little while ago," explained Cox, "we gave him the choice of putting the gloves on with you tonight or getting out of our cabin."

Red grinned. "I don't think he'll fight, but it's all right with me." The boys on the diving platform evidently forgot about the contest; they were having too much fun recalling incidents of the fight. Soon they began to give imitations of what they had begun to call "Dixon's last stand," just before he tumbled into the lake. It made a new dive. Everybody, St. Mary's boys and Gleaners, seemed to be delighted that Red had so decisively whipped the unpopular braggart, Dixon.

When Red and his friends were dressing after the swimming period, Jackie appeared at the door of the cabin. "Nice going, Red," he called out cheerily. "Dixon's gone home."

"What?" cried Red and his cabin-mates. "Gone home? Why?"

"Yes, he has," continued Jackie. "He packed up right after you licked him and sneaked out around the back of the cabins."

"Does Father Walsh or Major Williams know?" asked Bill Harte.

"Major Williams does. He saw him going and just laughed," answered Jackie.

"He'll hitch-hike to the city," said Steve Nolan. "Well, good riddance. He'll always be just an egg."

Dixon, however, did not hitch-hike back to the city. He started home in that modern tramp fashion, but when the autoist who favored him with a ride stopped at a gasoline station to get some gasoline and make a telephone call, he neglected to take the keys of his car with him. Dixon, seeing his chance, slid into the driver's seat, and in an instant was speeding down the road. Within an hour he had been stopped and arrested by a squad of state highway police, notified by telephone of the theft. When the boys of Camp St. Mary next heard of him, he had been tried by a village Justice of the Peace and sentenced to the State Reformatory. That was the last the Gleaners heard of him.

Camp St. Mary's present session, that brought so much fun to the boys, was soon to close. There were only two days left. Then the train carrying them home would pass another train bringing a new crowd, under Father Sexton's care, out to the camp to enjoy the activities now drawing to a close for Red and his friends.

Saturday morning Father Walsh called Red to his cottage just after inspection. "I was pretty busy last night, Red, and didn't have a chance to talk to you about your fight with Dixon," began Father Walsh. "I heard all about your refusal to fight him yesterday morning out on the campus. To stand there, Red, and let him call you yellow was pretty hard to take, wasn't it?"

"And how!" declared Red, shaking his head solemnly. "Father, that's why I had to get away from him. I was afraid I couldn't take his chatter much longer."

"You did fine, Red," said the priest; "that was a real test of courage."

"Thank you, Father," said Red, smiling.

"Major Williams told me something that I don't think you know yet," said Father Walsh, smiling. "I mean the plot of those fast working friends of yours to entrap Dixon in the act of hitting Jackie Barnett, with you on the scene to protect him, and ah—incidentally giving you a chance to prove that you were not afraid of Dixon."

Red looked at Father Walsh in open-mouthed amazement. "You mean they framed Dixon for me?" he asked.

"Yes, Red," explained the priest, "if you want to put it that way. Jackie Barnett was quickly coached by some of the Gleaners and some of your own crowd. He was merely acting his part when he baited Dixon. The boys on the diving platform with you sent you on a race to the pier just in time to be there when Dixon lost his temper and hit Jackie. Hasn't it occurred to you that that race was never finished? The rest of it didn't matter. Some of the boys managed to take the councillors out of the play; they had them in the boats or on the diving platform and on the raft." Father Walsh looked out over the campus, smiling as he added, "I suspect, however, that a few of the councillors were in on the plot, too. I understand they 'hastened slowly' getting to the pier."

"Well, what do you know about that?" exclaimed Red.

"See that bunch out there on the grass, Red?" asked Father Walsh, as he pointed to a group of Red's friends, Gleaners included. "They are looking over here laughing. They know that I'm telling you about it." Red broke into a cheery laugh.

"Well, what do you know about that?" he exclaimed again.

Now, another thing, Red," continued Father Walsh. "They tell me that you were smiling during your fight down there on the pier."

"I guess I was, Father," said Red. "He tried to box." Red laughed.

Well, perhaps that was part of it, Red," said Father Walsh, somewhat seriously, "but the big reason was that you were in complete control of that fiery temper of yours. Weren't you?"

Red blushed. "I...I thought of that too, Father," he said with a grin.

"Any teasing lately, Red?" asked the priest.

"Aw, that bunch," answered Red, good-naturedly, swinging his arm in the direction of the group waiting for him out on the campus. "They're always riding somebody. And Major Williams, too." A look of surprise crossed Red's face. "Say, Father," he asked quickly, "was the Major in on that frame-up?"

"He certainly was, Red," answered Father Walsh, "from the very beginning."

"He was?" exclaimed Red, the look of surprise gradually giving way to a weak grin and a deep blush.

Father Walsh noticed the change, and asked, "Now, what's wrong?"

"Major Williams," said Red, reflectively. "And, boy, did I fall for it?"

"For what, Red?" asked Father Walsh, pretending to be ignorant of something over which he and Major Williams had laughed heartily after taps the previous evening.

"Aw, last night, Father," explained Red, embarrassed, "Major Williams, with a whole crowd of the fellows around, almost made a speech about me; my sudden appearance seemed 'truly providential.' He laid it on thick about what would have happened to Jackie if I had not appeared in time to defend him. He had us all talking about how strange it was that I, of all the boys in camp, should be the one to appear just at that particular moment. And, Father, I swallowed it, no fooling." Red clinched his fists, a pretended threat. "Just wait till I see the Major," he declared, with a vigorous nod.

"Major's teasing never leaves a sting in it, though, does it, Red?" remarked Father Walsh, conveying a kindly hint to Red.

"No, Father, you can't get sore at him," agreed Red, emphatically.

"You like him a lot, don't you, Red?" asked the priest.

"Yes, Father. Everybody does," answered Red.

"He's a lot like Lieutenant Carroll, Red, isn't he?" said Father Walsh, quietly. Red looked quickly into Father Walsh's face; the priest was smiling. Red's cheeks slowly crimsoned. Before he could answer, Father Walsh said, "Well, Red, I just wanted to let you in on that little camp secret about the fight on the pier. Now, send me a councillor. I have a lot of letters I must get into the mail right away."

Red left the director's cottage—thinking of Lieutenant Carroll. The recollection of that last interview in the Engine House brought to him now, not a feeling of resentment, but the conviction that he had acted like a baby, had gone into a pout. This realization caused him to blush with a humiliation he had not felt before when he happened to think of Lieutenant Carroll.

His face was still red and solemn when he reached his friends. "Bert," he said, addressing his own councillor, "Father Walsh wants a councillor right away." Bert arose from the ground and started toward the cottage. The other boys grinned at Red, expecting him to say something about his visit to the director. Red looked them over, shaking his head; then, grinning back at them, he said, "Nice going, fellows. I mean it. I'm much obliged to you. No fooling." The boys laughed aloud.

Then, glancing toward the director's cottage, he asked, anxiously, "Who's got a postal card? A camp postal?" But before anybody could answer, Red turned and ran after Bert. "Hey, Bert, wait a minute," he called.

The boys saw him walk to the cottage with Bert and wait, sitting on the steps of the cottage, until Bert appeared with postal and pencil. He wrote for a minute or two, then handed the card to Bert and trotted back to the crowd.

"A card to the girl friend, Red?" asked Charlie Russell, laughing.

"No," Red answered. Then looking at Jack Clemens and Steve, next to him, he said significantly, "I sent a card to Lieutenant Carroll." Jack and the St. Mary boys smiled, but said nothing. The breach between Red and the Lieutenant was their secret, and there were Gleaners present. "I told him we'd be over to see him Monday night." Then, turning back to the rest of the boys, he said to the Gleaners, "Lieutenant Carroll is a friend of ours at the fire station in our neighborhood. He's a lot like Major Williams."

CHAPTER XIX

Bonnie Visits Camp

THE boys had just gone down to the lake for the Saturday afternoon swimming period when their attention was called to the noisy arrival of Ken Hobart, Barry Willis, and Bonnie Porter in Bonnie's automobile. As soon as the boys from St. Mary's recognized the visitors, some of them hastened to welcome Ken and Barry. They were somewhat surprised to see Charlie Russell running up to the car and exchanging greetings with Bonnie, and soon learned that Bonnie was evidently acquainted with several of the Gleaners.

The visitors did not notice the lack of warmth in Red's greeting. Although the boys had told Red that they might drive out to the camp, Red was rather surprised and quite displeased to see them. Instinctively, he blamed them for all of his unpleasant experiences of Thursday.

"Take your visitors to the director's cottage, fellows," said Bert Cooney, reminding the boys of the camp rule that required all visitors to report to the camp director upon their arrival on the grounds.

Red, Steve, Jack, and Russell started toward Father Walsh's cottage with the three boys, but Red stopped and, without a word, turned back to join the boys scampering down the pier to resume their swim.

"I suppose they'll stay overnight," remarked Bert.

"I guess so," said Red, without spirit. "Hobart and Willis were here last year."

Before the swimming period was over the boys reappeared in bathing suits. They had seen Father Walsh and were to be guests of the camp until tomorrow; just now they were eagerly trying to get the most fun out of the few minutes left of the afternoon swim. After their long ride from the city, a refreshing swim was more than welcome. None of the campers noticed that Red, standing on the platform with them, was not taking much part in the general hilarity. He was busy with his thoughts, and they were not pleasant. He was wondering whether his old friends, Ken and Barry, both expert swimmers, were cavorting in such glee and taking what to his mind seemed reckless chances with their lives by "their crazy diving stunts," without any thought of the sinful state of their souls. He noticed, without any qualm of conscience, that he was not much concerned with the spiritual welfare of Bonnie. "But...Ken and Barry," he reflected. "They are Catholics; they *knew* they were doing wrong...they *knew* it was a grievous matter, with sufficient reflection, and full consent of the will."

The swim over, the boys returned to their cabins. As they were trudging up the path, a hopeful thought came to Red. "Maybe they went to confession at home for the First Friday, too." He resolved to find out at the first opportunity.

Bonnie had been assigned to Cabin Seven, to occupy the bed left vacant by Dixon's departure, and had gone to that cabin with some of the Gleaners. Ken and Barry had been given places in an unoccupied cabin, but were now changing their clothes in Cabin Nine, with Red and his friends.

Red was trying hard to enter into the lively chatter about the doings at camp, but at the same time he was trying his best to find some way of putting into execution a resolution that at first seemed to him wild and impossible, but which, the more he thought about it, seemed to be the manly thing to do. Neither Ken nor Barry had made any reference to Red's ride with them Wednesday night. In fact, to Red's surprise, they did not now seem to be the same boys with whom he had ridden. There was not the slightest hint in their conduct or conversation of the evil that Red feared was hidden in their hearts. Bert Cooney seemed to be very much interested in them and in the incidents they recalled of camp life the previous summer. With unfeigned interest, they, too, asked Bert about the councillors of former years, who were now at the seminary's summer villa.

"Well, Barry," said Ken as the boys had finished dressing and were ready to dispose of their wet suits, "let's pick up our things and put them in our cabin." Turning to Bert Cooney, he explained, "Father told us to take Number Twelve. We'll be right back."

Red saw the chance he wanted. "I'll give you a hand and see that you have everything you need over there."

Red was silent as the two boys, pleasantly commenting on what they saw around them, walked with him the short distance to the designated cabin, but as soon as they entered, he said, "Let's see. Have you got soap and towels?"

"Yes, I guess we are all fixed; this isn't our first trip to Camp St. Mary, you know," said Barry, smiling.

Red looked out of the rear door. "No water bucket or basin. I'll get those for you later," he said. He was now very nervous, trying eagerly to find some way of broaching the subject uppermost in his mind.

Ken and Barry dropped on the beds what few belongings they had brought with them, hung their bathing suits outside the cabin, and returned. "Well, let's go," remarked Ken. "I'm almost starved. It must be almost time to eat."

Red saw his opportunity to speak slipping away, and as Ken started toward the door, Red instinctively laid his hand on the other boy's arm, saying nervously, "Just a minute, Ken. I want to speak to you, to both of you, ah…ah…privately."

Ken and Barry grinned. "Sure, what's it all about?" lightly asked Ken.

"Well,"began Red,"it's about the other night." Poor Red felt himself blushing as Ken and Barry, amused at his nervous earnestness and embarrassment, waited for him to continue.

"Yeh," prompted Ken. "What about it?"

"Well,—those—those jokes, and…" continued Red haltingly.

Barry and Ken frowned. "What's it going to be, a lecture?" asked Barry, with displeasure. "C'mon, Ken," he added sharply, as he moved toward the door.

"Wait a minute, Barry," said Ken, calmly. "Take it easy."

"Please wait, Barry," pleaded Red. "I want to tell you something." Barry turned; evidently it was not going to be a "lecture." Red closed the door and slipped the latch into place. "Sit down a minute," he said to the two boys, watching him with puzzled eyes. Barry and Ken seated themselves on the bed nearest them; Red sat opposite them on the next bed.

"When I got on the train that night, I got to thinking …and…praying…and the more I thought about it, the more it…seemed to me…we had committed mortal sin."

"Aw," began Barry, rising impatiently, but Ken silently pulled him down beside him.

"I was ashamed to tell Father Walsh when I went to confession for the First Friday, and…I guess…well, I made a bad confession," Red said quickly. He noticed Ken glance at Barry in surprise when he mentioned the First Friday, and saw from that glance that neither of the two had been to confession Thursday. "It was all over before I knew it," Red continued. "Then that night Monsignor Mallon, from the seminary, was here and talked to us. Fellows, I'll try to tell you what he said."

Then Red began to tell Ken and Barry, as closely as he could remember the Monsignor's talk, the story of Christ, the Boy among boys; how much at home He would be in camp with them; the Man among men, the carpenter who was the favorite of the boys and men of his village. Red hurried along, anxious to get to that part of the Monsignor's talk that told of the group of boys who visited Our Lord and of the poor fellow who was, one evening, too much ashamed to come with them. The boys noticed how Red's halting manner changed, how easily and earnestly he spoke, how his eyes glistened as he told them the story.

"I never felt meaner in my life," declared Red solemnly, "than when Monsignor reminded us that— well, all our sins are really deliberate insults to Our Lord, and He cares for each of us like that." Red found himself speaking now without the slightest trace of nervousness. His eagerness impressed the boys and lent him new powers of eloquence. Ken and Barry were listening to him with sober faces.

"Then, that night," Red continued, "I had a dream, a dream about you fellows and me...and Bonnie. Red frowned as he pronounced Bonnie's name. "You remember, when you were here last year, we were working pretty hard on bird-houses. Well, I was almost afraid to go to sleep, for fear I'd die during the night. But, I did fall asleep, and then…the dream came." Then Red told the two boys listening intently to him and totally oblivious to the noisy camp outside the cabin, of the dream-visit to the carpenter shop of Mr. Joseph, and of finding, instead of Mr. Joseph, no one else than Our Lord, at His work bench in the carpenter shop at Nazareth.

"Fellows," said Red softly, and the boys noticed that his eyes were blinking, "if you could only have seen His face when He said to me, 'I know…I'm sorry.'" Red sighed. "Well, I woke up…crying. I'm not ashamed to say it, and before I knew it I was at Father Walsh's cottage, right in the middle of the night. I went to confession then and there…the best confession of my life."

"Did you tell him we were with you?" asked Barry quietly, all trace of objection gone from his attitude and voice.

"No," said Red, then, suddenly realizing the import of the question, he declared more firmly, "Of course not. But I told him everything else, and, believe me, I'll never have to do anything like that again as long as I live."

Then Red suddenly thought of his purpose in speaking to Ken and Barry. He stood up before them quickly. Ken and Barry remained seated, their eyes on Red.

"A little while ago, when I saw you fellows taking chances with your lives, diving out there, without a thought of what might happen to you if you were to drown...when I think of what swell fellows you used to be...how you were up here last summer...and now, running around with that Bonnie...I just had to tell you this. Ken, Barry," Red pleaded, "why do you do it? What does it get you? Why..."

Ken interrupted him. "You win, Red," he said simply. "Barry, I'm going to confession tonight."

Barry said nothing; he arose and walked to the other end of the cabin, looking out the window, but seeing nothing. Red walked to the door, unlocked it, and swung it open.

Just then loud peals of laughter came from the vicinity of a nearby cabin. Ken hastened to join Red at the door and saw his friend Bonnie in front of one of the Gleaners' cabins, surrounded by a howling circle of Gleaners. Bonnie was going through the painful task of removing a large patch of adhesive tape from his face. It was spread cheek to cheek across his lips. His face was flushed with humiliation and anger. The three boys hastened to the scene; most of the campers were doing likewise, from all parts of the camp.

Only a short time before, Bonnie had been pleasantly received by his old friends. But, in the course of their conversation, in the cabin after the swim, his familiar use of obscene expressions disclosed itself. Instantly, Charlie Fowler warned him. "Go easy with the bad language, Bonnie. That stuff doesn't go here."

"What do you mean?" demanded Bonnie, surprised at the rebuke.

Then they told him. Bonnie listened with an expression of amusement on his face that plainly nettled some of the other boys.

"So, you've all gone sissy, hey?" he asked, with a snort of derision.

Bill Weston, one of the Gleaners who had not known Bonnie, arose from his bunk and silently set out a roll of tape. Bonnie, seeing in that act a challenge, sprang to his feet and angrily dashed the roll of tape to the floor.

"Pick it up," snapped Weston. "That's mine."

"Who the—?" began Bonnie, but no longer so sure of his security, he stopped short. Then he began again.

"Who are you?" he demanded.

"I'm the guy that owns that tape," answered Weston, calmly. Over Weston's shoulder, Bonnie saw that the other Gleaners were grinning at him.

"Think you can make me pick it up?" demanded Bonnie.

Weston's answer was a quick right hook, that, catching Bonnie flush on the chin, jarred him to his heels and sent him backwards to a sitting position on the nearest bed. Before the surprised fellow could collect his wits, Weston declared, "Listen, fellow. You're perfectly welcome to this cabin, and we don't want any fighting. You can obey our rules or get cut—after you pick up my tape."

Bonnie silently recovered the tape, placed it where Weston had put it, and started toward the door. Charlie Fowler moved to detain him.

"Aw, c'mon, Bonnie," he urged. "Be a sport. Don't get sore. It's one of our own rules, and we all have to obey it."

By that time Weston had stepped up behind Bonnie, now almost at the door. He placed his hand firmly on Bonnie's shoulder and turned him around. "Now cool off, mister," he said pleasantly. "We…" Bonnie angrily slapped Weston's hand from his shoulder. Weston just laughed and walked out of the cabin.

Then Bonnie turned to address his friends, but before he could speak, they laughingly warned him, "Now, be careful." Bonnie was too angry to see any humor in the situation. "I'm getting out of here," he almost yelled. "You're a fine bunch of molly-coddles. Of all the…" Bonnie intended to use a string of his usual expressions that by their very rottenness were supposed to be emphatic, but at his very next word, Charlie Russell leaped for the tape, and the others leaped for Bonnie. It was all over in a minute; then, in high glee, they pushed and pulled the well-taped offender out into the public view.

Supper was forgotten as the waiting campers rushed to the scene to enjoy the distress of another unfortunate who had broken the clean-speech rule of the Gleaners.

"Boy," exclaimed one of the lads, "they pasted plenty of tape on that fellow; he'll never get it off; look, it's all over his face." Indeed, he was right. To make the lesson more effective, the Gleaners had been most lavish in spreading the tape well over Bonnie's face.

Red saw the angry look that flashed into the faces of Ken and Barry, as they ran to the scene, quickly explained to them the situation, and urged them not to attempt to interfere. Red had no desire to see Ken and Barry taped for trying to rescue Bonny; he knew well that the Gleaners would do just that if Ken and Barry provoked them. "He had it coming to him," Red declared firmly, "or Charlie Russell and some of the rest would have stopped it."

Ken and Barry hesitated. Then, before they could decide what to do, Bonnie jerked off the last bit of tape from across his lips, and, with an angry oath started for his car. A few Gleaners, with a yell, started after him, but when Bonnie ran, they laughed and let him go. Almost at the car, Bonnie looked around and saw Ken and Barry walking rapidly after him.

"C'mon, you two," Bonnie called angrily. "Let's get out of here. I'm going back."

Suddenly Ken stopped and laid his hand on Barry's arm, stopping him, too. "I'm going to stay, Barry," Ken said, looking intently at his friend.

Barry turned toward the car. "We're going to stay, Bonnie," he called. "Wait a minute."

Red, dismayed by the thought that Bonnie might influence his two friends to return with him to the city, ran to join them.

"Let him go," he said earnestly. "You can go back with us." One of the younger campers dashed past the three boys carrying to the departing Bonnie the few things he had brought with him for his intended stay in camp. Bonnie snatched them and climbed into the car.

"C'mon, if you're coming," he called angrily to Ken and Barry.

"We're not going," Ken answered. He and Barry were now the center of a group of Gleaners and St. Mary's boys, all eagerly urging them to stay.

Without another word, Bonnie backed the car into the road and drove out of the camp.

Father Walsh and Major Williams, unnoticed by the campers, had watched the whole proceeding from the porch of the director's cottage, and now, as the bugle sounded for supper, they came down the stairs of the cottage, evidently well pleased with all that they had witnessed. Several of the smaller boys hastened to them to give them the details of what had taken place. The rest of the camp was quickly falling into formation for "Retreat." When the flag was lowered, the campers moved, in twos, toward the dining hall.

Ken and Barry whispered to each other and stepped out of line. As Father Walsh and Major Williams drew near, Ken asked politely, "Will there be confessions tonight, Father?"

"Certainly, if you wish," answered Father Walsh. "Immediately after supper."

"Thank you, Father," said the two boys, as they passed into the dining-hall.

Red had already taken his place at one of the tables, and as the boys passed him, Ken smiled and whispered,

"Confession right after supper, you old red-head." Red beamed. "Nice going," he exclaimed.

The Major stopped at one of the Gleaners' tables. The boys were still laughing and chatting over what had just happened to their visitor. "It seems that fellow couldn't take it, eh?" the Major exclaimed.

"Oh, he took it all right," they assured him, laughing heartily.

"And how," added the Major, as he passed on to his place at the head table.

After supper Red waited outside the chapel for his friends. "Well, that's over," exclaimed Ken cheerily, as he and Barry joined Red, "and I feel like a new man."

"Me, too," added Barry; then, as the boys started toward the baseball diamond, he said, with a serious note in his voice, "Red, tell us about that dream again— all of it."

Red did, slowly and quietly, as the three boys walked slowly across the campus. Ken and Barry listened silently until Red had finished; then Barry said solemnly, "I hope I never forget that."

Ken and Barry tried to cram into their short stay at camp all the fun possible. They seemed to be wherever anything exciting was taking place. Saturday night and Sunday passed all too quickly for them. They showed themselves to be excellent campers, capable and willing to do more than their share in the many little tasks that had to be done in order to leave the camp premises in ship-shape for the new crowd coming out Monday.

Their fine spirit and general popularity attracted the attention of Major Williams.

"Those are two fine boys, Father," he remarked to Father Walsh, as they watched the pair toward nightfall Sunday evening, making their way from the pier to the boathouse, both heavily laden with oars that were to be put under lock and key until camp opened again.

"Yes," agreed Father Walsh, "they match up pretty well with most of our lads."

"I wonder how they got in with that other fellow, the lad my boys taped up last night," remarked the Major, laughing as he recalled the scene. "Why, even some of the Gleaners have no use for that fellow."

Father Walsh did not make any explanation. His brief interview with Ken and Barry on that point had taken place under the sacred seal of confession. "Barry was baptized Francis," said Father Walsh, "but his dad always called him Barry in honor of the famous Commodore Barry of the American Navy, to whom the Willises claim some distant relationship."

"I think I'll have a chat with them," said the Major, starting toward the boat house.

The boys saw Major Williams approaching and greeted him with a pleasing deference. "Why didn't you fellows come out here two weeks ago?" asked the Major. "We would all have had a lot more fun if you had been with us."

Ken and Barry sat down on an old overturned boat. "Well, we wish we had come, now," said Barry, rather wistfully. "How about it, Ken?"

"I'll be here next year, the full term," declared Ken.

Major Williams flicked the ashes from his cigar. "That fellow you came with," he began questioningly. "I can't put you together very well. I've been asking my boys about him, but I can't find anyone to recommend him very highly. He doesn't seem, from what I can learn, to be your style at all. He's two or three years older than you fellows, too, and—well, he just doesn't seem to belong, that's all."

Major Williams quickly saw that the two boys were rather embarrassed. "He reminds me of a mutt that I fell in with for a while when I was about your age," he continued, smiling. The Major seated himself on a wooden sawhorse opposite the boys. "My parents were pretty strict with us when I was a boy. At least, that's what I thought then. Pocket money was scarce; a nickel looked like a cart-wheel. Then this fellow moved into our neighborhood. He seemed to have plenty of spending money—and that was what I wanted most."

The Major saw from the smiles of Ken and Barry that they understood the situation perfectly. "I can remember my first cigar with that fellow, and also the trouncing I got when my dad found me doubled up in misery on the back steps that night, with this fellow standing grinning at me. Dad came out to look for me to send me to the store, and there he found me. As soon as my dad came through the kitchen door, my new pal went out the back gate like a streak, back into the alley, where only a few minutes before I had 'inside information' that I was going to be very, very sick in a very few moments. In his flight, my friend dropped his cigar, or what was left of it, and that, of course, gave my dad the key to the whole situation."

Ken and Barry were laughing now. That was what the Major wanted. He continued. "I just turned my head and looked up at my dad. Now, boys, my father must have read somewhere that ambiguous caution not to slap a child on an empty stomach, so he turned me over, and for a time the misery of a sick and empty stomach was forgotten entirely in the rush of acute sensations of sharp and repeated pains that only a policeman's belt, doubled and wielded by a good strong arm, can inflict. And then, boys—I still almost tremble when I think of it—my dad sent me, sick and sore, to the cigar store! He happened to be looking for me because he wanted—of all things—some cigars. I carried them home behind my back; the very sight of them made my poor stomach do tail spins." The Major and the boys were laughing heartily. Then the Major said, "I guess that's about the way it was with you fellows. Like every lively boy, you wanted adventure and excitement, and this fellow happened along with a car and provided them. Wasn't that it?"

"I guess that was it, Major," agreed Ken, slowly.

"But," added Barry, "we got more than we were looking for, and I guess we didn't have sense enough or nerve enough to back out when we should have. We kept going with him, and—well, I guess, getting like him."

"Only for Red," began Ken, but he stopped short. He might say too much. No use dragging Red's name into it.

"Red?" asked the Major, trying not to show his surprise. He had judged Red too timid, too bashful, even to attempt what Ken's remark led him to believe he had effected.

"Yes," said Barry. "Red got a taste of the way we were heading last Wednesday night, when we met him in the city. He didn't like it, and he told us so last night."

"That certainly was fine," said the Major quickly. "Boys, I wonder if you realize how hard that must have been for Red. It takes a lot of courage for a boy to speak up to other boys like that. Yes, sir, the finest kind of courage."

Ken laughed lightly. "Well, he didn't waste any time about it, Major. He got us before we went to supper last night."

"That's why you saw us ask Father Walsh about confession," added Barry, smiling.

"Well, well," exclaimed the Major, rising. "Now I don't know whom to admire most: Red for speaking to you, or you for being so sensible and taking it the right way, and—best of all—almost jumping at the chance to make a clean breast of things to Father Walsh like that, squaring yourself with God and your conscience. The whole affair is about the most manly thing I can think of right now."

Ken and Barry smiled; they were very glad to hear the Major put their reformation in that light.

CHAPTER XX

Nice Going, Red

SHORTLY after breakfast the next morning, Father Walsh and the councillors made a final inspection of the camp. Satisfied that everything was as it should be, Father Walsh instructed the senior councillor to have the last bugle call—the signal to assemble for the hike to the railroad station—sounded. In more or less orderly fashion the boys soon wended their way out of the camp and to the station, and were soon on the train, homeward bound.

The Gleaners and Red's friends from St. Mary's were no longer two groups separated by suspicion and dislike. Their two weeks' stay in camp had changed all of that. Now, on the train, they were intermingling freely, laughing and chatting over incidents of the past two weeks and planning more fun together in the city. The Major's experiment had been eminently successful, and he was well pleased with the marks of friendliness exchanged between boys of the two groups as the train sped toward the city.

Father Walsh and Major Williams were sitting together in the rear of the last car. They had just walked through the "specials" added to the train to accommodate the campers. "They are pretty well settled down now, but there will be a lot of excitement when the sandwiches are distributed about noontime," said Father Walsh, laughing. "That is always an interesting time."

Major Williams smiled. "Father," he said. "I think the camp has done these chaps a lot of good. It has given my crowd a new outlook on life, I'm sure. It has given them some new ideals."

"I think, Major," said Father Walsh, "the principal thing it has done is to have brought into their lives, just at the right time, the strong treasures of religion. It has brought them closer to Christ. I think that they understand now that they can have a lot of fun and still stay clean, decent, and manly. They owe you more than they'll ever be able to repay. Think of them as you found them. Where would they be right now if you hadn't picked them up and put them on the right path? It was your interest in them that started it all. And I think that your compliment in naming them the Gleaners in honor of those fine fellows who were with you 'over there' has inspired them to try to be worthy of that name."

"Well, Father," said Major Williams, "I'm satisfied. I think that, so far, they have done nobly And as for what they owe me, why, I've not enjoyed anything in a long time as I have working with those boys." Father Walsh smiled; he knew that.

Just then, Red appeared at the door of the car, evidently looking for one of his friends. "By the way,

Father," said the Major, "you've got a dandy boy there. I can't get over the way he turned those two boys away from that fellow my lads taped up. From what the Gleaners tell me, that fellow is trash. Red evidently objected to Hobart and Willis running around with him, and, whatever he said to them, he surely made an impression. At least, that's what I gathered from my chat with Hobart and Willis last night." The Major smiled, then continued: "Shortly after we landed at camp, one of Red's friends told me that he was very sensitive and bashful. He told me that the only thing Red feared was teasing. That means a lack of moral courage, it seems to me; but to stand up to two boys of his own crowd and lay the law down to them and make them like it—that's moral courage to a pretty high degree. Don't you think so?"

Father Walsh smiled. "Red is all right," he said. "He is entering our preparatory seminary when school opens. He and Steve Nolan hope to become priests. They were rather undecided when school closed in June, and their decision is still something of a secret. They haven't spoken to me about it yet, but Bert Cooney, their councillor, told me last night that they had made up their minds at camp."

Before the ride was over, Red and Steve managed to get Father Walsh's ear for a moment to tell him of their decision. "Well, boys," he said, "I would have been surprised if you had decided not to enter the seminary. That's where you belong, both of you."

Special trolley cars were waiting for the boys when the train rolled into the depot, and, after a short ride, Red and Steve were soon walking down the street to their homes.

"Will you be out for a while, Red?" asked Steve, as they reached the Nolan home.

"Yes, Steve," answered Red, with a smile, "but I've got something to do alone."

Steve looked at his friend in surprise. Red smiled. "I'm going over to the Engine House and square myself with Lieutenant Carroll."

"Nice going, Red," exclaimed Steve, grinning. "That's swell."

Red ran across the street to his home. His mother, Rita and Bobbie greeted him effusively. They had missed him.

"You're as brown as an Indian, Frank," declared Mrs. Devlin.

"They all are, Ma," he declared. "We had a wonderful time."

"Did you have any lunch?" asked Rita.

"We had some sandwiches, but am I hungry!" he exclaimed.

"As usual," said his mother, "and you're just in time to go to the store for me."

"O.K., I'll go right away," said Red, enthusiastically. He wanted an opportunity to get away for a little while anyhow.

Red hurried, but he did not go directly to the store. He went to see Lieutenant Carroll. He entered the

Engine House and walked directly to the Lieutenant's desk, rejoicing that his big friend was on duty today.

"Well, Red," exclaimed the Lieutenant genially, "I got your card. Did you enjoy your stay at camp?"

Red ignored the question. "Lieutenant," he began manfully, "I just got home, not ten minutes ago, and came right over to apologize to you for getting sore when you told me to keep away from White and Stone. I'm sorry I acted the way I did, and I don't think you'll have to speak to me about anything like that again—ever."

Lieutenant Carroll smiled, as he grasped Red's outstretched hand. "I knew you'd come around after a while, Red. I was sure you would. Let's forget it. How did things go at camp?"

"Fine," exclaimed Red. "We have a lot to tell you, but I'm on my way to the store now. The other fellows will tell you some of the things that happened, but," Red looked around and lowered his voice, "Lieutenant, I've got something to tell you that they don't know anything about. Then you'll know why I came right over to square myself with you, and why I'm so sure that nobody will ever catch me with the wrong kind of company again."

"That's fine, Red," exclaimed Lieutenant Carroll, heartily. "I'll be more than glad to hear about it. It surely must be something interesting."

"It is," said Red, solemnly. "It's a dream I had about Our Lord. But I must be on my way now. I've got to go to the store."

"All right, Red," said the Lieutenant kindly, as he watched Red hurry out and down the street. Then, smiling, he turned back to his work.

Steve called Red shortly after supper and the pair picked up other St. Mary boys as they walked toward the Engine House. They all wanted to see Lieutenant Carroll and knew he would be expecting them.

"I wonder if Lieutenant is on duty today," said Bill Harte.

"Yes, he is," said Red. "I dropped in to see him this afternoon on my way to the store."

"You did?" exclaimed Bill, in surprise.

"Yes," answered Red. "I told you I sent him a card. I wanted to square myself with him. I was plain goofy to get sore, anyhow."

"Nice going, Red," cried the boys almost in unison. "We told you that."

"Let's see if any of the Gleaners are in their club-room," suggested Steve. "It's not much out of our way."

The Gleaners were at their club-room, busily wiping the dust of the past two weeks from tables, chairs, and equipment.

"You're just the fellows we wanted to see," called Charlie Fowler, as the boys entered. "Major Williams and the Gleaners invite all you fellows and Father Walsh, of course, if he can come, to a party here tomorrow night. Fun and eats and plenty of both. How about it?"

"How about it?" cried the boys, delighted with the invitation. "We'll be here. That's swell." Then Red asked, "How about us bringing Ken Hobart and Barry Willis?"

"Fine," exclaimed several of the Gleaners. "But," added Charlie Russell, "tell them not to bring Bonnie, though. I don't think the Major goes for him, you know."

"Oh, Ken and Barry are through with him, too," said Steve. "I heard them mention that on the train when they were making plans for tonight. I think that they'll be drifting in here later on tonight. They want to see your club-room."

Ken and Barry met Red and his friends as they were on their way to the Engine House. They told them of the invitation, and of Bonnie's exclusion.

"Oh, we're through with him, anyhow," said Ken.

"You mean he's through with us," corrected Barry, laughing. "He told some of the fellows that as long as we did not come home with him, he didn't want to have anything to do with us anymore. So that makes it easy for us."

The boys from St. Mary's spent a delightful hour chatting with their friend, Lieutenant Carroll, and with the firemen on duty at the station. While they were there, Major Williams telephoned to invite the Lieutenant to the Gleaners' party.

And what a pleasant party it was. Among the adult guests were Captain Meadows and some of the policemen from the local station. They, too, found a new and praiseworthy spirit animating the Gleaners. The policemen were welcomed with sincere enthusiasm by the boys, and they returned the welcome by a fine display of friendship and good will.

Major Williams had secured for the party the services of a few professional entertainers: a magician, a comedian, with a seemingly endless fund of good stories and songs, and two of the city's best professional lightweights, who staged a three-round boxing exhibition. Then they dressed and took charge of a few bouts between members of the club.

Just as Charlie Russell and a few helpers were arranging to serve the refreshments generously provided by the Major, to the surprise of everybody but Father Walsh and Major Williams, in walked the Mayor of the city, who, like Major Williams, had been an officer in the American Army in France. The high point of the evening came when each of the boys was introduced personally to the Mayor.

The party came to a close about eleven o'clock, with everybody singing, at the suggestion of the Major, "The Star Spangled Banner."

As the boys started toward their homes, Father Walsh called Red over to his car. "I thought, from some things I accidentally heard some of the boys say a few weeks ago, that you were not on speaking terms with Lieutenant Carroll" said the priest. "You seemed to be very friendly toward each other tonight. Were the boys mistaken?"

"No, Father," answered Red. "Lieutenant Carroll sent for me the Sunday morning after he saw me in the alley with those fellows you got the letter about. I lost my head when he scolded me." Red smiled. "I couldn't take it, Father. You know." Father Walsh nodded. "Now, well, I guess I grew up while I was at camp," continued Red, "and as soon as I got home yesterday, I went right over to the Engine House and apologized to the Lieutenant. Now, Father, I'm square with everybody."

"Well, I think you've grown up, as you say, quite a bit, too," said Father Walsh, as he started the motor. Then he added, smiling, "Now you and Steve hurry home to bed; future seminarians, you know, should be daily communicants, even in vacation."

"We'll be there, Father," said Red, as with a light heart, he hurried to rejoin his friends.

Mr. Devlin and Arthur had been out of town for a few days and had not yet seen the returned camper. They were waiting on the porch for him, as Red had only a few weeks ago waited for them. Red greeted them affectionately, and then said, "Boy, have I got a lot of things to tell you!" Mr. Devlin patted Red on the shoulder as he said, "But you must get to bed now. You can tell us all those things tomorrow." They could see that Red was supremely happy. Arthur was laughing, as he said, "Well, it certainly must be great news. You look like a different fellow."

Red had started upstairs to his room. He suddenly stopped and turned. Arthur was coming up behind him; his father was locking the front door. Red looked at them a minute; then he said solemnly, "I am a

R ed had started upstairs to his room. He suddenly stopped and turned...then he said solemnly, "I am a different fellow, Art. I've grown up."

different fellow, Art. I've grown up." Mr. Devlin and Arthur laughed heartily, as Red took the stairs two at a time.

Red knelt long at the side of his bed that night with a heart full of gratitude and happiness as he prayed to the Christ of his dream. Indeed, it would not have surprised him if he heard the Christ who then said, "I'm sorry," whisper to him now, "Nice going, Red."

Books for Boys
By Msgr. Raymond O'Brien
(1891-1963)
A Chicago Priest,
Chaplain at the County Jail
and Friend of Troubled Youth

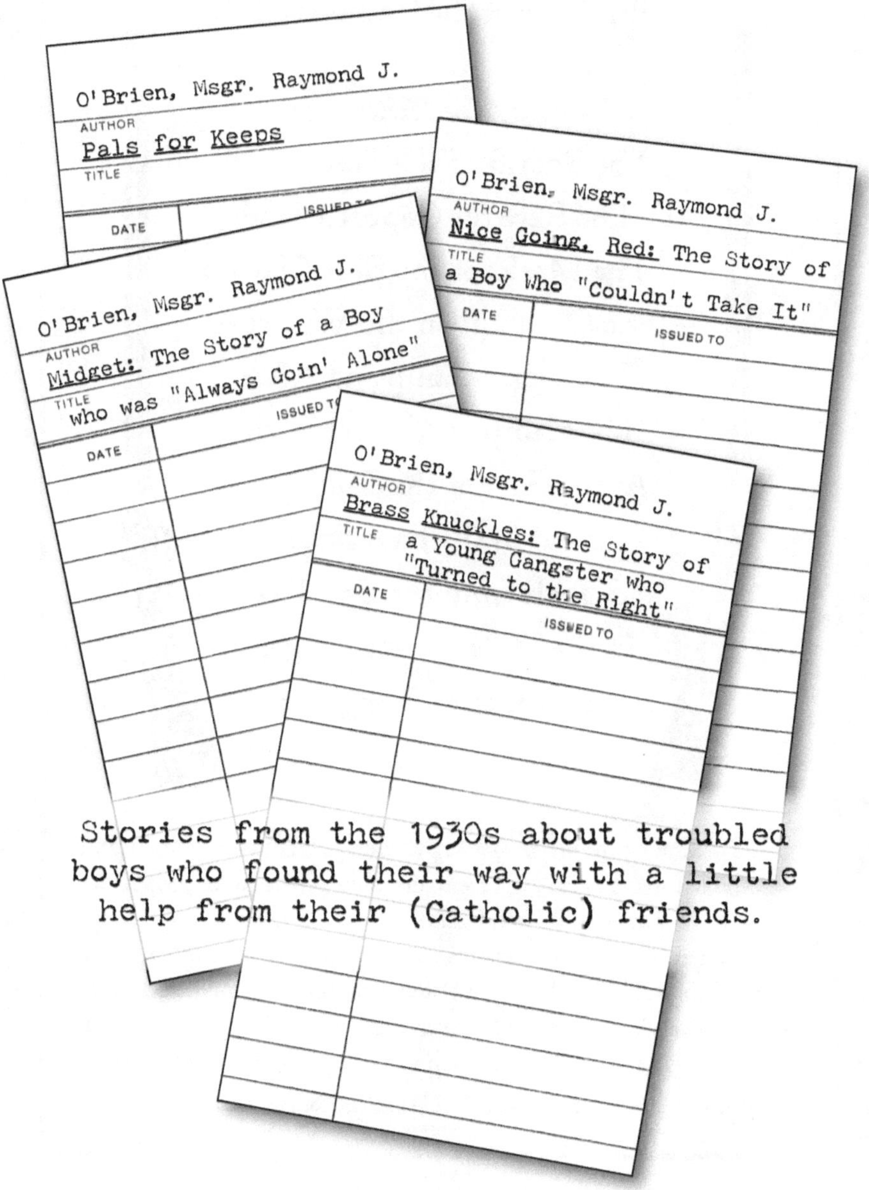

O'Brien, Msgr. Raymond J.

AUTHOR

Pals for Keeps

TITLE

DATE	ISSUED TO

O'Brien, Msgr. Raymond J.

AUTHOR

Nice Going, Red: The Story of

TITLE

a Boy Who "Couldn't Take It"

DATE	ISSUED TO

O'Brien, Msgr. Raymond J.

AUTHOR

Midget: The Story of a Boy

TITLE

who was "Always Goin' Alone"

DATE	ISSUED TO

O'Brien, Msgr. Raymond J.

AUTHOR

Brass Knuckles: The Story of

TITLE

a Young Gangster who
"Turned to the Right"

DATE	ISSUED TO

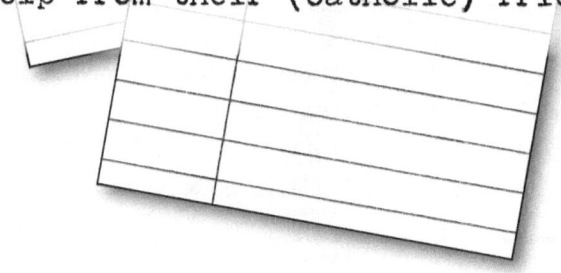

Stories from the 1930s about troubled
boys who found their way with a little
help from their (Catholic) friends.

Adventure Books for Boys
by Father Henry S. Spalding, S.J.

Stories that combine the Love of Country
with Love of the Catholic Faith

Cave by the Beech Fork
The Sheriff of the Beech Fork
The Race for Copper Island
The Marks of the Bear Claws
The Old Mill on the Withrose
The Sugar Camp and After
The Camp by Copper River
At the Foot of the Sand Hills
Held in the Everglades
Signals from the Bay Tree
In the Wilds of the Canyon
Stranded on Long Bar

"In *The Cave by the Beech Fork* a new genre is credited in American
Catholic Literature...all the fresh air books provided for boys had
hitherto been written by non-Catholics, and the lessons taught were
the commercially virtuous maxims of Benjamin Franklin, which are so
devoid of spiritual life as those of Polonius in his famous counsels to his
son Laertes...A dozen more books as true, as interesting, as honestly
religious, as manly as that, are, we hope, to be expected from his pen."

—Maurice Francis Egan (1852-1924), American Catholic Writer and Diplomat

www.ingramcontent.com/pod-product-compliance
Lightning Source LLC
Chambersburg PA
CBHW030956260626
47169CB00002B/556